PRAISE FOR THE DA

Killer Listing

"Sexy, savvy, and entertaining. Real estate agent Darby Farr solves the crime, nets the commission, and looks great doing so. Vicki Doudera displays a deft hand with story and characters. *Killer Listing* is a real showcase."

—Julia Spencer-Fleming, author of *One Was a Soldier*

"A hot property! Multi-million dollar deals, mojitos, and murder —real estate brings real trouble to this smart and savvy heroine. Scheming, speculation, and a scary bad guy will keep you turning the pages of this suspenseful and cleverly plotted mystery. Readers beware: though the setting is sunny, there's a twist around every corner."

—Hank Phillippi Ryan, Anthony, Agatha, and Macavity award-winning author

"A touch of romance, a hint of danger, and a mystery that keeps you guessing spice Darby's second case."

—*Kirkus Reviews*

"This is a good, Southern mystery. Colorful characters abound and mysteries keep you guessing!"

—*Suspense Magazine*

A House to Die For

"[Doudera] expertly weaves a tale of suspense on a Maine island, where murder and real estate are an explosive combination."

—Tess Gerritsen, bestselling author of *The Mephisto Club*

"The cutthroat world of luxury real estate is the perfect setting for a murder mystery, and Vicki Doudera's *A House to Die For* doesn't disappoint. Here's a fast-paced and well-told story with a smart, savvy real estate agent as the heroine, solving crimes while making sales. Bring on the next one!"

—Barbara Corcoran, real estate contributor for NBC's *Today Show* and author of *Nextville: Amazing Places to Live the Rest of Your Life*

"An appealing debut . . . the author does a good job portraying Darby in her efforts to make peace with her childhood past and solve a murder on a picturesque Maine island."

—*Publishers Weekly*

"A superb prologue, wonderful story, atmospheric with a good plot."

—*Crimespree Magazine*

"This gentle cozy with some unexpected plot twists is sure to please fans of Sarah Graves."

—*Library Journal*

"Light and entertaining . . . a fun mystery and fantastic way to spend an evening!"

—*Suspense Magazine*

A *Suspense Magazine* "Best of 2010" Selection

DEADLY
OFFER

DEADLY OFFER

A Darby Farr Mystery

Vicki Doudera

MIDNIGHT INK
WOODBURY, MINNESOTA

FIRST EDITION
First Printing, 2012

Book design by Donna Burch
Cover design by Lisa Novak
Cover illustration © Dominick Finelle/The July Group
Edited by Connie Hill

Midnight Ink, an imprint of Llewellyn Worldwide Ltd.

Library of Congress Cataloging-in-Publication Data
Doudera, Vicki, 1961–
  Deadly offer : a Darby Farr mystery / Vicki Doudera. — 1st ed.
    p.   cm.
  ISBN 978-0-7387-1980-1
1. Women real estate agents—Fiction. 2. Wineries—Fiction. 3. California—Fiction. I. Title.
  PS3604.O895D43   2012
  813'.6--dc23   2011044394

Midnight Ink
Llewellyn Worldwide Ltd.
2143 Wooddale Drive
Woodbury, MN 55125-2989
www.midnightinkbooks.com

Printed in the United States of America

To my brother, William von Wenzel, and his wife, Lucia Razionale. Thanks for all of the wonderful times in California.

ACKNOWLEDGMENTS

I'm thankful for the assistance of many who helped with *Deadly Offer*.

First, a big thank you to my faithful manuscript readers Lynda Chilton and Ed Doudera, whose comments and careful edits are so appreciated, and to Jane Lafleur and Jane Babbitt for proofreading. Thanks to Robert Merrill, MD, and Eric Schenk, DO, for their advice on chronic illness, as well as Luci Zahray, a.k.a. "the Poison Lady" for her excellent ideas.

I appreciate the help of wine pro Ken Churchill of Churchill Cellars for his thoughts and several glorious bottles of wine. Right here in coastal Maine, Cellardoor Winery's beautiful vistas helped with the creation of the imaginary Carson Creek Estate & Winery. Thanks to Bettina Doulton for her transformative work there.

I'm grateful to Aikido expert Sensei Gordon Muller of the New Jersey Police Academy for his technical guidance and helpful videos on gun disarming strategies. For suggestions regarding California law, thank you to Kenneth Horowitz, Esq., of San Mateo. Thanks also to Lee Scheuer of Camden and California for his assistance.

Much appreciation to my fellow real estate agents in Maine, above all, Scott Horty and the team at Camden Real Estate Company, including the extremely talented trio of Christopher Brown, Jeanne Fullilove, and Brenda Stearns.

Big thanks to everyone on our September 2010 Backroads Bike trip through Sonoma and Napa: Paul and Robin Giddings, Bill and Kathy Storm, Robert Takla, Joseph Akouri, Paul Kalekas, and Pamela Mann, including fearless leaders and super cyclists Bryan Rees and Cynthia Sullivan. Great doing research through wine country with all of you!

Thank you to my literary agent, Tris Coburn, and to all the good people at Midnight Ink, including editors Terri Bischoff and Connie Hill; my patient publicist, Marissa Pederson; and book designers Donna Burch and Lisa Novak. Thanks to illustrator Dominick Finelle for a beautiful cover as well.

I'm extremely grateful to readers of this series everywhere, especially those who helped me to choose Darby's vintage "ride"—Nadia Salemi, Peter Russell, Nancy Lubin, Cecilia Salas, Julia Levensaler, Jane Dagley, Karin Rector, Heidi Nason Hawk, Kit Parker, Patty Albany, Heidi Karod, Alison Dyer, and Nancy Lawson. Special thanks to Terri Mackenzie, who pushed me toward the "Karma of the Ghia" with her comment: "The wind in your hair, the feel of the road, the threat of imminent breakdown at every curve sharpens the female mind like nothing else." Thanks also to Richard Troy, Founder of The Karmann Ghia Club of North America, for his expert assistance.

Finally, nothing I do would be possible without the support, love, and encouragement of my family. Thank you Mom, Matt, Nate, Lexi, and especially, Ed.

PROLOGUE

"I WILL KILL YOU."

The words were uttered calmly, casually, the way one might order a glass of Chardonnay at a wine bar, but Selena Thompson knew from experience the cold fury lurking behind the benign tone. She blinked, hoping the nightmare would dissipate. Her life was in mortal danger, and there was precious little she could do.

The scythe...

She took a step backward, pushing her thin frame up against the corner of the vineyard's old barn. Here a collection of weathered tools gathered dust, their time as useful implements long a thing of the past. Selena groped behind her back, wincing at the effort even this small movement took, until she fingered the smooth wooden handle of the antique scythe. The blade was rusted, but it was deathly sharp.

Sunlight slanted through small slits in the barn's roof. A fly buzzed by her head, its flight a meandering circuit through the dusty air. She moved her head a fraction and felt her long black braid just grazing the top of her forearm. Beneath her thin cotton blouse her heart was pounding, so loudly she was sure he could hear it.

She prayed he could not see her hand grasping the tool.

"I swear, I could do it…" he took a step forward, the barn floorboards creaking beneath his weight. Selena's every muscle tensed, sending thin slivers of pain that pierced what seemed like every cell.

Running was out of the question. In her condition, at this stage of the game, it was remarkable that she could still walk. She tried to quell her trembling muscles. There was only one option.

I have to fight him off.

Swinging the rusty implement would be excruciatingly difficult. The scythe was unwieldy as a weapon—she had used it once, back when she was healthy, to hack down some weeds—but it was her only chance. Her attacker had only to move one step closer, and he would get a taste of the burnished steel. *I'll slice his carotid artery…*

A long second passed in which neither of them moved. Off in the distance, a rooster crowed, a sound Selena normally found comical at nearly five in the afternoon. She wondered how much longer her legs could support her. Already they were tingling, as if on fire from a thousand ant bites.

He lifted his big hands, palms towards her, and she stiffened.

"Leni, I beg of you." His throat was suddenly hoarse. "Show compassion. I am a changed man."

She said nothing and watched as his hands sunk to his sides. Was this when he would pounce, when he looked his most submissive? After several seconds, he gave a slow shake of his head.

"Is this it, Leni? You won't even give me the courtesy of a discussion?"

Selena's black eyes flashed.

"There is nothing to discuss. I told you, this isn't about you and me, it is about the business. It's about who is right for the vineyard."

"And how am I not right? I will love this place, you know that."

"It's not enough to love it," she muttered. Suddenly she was so exhausted, so drained of what little energy she possessed these days, that she nearly didn't care anymore. She let her hand fall from the scythe and summoned every ounce of strength to continue talking.

"I have poured the last five years of my life into Carson Creek. Choosing the new owner is the most difficult thing I have ever done."

"Then you have decided?" His jaw tightened. "You have chosen?"

Selena nodded. She tried to lift her hand back to the scythe and failed. A fragment of a prayer she'd learned as a child flitted through her brain. *If I should die before I wake . . .* She gave a small smile.

He balled his hands into fists. "Then there is nothing to discuss." His words shot through the air like bullets.

I am about to die.

He took a step backward, and then another. Selena pictured an angry boar, preparing to charge and gore his hapless victim. She'd come upon one once, years ago on a trip to Italy, as it tore into the flesh of a still-kicking rabbit. She'd seen the look in its eyes: cold, calculating, deadly. The same look she saw now in his.

Another step backward. Selena braced her aching body.

"God have mercy on you," he spat. Selena felt what she was sure was a ridiculous trickle of hope. She opened her eyes. Was he ... leaving? Was he really going to leave her alone?

He saw her baffled look and gave an ugly sneer. "I told you, Selena Thompson, I am a changed man." She watched as he retreated from the barn, his broad back blocking the sun.

She sank to her knees in exhaustion.

———

Fifteen or so minutes later, Selena felt able to rise to her feet. Grabbing the old wooden walls for support, she eased herself upward, waiting until she was steady before taking a step. She shuffled slowly past the rusty scythe. The terror of the encounter was behind her, and her heart felt lighter than it had in weeks. Even the pain, her ever-present yet unwelcome companion, seemed to have subsided.

She walked slowly out of the barn, surveying the acres of vines heavy with fruit and the rolling brown hills and meandering Carson Creek just beyond. The sun was warm on her face, a golden caress. This was her favorite time of day: the heat of the afternoon fading to pleasant warmth, the golden ball of the sun just starting to move with purpose toward the west. Years before she'd cycled at this hour, pumping her slender legs up the hills and relishing the feeling of freedom as she coasted down. Those had been wonderful rides, solo times when she'd sorted out her problems and cleared her head, returning to the winery pleasantly tired and ready for a shower and simple dinner. She missed those days, and suspected that she'd taken them for granted. *I was always such a health nut,* she remembered. *I was the last person anyone would think could become chronically ill.*

She stopped at the doorway and fingered the burgundy blooms of a late flowering spice bush. She remembered the scent as reminiscent of red wine, even if she could no longer smell it. That sense was gone, along with taste, the reason she had shed nearly twenty pounds from her already slender frame. *Try the Selena Thompson Diet*, she thought with a touch of sarcasm. She pushed open the door and stepped into her kitchen. *Lose weight because you can't taste your food …*

And yet, despite the disabilities brought on by her cluster of illnesses, she refused to become morose. There was still so much for which she was thankful. *My house,* she thought, looking around her comfortable farmhouse kitchen, the gleaming appliances once such a pleasure to use. *My business.* Carson Creek Estate & Winery was her pride and joy, the result of years of hard work, careful management, and good old-fashioned luck. *My brothers.* They had hovered over their little sister for years, acting like protective parents, even though she was a grown woman and perfectly capable of running her own life, but she knew that they loved her deeply.

Selena thought back to the day when she'd finally put an end to their constant meddling, nagging phone calls, and endless questions. "Do you still want to see me?" She'd hated to give Carlos and Rico an ultimatum, but it had come to that. "Then you've both got to leave me alone!" She suspected that they'd discussed what they undoubtedly referred to as her "meltdown," but she didn't care. It had worked.

And just in time. Her diagnosis had come a few months later, and with it, shock, confusion, and then—an odd sense of freedom. Besides her doctors, she was the only one who knew of her condition. She was free to let it define her, or let it be something she dealt with in confidence. She'd chosen the latter and adopted a characteristically defiant attitude. *I'm more than a bundle of symptoms. I am still me.*

Selena took a small ceramic plate from a cupboard and placed a few crackers and squares of cheese on it. Wincing, she reached up for a wine glass and set it on the counter. She pulled a decorative stopper from an opened bottle of Carson Creek Pinot Noir and poured herself a generous glass. The bottle was empty but she'd deal with it later.

While the wine was breathing, Selena made her way slowly toward the downstairs bathroom where her bathing suit hung on the back of the door. The material felt thin in her hands. She regarded the seat of the one piece and saw that it was becoming threadbare. *Not that I'm at a Beverly Hills Beach Club,* she thought. *No one sees me but the cat.*

Speaking of Jasper, where was he? Usually the independent feline would have sidled up by now, rubbing against her calves with a hopeful nudge or two. Selena glanced out the window. He was probably prowling between the vines, stalking a field mouse or an unsuspecting cricket. *Jasper will show up poolside, wearing a smug little look on his face.* She reached up for a towel, then sank onto a nearby chair and began the slow process of putting on her suit.

———

The blue and green tiled pool was one of Selena Thompson's few indulgences. She'd splurged on it the year after buying the winery, back when she was still doing some consulting work for several San Francisco clients, back when the majority of her income didn't have to pay for medical treatments, prescriptions, and paid help. For years she swam laps in this water, challenging her body to go faster and farther with every session. Now, as she placed a float around her waist and eased herself into its warmth, she felt a profound gratitude for the aquamarine haven. She let the water surround her like an embrace, cradling her sore limbs and giving her the illusion that the pain might someday pass. Someday...

She managed a few gentle kicks with her legs, focusing on the caressing sensation of the water against her skin. *This is heaven*, she thought. She floated aimlessly for another ten minutes, keeping her mind as free as possible, opening herself to a healing, meditative state. When at last a cloud passed over the sun and goose bumps formed on her arms, Selena kicked slowly to the pool's edge. *Time for that glass of Pinot*, she thought.

She had only to negotiate three stairs, but climbing them was becoming more challenging with each swim. Selena reached for the sides of the pool, her hands gripping the smooth tiles. In the distance, a hawk cried, its shrill voice startling against the quiet.

She brought one leg to the first step and steadied herself. *You can do this*, she told herself. *Just go slowly*.

Selena eased her body upward, hanging on to the metal rail for support. So far, so good. She began bringing her other leg to the stair, aware suddenly of a new pain shooting through her calf muscles. She yelped in surprise at its severity, swayed, and felt her feet buckle under her. A second later she slammed into the concrete.

Overhead the live oaks shook with a sudden breeze. Selena groaned and gingerly pushed herself up. She inhaled cautiously, hoping nothing was broken. Sore ribs—perhaps a nice black and blue bruise would be the only result.

Tears sprang to Selena Thompson's dark eyes. *Dammit!* It wasn't fair, it just wasn't fair. Her body had become her betrayer.

It's time you got a cane. The sober advice of Jenna Yang, her primary physician, came to her with the force of a blow. *It's time for that,* she realized. *I can't take any more chances.*

By the time she was out of the pool and had crossed the lawn to the patio, she'd stopped feeling sorry for herself. Her legs felt stronger, the strange shooting pain now merely a memory. And yet the incident had frightened her. *Tomorrow I'll get a cane.* Dr. Yang had made it sound like a fashion accessory, describing the many styles and colors. Selena sighed. *And if I have to start telling people about my illness, so be it. Even Rico and Carlos.*

Wrapping the plush pink and white striped towel more tightly around her narrow hips, she eased herself onto a cushioned teak chair. Beside her was a matching teak table, her plate of cheese and glass of wine in its center. She'd draped the glass with a cloth napkin against the tiny gnats that flew in and then drowned, rapturously, in the red liquid. She removed the napkin and lifted the glass.

"Here's to the end of another beautiful day," she said aloud. She raised the glass higher and considered the Pinot Noir with a critical eye. Ruby red—a perfect shade. The valley's cool climate offered optimal conditions for growing the little purple gems. She swirled the wine and took a sniff. *Blackberry, cherry—that's what I should smell.* She took a taste. This vintage was known to be bold and full of life, with a black licorice finish, but Selena detected none of these notes. She gave a little shrug. *Never mind.* The wine was cool on her tongue and throat and she took several sips.

She let her head and neck relax against the chair's cushion. Her day had been, on balance, a productive one, the only episodes marring it the pre-swim encounter in the barn and her poolside fall. Selena thought once more about the wooden scythe, and how its lethal blade would have whistled through the air.

She shuddered. *It doesn't matter now,* she thought, looking out at the fields and distant mountains. Her stumble at the pool was more worrisome. She pictured a cane and sighed. *Time to let go of your vanity,* she thought. *It's just a cane.*

She lifted the glass and took another sip of wine, letting her eyes drink in the scenery. Row upon row of neat vines rose from the brown earth as if to kiss the setting sun. Behind them, the small grove of olive trees Selena had selected years before opened their branches toward the heavens as if in supplication. Dark shapes darted amongst the trees. Were they bats? Selena couldn't quite be sure.

There is a magical serenity to this place. Such a small vineyard— only twenty acres—and yet it held an irresistible attraction. Selena had witnessed that attraction firsthand, had seen the desire on each prospective buyer's face; their determination to own Carson Creek at just about any cost. *It is special,* she thought, taking another gulp of the wine. *It's a little piece of paradise. And tomorrow I will tell the lucky buyer…*

She lowered the glass onto the teak table with a trembling hand. *That's odd,* she thought. *Another symptom to add to the list.* She placed her hands on her lap and sighed. *Face it; you're like an old mare out in the pasture. But I'm not old,* she couldn't help but protest. *I'm only forty-four.*

She picked up a cracker, placed a cube of cheese atop, and took a nibble. She swallowed and felt an uncomfortable pressing sensation on her chest, bearing down hard against her ribs, as if a huge piece of furniture was being lowered onto her midsection. She shook her head, determined to ignore it. Perhaps a soak in the hot tub.

She rose to her feet, waited until she had her balance, and walked the few steps to the hot tub, her wine glass in hand. The jets were off, as usual, the surface of the water a placid pool. Placing the glass on the side of the tub, she eased herself in, smiling in gratitude at the water's warmth. She let it engulf her body until only her head bobbed on the surface.

The hot tub was as soothing as ever, and yet the pressing sensation continued; in fact, it was intensifying with alarming rapidity. She took in a sharp breath. *I'm overwrought*, she thought. *That whole thing in the barn took more out of me than I realized.*

She reached with a shaking hand for her wine and took a long sip. Suddenly the pain in her chest seemed to seize her whole midsection and she doubled over, her face hitting the hot tub's warm water. She drew in a huge, frightened breath but the pain was upon her once more, even stronger, like a tidal wave swamping the tiny craft of her. *What is going on? This feels like...*

Before Selena could finish her thought she was seized with a crippling cramp. She forced herself to stand up. *I've got to get out of here.* Dizziness engulfed her and the trees surrounding the hot tub began to spin. She gripped the edge of the tub in terror.

Blood drained from Selena's face in a quick rush. A terribly cold chill swept down her body and her vision became a wavy tangle.

The bright afternoon dimmed and then went black as she slumped to her knees.

All pain was forgotten as the unconscious Selena slid slowly under the water. As she sank, her braid floated up, coiling on the surface like a dark water moccasin. Air bubbles from her mouth and nose rose languidly for a few minutes, and then subsided. The surface of the water grew deadly calm.

The air took on a chill as the light of day faded. The birds and small mammals living in the vineyard's underbrush were still, so that the only sound was a light wind rustling the leaves on the vines and olive trees. A figure emerged from the shadow of the cabana and crept toward the hot tub. With a gloved hand, the intruder nudged Selena's wine glass into the water. It splashed and then sank, coming to rest on her mottled white thigh.

ONE

"DROP DEAD GORGEOUS." DOUG Henderson ran a hand through his bushy hair, still mussed from rolling out of bed, and shook his head. "I tell you, Darby, she is just beautiful—inside and out." He gave a shy grin and then hefted a box full of record albums and carried them to the front porch. "Whew. Look at these old things. Wish I could part with stuff like this, you know? Had a guy in L.A. offer me two thousand bucks, but that just made me want to hang on to them. You know how it is."

Darby Farr pushed her long black hair back from her face and smiled. Her neighbor was not only in love, he was in the throes of moving, and having a hard time parting with his possessions. It was a process with which Darby was very familiar. As a top real estate agent for San Diego's Pacific Coast Realty, the young star had seen it all with her many clients over the years. The ones who couldn't part with their size-four wardrobe, even though they were now a size ten, or the parents who held on to box after box of children's toys although their "children" were having kids of their own. There had even been a few clients who stayed put in houses they no longer wanted because they could not deal with paring down their possessions. She knew all too well her friend Doug's dilemma.

Darby lifted a box of albums labeled "Tony Winners" and followed Doug to the porch, where the morning sun was just starting to creep in the old windows.

"You can't part with your collection of old show tunes, and I'm sure Rhonda wouldn't want you to. They're so much a part of who you are." She gave him a teasing look. "Plus, how will she hear you singing 'Wouldn't it be Loverly?' at the top of your lungs if you can't play the album?"

His look was sheepish. "Come on, you never heard me singing." Frowning slightly, he asked, "Did you?"

Darby laughed. "I did, and I enjoyed every rendition." She plunked the box down and wiped her hands on her jeans. "Okay, the living room is looking good. What's next?"

"I'm not sure, but let's head to the kitchen." He thumped through the Arts and Crafts style home and sighed. "I'm going to miss this place, you know? It's been a great house."

"Yeah, if only you'd had better neighbors, you might be sticking around." Darby grinned, grabbing an empty box and heading toward the kitchen.

Doug Henderson stopped and faced her. "The neighbors are wonderful, and be sure you tell anyone looking at the place that they won't find a better street in all of Mission Beach, or San Diego for that matter." He entered the sunny kitchen and opened a cabinet. "You do think it will sell, right?"

Darby nodded. She'd been through this with Doug many times, but knew he needed to be reassured once more. "It is a fabulous house, Doug. Authentic and yet updated with a great sense of taste and flair." She ticked off more selling points. "You have terrific curb appeal and your price is fair. I think we'll have it sold by this fall for sure."

"Good." He clinked together two china teacups as he pulled them from the cabinet. "I think we've earned a cup of tea on this lovely Friday morning." He lit the gas flame under a kettle of water. "Okay with you?"

"Sure." She perched on a small oak stool at Doug's formica-topped kitchen table. Picking up a postcard with a glossy photo of a palm-tree dotted beach, she saw a scribbled message and the signature of Doug's new girlfriend. She flipped it back over to the photo.

"So Rhonda is beautiful—drop dead gorgeous, as you say. What else can you tell me about this mystery woman?"

Doug plunked a rose-patterned sugar bowl on the table.

"She's a surfer, big time, and runs a small gift shop in one of the tourist towns, Sunset Beach. We hit it off instantly."

Darby nodded. Doug had met Rhonda on a computer dating website only a month before, and their on-line relationship had escalated at lightning pace, so quickly that he was selling his home and moving to Hawaii to live with her. She glanced again at the postcard. "Looks like a pretty place. How big is her house?"

"It's a three-bedroom ranch. Did I tell you that it's only a few blocks from the beach? Just like what we've got here." His sandy hair fell in his face and he brushed it back in a boyish gesture. "Can you believe that at fifty years old, I've finally found the woman of my dreams?"

You may have found her, but you haven't met her, Darby wanted to say, but she bit her tongue. Instead she looked into his eyes and gave a gentle smile.

"I'm so happy for you, Doug." She paused, choosing her words with care. "I'll miss you, but I am absolutely thrilled that you are embarking on this adventure. My only suggestion is that you wait to list your house. What's the rush? Get settled in Hawaii, and then I'll put it on the market for you."

"I don't see the point, Darby. It's crazy to have it sit here empty."

"Let me rent it for you then. At least until you're sure you want to stay."

"I am sure." He frowned, and then glanced at the kettle of boiling water. "Ready for your test?"

Darby groaned. "It's seven-thirty in the morning. Can't a girl just have a nice cup of tea without being quizzed by her neighbor?"

"Not when that girl has super-duper powers." He chose a gleaming silver canister from a cupboard and spooned some tea leaves into an infuser. He added water, let it slowly steep, and then strained it into a cup. "Let's see if your famous palate memory can figure this one out with a blind taste test."

"Blind?"

"That's right. You have to close your eyes."

Darby shook her head and complied. Doug's little tests were nothing new. He was fascinated with her extraordinary ability to discern tastes and smells, and was forever playing "stump the neighbor."

She felt his rough fingers press a warm china cup into her hands. She bent forward, eyes closed, and inhaled the scent of the tea. A heavy smell of overripe fruit, bordering on unpleasant. She pictured acres of tea fields in a far off place ... Asia? India? Africa?

Africa! That was the origin of this unusual brew. She took a tentative sip, letting the liquid linger on her tongue. Sweet, slightly nutty—definitely more appealing than its fragrance, thank goodness. She took another sip and smiled.

"I ought to disqualify this entry, Doug, but since you're moving I'll let it slide." Raising the cup to her lips for another sip, she smiled again. "Technically, what I'm drinking is not a true tea. It comes from the plant *Aspalathus linearis*, rather than the *Camellia* plants that produce traditional brews. It's from Africa—South Africa to be precise—and the reason you did not let me look at the tea is because of its distinctive red color." She paused. "This is Rooibos tea, also called Red Rooibos. Can I open my eyes now?"

Doug shook his head in amazement. "Darby Farr nails it again. That's what this is alright, Red Rooibos." He poured himself a cup of the bright red liquid and took a sip. "Smells a little funny but it tastes good, and it is supposed to be very healthy. Rhonda told me about it."

Darby smiled. "She's going to have her work cut out for her, changing you into a healthy eater. Does she know about your addiction to Sugar Babies?"

He colored. "No, and she never will. I'm done with processed sugar."

Darby put down her tea cup. "I see." She decided to change the subject. "Does Rhonda have family in Hawaii?"

"No. She moved out there a few years ago, from the Midwest of all places. Chicago, I think. Anyway, she says the laid-back lifestyle is just great. She runs her store, surfs every day, and tends a little garden. It's a paradise on earth."

"It certainly sounds idyllic." She glanced at her watch, a slim silver old-fashioned piece of jewelry that was a gift from a family friend in Florida. "I've got about half an hour, Doug, and then I need to head into the office. It's Friday, and I'd better get there on the early side. Shall I start with the upper cabinets?"

"I think we can skip the kitchen and go to the basement. I'm only bringing a few things from here."

Darby rinsed her teacup in the kitchen sink and turned to face her friend. "Why's that?"

"Rhonda said she's got a kitchen full of stuff already." He pushed his hair out of his eyes. They were a brilliant blue against his tanned face, and framed by laugh lines that gave him a friendly, open appearance. "Man, I've accumulated a lot of stuff in my five decades, haven't I? It truly boggles the mind."

Darby pulled a ponytail holder from the pocket of her jeans and pushed her long black mane into a messy bun. She put a hand on her slim hip and surveyed Doug's glassware. "Your possessions aren't just 'stuff'; they reveal who you are. Your collection of shot glasses, for instance. How many have you got?"

"Sixty-one, last time I counted." He opened the cabinet and pulled out a clear glass with a red hammer and sickle emblazoned across the front. "Take a look at this one. I drank a fair amount of vodka in this baby."

Darby peered at the shot glass. "This is from your student days?"

He nodded. "1985. Just as the whole thing started unraveling."

"You mean *glasnost*?"

"The dissolution of the USSR into separate states." He replaced the shot glass and closed the cabinet door. "It was an amazing place to be. To watch a country—an empire, really—in transition like that. Scary, but fascinating, too." He sighed. "I can't get rid of these, so I'm renting one of those storage units out on the freeway until I decide what to do with them. I'll probably put the albums there, too."

Darby nodded. She hated the thought that people had to spend good money to rent space to store things, but in Doug's case it made some sense. She glanced at her watch. "You know, I think I'd better head out after all. See you tonight to pack up some more."

Doug gave her a grateful look. "Dinner's on me, okay?" His voice grew louder as she jogged across the yard and toward her own bungalow. "My last night in California. I'll order in from the Thai place. *Chicken Mas Sa Man.*"

Darby smiled as she entered her bungalow and yanked off her sneakers. Her friend had her favorite yellow curry dish just right.

———

Dan Stewart maneuvered his ancient Jeep up the twisting road to Carson Creek Estate & Winery, frowning at the time on the dusty dashboard's clock. Eight-thirty. Normally he liked to be at work by eight: have a quick cup of coffee with Selena, and then get right to work. But today it had been a challenge to get out of the house at all. He gritted his teeth and the image of Sophie Stewart, long and lean, her sandy brown hair hanging to her shoulders, and that teeny-weeny little red skirt that just barely covered her butt ...

He slammed the steering wheel with his fist, still furious over his teenaged daughter's choice in dress. Didn't she know that skimpy scrap of fabric was like a red flag to all the hormone-flooded boys of Valley High School? A little voice piped up in his ear: *Isn't that the point?*

Ugh! He took a deep breath and tried to let their shouting match over a piece of clothing become a memory. She'd changed and still managed to catch the bus, but Dan suspected that the miniscule skirt had been tucked into one of the pockets of her backpack and was probably already on her slender frame. Really, how could the teachers let their students wear clothes like that? Didn't Principal Horowitz care that his daughter's backside was nearly exposed for the whole student body? Dan exhaled, and tried relaxing again. Maybe he could tell Selena about it with some humor, get her to laugh a little, and she'd help him to see the funny side of it as well. *She has a knack for seeing the bright side of things.*

He rounded the bend, downshifted, and took in the rows of grapes shrouded in mist, the sun just starting to peek through the Ventano Valley's cloud cover. He grinned at the beauty of the place, the ancient stones that dotted the landscape and the fertile soil surrounding them. There was always much more to do than he could fit into the day, but that was why he loved working at Carson Creek. It was a beautiful, rewarding, never ending project, the closest he would get to actually owning his own vineyard. Selena Thompson understood his feelings, and he prayed that the new owner would as well. *If not, there are plenty of other vineyards in this part of California*, he told himself. *Yeah, but none as pretty as Carson Creek.*

Nor were there many vineyards with owners as special as Selena, a woman who had taught him how to be brave in the face of adversity, who epitomized grace under fire.

He parked the jeep and jumped out, running a hand through his hair. Once the same shade as his daughter's long tresses, it was now several shades lighter, thanks to the growing number of gray strands she was causing him to acquire. Teenagers! It was difficult enough to raise them in the most perfect of conditions, never mind as a single parent.

Dan Stewart took long strides across the pebbled driveway, his body fit and muscled from years of fieldwork and his daily routine of jumping rope and sweating through pushups and crunches. The air was still, without the usual hum of the cicadas, and the unnatural quiet unnerved him. He whistled a few lines from an old Cat Stevens song, "Morning Has Broken," more to interrupt the silence than because he actually liked it.

He entered the old farmhouse, restored to perfection, and glanced around the immaculate kitchen. "Selena?" he called out, not wanting to startle her with his sudden presence. He glanced at the butcher block counter. No coffee in the pot, which was odd, as it was his employer's habit to have it ready before eight. He lifted the empty glass carafe from the drip-brew machine. His eyes and nose told him that she had not made coffee since yesterday.

Probably on an errand, he thought, grabbing the bag of beans from the freezer and pouring some into the grinder. The appliance's harsh staccato startled him with its severity. He finished grinding, found a filter, and was pouring in the ground coffee when his legs were brushed by something furry.

"Jesus, Jasper!" The cat was like a stealth bomber, never making a sound, and sneaking up to rub against calves when least expected. Dan glanced down at the black and white animal in relief. Jasper gave him a penetrating look, his amber eyes unblinking. "What is it?" Dan glanced at the feline's hand-painted food and water dishes and his heart skipped a beat. They were empty.

No coffee, and her beloved pet had not been fed. Even if Selena had left early for some reason, say a doctor's appointment in the city, she would have taken care of Jasper. Dan swallowed. His throat was tight and he could feel his heart thumping in alarm. Something was wrong.

"Sorry, Jasper, you'll have to wait a few more minutes." The cat seemed to consider his words and then turned and crept soundlessly out of the kitchen. Dan put down the filter full of coffee and followed the feline into the dining room, his boots making the wide floorboards creak. Nothing amiss in here—the long farmhouse table graced the center of the room, a mismatched but pleasing assortment of old press back chairs on either side. He entered the casually furnished living room where Jasper jumped on an overstuffed yellow loveseat and prepared for a nap. *Nothing.*

Dan licked his lips and mounted the old farmhouse's narrow stairs. They were stenciled in a simple pattern of grape leaves, grapes, and words, the letters spelling out a winemaking adage as one climbed the stairs. *With wine and hope, anything is possible.* Selena herself had stenciled the saying. It was an old Spanish proverb that had been her mantra since the early days of the business.

There were four small bedrooms upstairs, a bathroom, and a cozy, bookshelf-lined study that Selena used as a private office. The vineyard's real office was in the new barn, where both Dan and Selena had computers and all of the associated office machinery—a copy machine, fax, and printer. He glanced in the study, and then checked the guest rooms. His heart thudding in his chest, he entered Selena's sunny bedroom.

The four-poster double bed was made up with a light-blue chenille bedspread and blue-flowered pillows. It had not been slept in. Dan wasn't aware how he knew this, but instinctively he felt sure it was true. He shook his head, uncomprehending, trying to reason where Selena could be. He'd taken yesterday afternoon off, but Selena had said nothing that morning about going out of town.

He scanned the room quickly, noticing a small dark mound on the floor. He took a few steps and smelled a foul odor. *Jasper!* The cat had left a little "present" for his mistress by the base of the bed. Dan gritted his teeth, strode to the bathroom for some toilet paper and a wet paper towel, and quickly cleaned up the mess.

That unpleasant chore completed, he wasted no time in bounding down the stairs and back outside. Had Selena left the property? Dan jogged to the old barn, a handsomely restored building housing equipment as well as Selena's small Subaru truck. He peered in a window. The truck was parked and empty. Dan Stewart felt the first pricklings of fear.

Where was she? Lying on some small corner of the property, her ankle twisted? Or worse?

Dan sprinted to the five-year-old building housing the vineyard's office, tasting room, and production room, a structure Selena called the "new barn." Designed to look as if it was original to the property, the new barn was painted red with white trim, and sported a cupola with a jaunty rooster weathervane atop. He tried the door. Locked, but Dan knew where Selena kept a hidden spare key. He opened the door and went in.

He glanced around the tidy room. The message light on the phone blinked and a fax waited in the basket of the machine. No sign of Selena. That meant she had to be somewhere on the grounds of the vineyard.

He raced out, his mind forming a quick search plan. Start at the house and work outward in concentric circles, he thought. Encompass the pool and the olive grove...

The pool. His body flooded with a cold dread as he remembered Selena's penchant for a daily late afternoon swim. Before he knew it, he was poolside, his adrenalin having carried him the one hundred or so yards without his even remembering. The water was clean, an unnaturally bright blue, and the surface and bottom of the pool were clear. *Thank God*, he breathed. *Thank God.*

He turned to start his methodical search. A raven, wings inky black against the sky, whooshed by his head. He twisted toward the bird and caught a glimpse of something pink and white draped at the side of the hot tub. *A towel. So Selena had been here for a swim.*

He crept toward the colorful piece of fabric, a feeling of impending doom settling upon his body like a wet, heavy blanket. He leaned forward, not wanting to look, but knowing he must.

A bathing-suit clad body lay curled in a semi-fetal position on the bottom of the hot tub. A long black braid strained upward toward the surface, as if the figure was a marionette on a string. Dan Stewart gasped. He knew that braid; he recognized the navy swimsuit.

He leapt into the water, struggling to get a grip on Selena's body, the Spanish proverb echoing like a bad dream in his head.

With wine and hope, anything is possible. He clasped his hands around Selena's water-logged corpse and pulled her to the surface. Her arms splayed out as the body rotated face-up.

Dan felt as if he would vomit.

Selena's lovely face was bloated nearly beyond recognition, her lips puckered and grayish blue. She was staring at him with glistening brown eyes, eyes that would never again catch his from across a room. Dan heard a throaty cry, low-timbered, like a lion's roar of intense pain, and as he struggled to heft Selena's streaming body up onto the cement, he realized that the primitive sound came from him.

TWO

DARBY FARR JUMPED INTO her red Karmann Ghia cabriolet and started the engine. Nearly nine a.m. on a Friday and she was in her characteristic morning rush. Impatient to be at the office and doing the work she loved, she first grabbed her smart phone and checked quickly for messages and e-mails.

Some were predictable: clients wanting to see property; clients wanting to sell property. As one of the busiest brokers in southern California, Darby was never without a long list of people to contact, and she scrolled through the myriad e-mails with practiced speed. A few messages were personal. Her friend in Florida, Helen Near, had written several chatty paragraphs describing a particularly challenging golf game; her friend in Maine, Tina Ames, announced in two terse lines that she and her long-time boyfriend were finally "getting hitched." Darby smiled and continued scrolling, vowing silently to respond later in the day.

The last message from an unfamiliar Japanese name puzzled her. *Kenji Miyazaki.* She clicked open the e-mail and checked the signature. Mr. Miyazaki was a senior vice-president of the mega-company Genkei Pharmaceuticals, headquartered in Tokyo.

Darby skimmed the e-mail, her stomach tight. Finally she shoved her phone in her pocketbook and backed out of the driveway.

Cruising through the laid-back community of Mission Beach, Darby hardly noticed the throngs of skateboarders, runners, and mothers pushing strollers. Instead, she thought back to her earlier dealings with the drug company's president, Mr. Kobayashi, and the shocking family secret he had helped her uncover.

It all stemmed from a book that described Japanese atrocities in China during the Second World War. Darby's maternal grandfather, Tokutaro Sugiyama, had been mentioned in the book. Mentioned? *Heck,* Darby thought, *he'd been named a war criminal.*

It was a secret Darby's mother had discovered as well.

And now someone else—Kenji Miyazaki—wanted to meet with Darby to discuss the "incident." She had never heard his name. Who was he, and why was he contacting her?

Her stomach clenched once more and the taste of acid rose in her mouth. Whether it was from the Red Rooibus or her anxiety, she wasn't sure. She took a deep breath, fighting the feeling of nausea, and accelerated toward the freeway exit.

It happened in Japan, more than fifty years ago, she told herself. *My grandfather is dead. My mother is dead. What does a mystery from the past have to do with me?*

Out of what seemed like nowhere, flashing blue lights appeared in Darby's rear view mirror. She slowed her Karmann Ghia to a crawl, looked back in the mirror, and groaned.

It was a car from the San Diego Police Department. The officer inside motioned, and Darby pulled over as soon as it was safe. A beefy, dark haired man in uniform emerged from the black-and-white vehicle and ambled slowly toward her car.

"Thought that was you, Darby." He had an affable grin, this young police officer, and Darby recognized him as a client she'd helped purchase his first home just the year before.

"Eric … it's good to see you." Embarrassed, she gave a small smile. "I guess I'm in too much of a hurry this morning, is that right Officer Sanchez?"

"Going twenty-five miles over the speed limit, so you might say that." Eric Sanchez's voice turned serious. "Wish I could give you a warning, but I've got you on the radar. What are you in such a hurry for? You late for a big closing or hoping to get a jump on the weekend?"

She shook her head. "No excuses—I'm just on my way to work."

"You're lucky you weren't a half mile farther down the road. You've got a school zone coming up, and that would be a criminal charge." He jotted a few things down on a pad. "I've got to go back to my vehicle and write this up."

Darby nodded and watched him walk away. Her throat was suddenly dry and she grabbed a water bottle from the back of the car and took a long swig. *A criminal charge would jeopardize my real estate license.* Her hands shook as she put down the bottle. *But I would never speed in a school zone, would I?*

Slowly she shook her head. *Why am I racing around like a madwoman?* Her career was going well, and even in the flagging market she'd had some impressively large sales. She was fit, thanks to her early morning runs, and reasonably happy. And yet she raced from appointment to appointment, in a kind of a fog, not even enjoying the ride. *I can't blame it all on my grandfather*, she thought.

She took a deep breath and let it out slowly. *That's it*, Darby vowed. *I'm going to slow my life down a little. I'm going to focus on the present and stop dwelling on the past.*

When Eric Sanchez returned with the ticket, Darby tried not to wince as she looked at the amount: Three hundred and twenty dollars. She sighed and put it on the seat next to her.

"I'm sorry, Darby," he said, his round face puckered with concern.

"Please, don't be," she smiled. "I think it was just what I've needed to get my life back on a slower track. Thank you for the wake-up call, Officer Sanchez."

He blushed a deep crimson. With dimpled fingers he waved as she pulled carefully back into traffic.

———

"You are looking more relaxed than usual," said Enrique Tomas Gomez, his dark eyebrows lifted in surprise. He plunked a stapler down on his desk. "Should I be concerned?" He was, as always, impeccably dressed in a Joseph Abboud designer suit, his black hair perfectly cut and styled. Darby swung her pocketbook onto a chair and turned to face her assistant.

"I got a ticket getting onto the freeway," she explained, grabbing a stack of mail and flipping through the envelopes. She paused, opened one, and handed him a check for twenty thousand dollars. "There's the second earnest money deposit for the Wymans' purchase of the lakefront house."

He glanced at the check and nodded. "Tell me more about your run-in with the law," he urged. "I'm not used to my boss being a 'bad girl.'" He made little air quotations with his tapered fingers. "You are always so squeaky clean. What some might call boring."

Darby laughed. Enrique Tomas Gomez, or "ET" as she called him, was an aging Ricky Martin with a sense of humor as big as his wardrobe, which was to say, vast.

"I was speeding. The officer was that young guy who bought the ranch over on Palm back in the spring."

"The man who was shaped like a little bowling pin?"

"Yup. Eric Sanchez." She tossed down the pile of mail and faced her friend. "I thought he'd let me go, but I was on his radar. The whole thing made me realize how much of my time is spent racing from one thing to the next. I'm going to slow down a little, see if I can't stop this frantic pace."

"Interesting idea," ET murmured. "We'll see how far you get, Speedy Gonzalez."

She laughed again. "Are we seeing Claudia today?" The mother of three school-aged children, Claudia Jones worked part-time as a sales agent at Pacific Coast Realty. She'd joined Darby and ET just a few weeks earlier to help them show property, and was a welcome addition to Darby's growing real estate team.

"No, today is the day she helps in the little one's first grade class." ET moved to answer the ringing telephone, leaving Darby free to think about her own day. Appointments with a few potential listings, but other than that, she was open. Of course, there was always desk work to do. Real estate was a never-ending, twenty-four-seven kind of job in which you could peruse listings endlessly, search the multiple listing system compulsively, contact clients constantly, and farm for prospects until the cows came home. Free time—now there was a concept that was new to Darby Farr.

I could check out an art museum. Something normal people do.

A harsh intake of breath from the other end of the room made Darby look quickly toward her assistant. Something about his posture—the way his back, always ramrod straight, was slumped—made Darby's heart tighten.

ET clutched the phone in one hand and held one of the wooden desks with the other, as if it was the only thing keeping him erect. Darby searched his face, normally so serene and smooth. What she saw made her wince.

His skin was ashen, his handsome Latin features twisted in an emotion that was clearly pain of the worst sort. Without warning he slid to the floor, taking the phone crashing down with him.

———

Dan Stewart felt trapped in a nightmare from which he could not hope to awake. First the discovery of Selena's lifeless, bathing-suit clad body, and then the arrival of the emergency medical team, and finally the call he'd known he must make to Selena's brother Carlos.

It had been, without a doubt, one of the worst things he had ever done in his life. Right up there with the day he'd told his little girl Sophie that her Mommy wasn't coming back—ever.

Thankfully Carlos had been at his studio, and not on the freeway stuck in traffic or in the middle of a business meeting. Dan gave him the news, as gently as he could, that Selena was dead.

"What?" Carlos' deep voice was unbelieving, as if he'd heard incorrectly and was trying to understand. Dan repeated his awful message, listening to hear if the words had sunk in.

"No…" It was a long, drawn-out denial, followed quickly by a painful "How?"

"I don't know. She was in her hot tub." Dan nearly choked as he said it, remembering the image of her bloated face, burned on his brain like a brand. Would he ever forget the horrible scene? Would it be his new—and final—memory of his employer and friend? "It may have been a heart attack. The paramedics weren't sure." He swallowed. "I'm sorry."

Carlos was crying, big, racking sobs that filled Dan with despair. Snatches of Spanish words peppered his cries, and Dan knew, without understanding, that they were phrases of anguish.

———

"I cannot believe it," ET murmured from the passenger side of Darby's vintage roadster. "I am trying to tell myself that it is true, that my sister is gone, but my heart will not listen." He was staring straight ahead and as Darby stole a quick glance at him, she felt her own heart constrict with pain.

She accelerated on the nearly empty stretch of highway. Despite the distance, they were driving from San Diego up the coast to San Francisco, and then inland to the Ventano Valley. They had departed immediately after ET's younger brother Carlos had called, stopping only to grab overnight bags and a full tank of gas.

Darby had called Claudia Jones from her cell phone, explaining over the din of chattering first grade voices about the tragedy.

"Poor ET," Claudia had clucked sympathetically. She admonished a child to share his Legos, and then switched to her professional voice. "I'll be at the office in fifteen minutes. Drive safely, and don't worry about anything on this end."

Darby thanked her and hung up. She glanced at her passenger, who was staring out the window. As if he felt her gaze, ET turned towards her.

"I can never thank you enough for doing this." His eyes were moist with tears. "I couldn't face the airport. Not today."

Darby nodded. "I understand." Her assistant was deathly afraid of flying, and although he had put his fears aside once or twice in recent years, she knew that in his present condition boarding an airplane would require more stamina than the poor man could muster. "It's a beautiful drive. We're cruising right along." She gave a small smile. "We'll be at Carlos' apartment in the city before you know it."

He gave a slow nod of his head and turned toward the window. Once again, Darby felt acute stabs of sympathy.

She thought back to what she knew about ET's youngest sibling, Selena Gomez Thompson. What was it ET had always called her? A free spirit, someone who took risks and was unbounded by society's conventions. Selena had defied her conservative Mexican upbringing and forged an independent life away from her family, even her brothers who loved her dearly but tended toward overprotectiveness. In her late teens she fled the Mexican town of Ensenada and settled in San Francisco, living with a group of cyclists in a rundown old Victorian near the Haight-Ashbury District. When the landlord mentioned he needed to sell the house, Selena borrowed the funds to buy it. "She fixed it up little by little, renting rooms to the other cyclists, and then sold it for a mint," ET once told Darby. "And then she bought the vineyard."

Calling the neglected acreage and ramshackle farmhouse "a vineyard" had been a stretch at first, but once again Selena had employed good old-fashioned elbow grease, ingenuity, and all of her savings to get Carson Creek Estate & Winery up and running. Her brothers offered to help, but their sister was stubborn, insisting she could make it on her own. She'd never borrowed a cent from them—until a month ago.

Darby recalled the phone conversation with ET in which he'd quietly requested fifty thousand dollars to help a family member in need. From her friend Helen Near's home in Florida, Darby had agreed to ET's appeal immediately and without any questions. She'd transferred money into his account, not knowing any of the details, because he was her most valued employee and friend. It was only a slip of the tongue that had revealed for whom the money was intended, but Darby still did not know why.

She used her directional and pulled off the highway toward a small gas station with two forlorn looking pumps. "We're about twenty-five minutes from the city," she said, unbuckling her seat belt. "I'm going to grab some more gas and a bottle of water. Can I get you something?"

He turned toward her. "A coffee would be nice."

"Sure." She climbed out of the car and began pumping her gas. A few minutes later she was in a dingy little convenience store, a water and large coffee in hand.

The woman at the counter's eyes were ringed with black eyeliner. Blush accented the sagging skin around her cheekbones. She yawned. "Forty-two even," she said.

Darby handed her a credit card. She glanced at the stack of newspapers on the counter and scanned the headlines, looking, as always, for the byline of a certain British reporter on assignment in Afghanistan. She flipped the paper over and waited for a receipt.

"Veronica's in town," the saleswoman said, plunking down the credit card slip for Darby to sign. She gestured toward the headline of the Style section. In bold print it trumpeted the sold-out "Angel Tour."

"Veronica?"

"Don't tell me you don't know who she is. Geez, I'm over sixty and I know her. Here." She thrust a brochure at Darby that depicted a tall, leather-clad woman with vibrant red hair sporting large pink feathery wings. "That song 'Heaven Bent' is about the only thing the radio plays."

"When does Veronica perform?" Darby asked, handing back the brochure.

"This weekend at the polo grounds. Then she'll be in the convention center in San Francisco." The woman sighed. "Wish I had even a tiny bit of her billions. But me? I can't even carry a tune."

Darby picked up the newspaper. Perhaps it would take ET's mind off his awful journey for a moment or two. She glanced at the price and handed the saleswoman a dollar. Then she grabbed the bottle of water and cup of coffee and turned to leave.

"Come again," the saleswoman called, in a tone that implied she didn't care one way or another. Darby pushed open the door and headed for her car.

———

Andrea Contento snipped another bunch of purple-leaved basil from the kitchen garden and added it to her willow basket. Once more she inhaled the herb's rich aroma and sighed. It was the scent of the growing season, of late summer, and she never tired of it. She rose from her kneeling position, wiped her hands on her jeans, and lifted the basket. Time to make pesto.

She strolled from the tidy garden to the stone patio, one of the many pleasing outdoor spaces at Contento Family Vineyards. An arrangement of weather-resistant furniture with plump cushions invited guests to sit, relax, sample one of the vineyard's famous flagship wines, or take in the lush scenery. This particular patio was private, off-limits to the hordes of visitors who poured from vans, cars, and busses nearly every day, but there were plenty of lovely public picnic spots elsewhere on the grounds. The whole property was a showplace, a testament to the hard work and vision of generations of Contentos who had poured their time and money into the Ventano Valley land.

Andrea paused before a hedge of rosemary that was growing vigorously in its sunny location by the rock wall. She admired the verdant spikes and broke off a small branch. Remembrance—that was what rosemary stood for. She glanced at the entire row and then frowned. One of the bushes was clearly sick, the tips of its needles an alarming shade of yellow. Aphids? Fungus? Or something else?

Without question Rolfe, the estate's gardener, would have some sort of non-toxic spray to counteract the disease. He was an expert and an expensive one at that, and the Contento family paid him well. After all, he was responsible for one of the most beautiful gardens in the valley. Andrea admired his skill, as well as the accolades her gardens received, but she had little patience with underperforming plants.

She scrutinized the yellowing bush once more, then grasped its main stem and tugged. After a few yanks, the plant's roots released their hold and surrendered to Andrea's will. A burst of fragrance assailed her nostrils and she smiled. The scent was truly magnificent.

A cleverly concealed compost bin hid near a blooming bougainvillea, and Andrea disposed of the plant, making a mental note to remind Rolfe to find a replacement.

Brushing the soil off her hands, Andrea continued across the patio and toward the kitchen. Located just steps away from the herb garden, the country kitchen was set up for serious cooking. On any given day there were famous chefs from the valley and camera crews encamped amongst the painted cupboards, stainless steel appliances, and gleaming granite countertops, but on the rare occasions when Andrea had the kitchen to herself, it seemed a cozy and creative refuge from the bustling estate. She pulled a sky-blue apron emblazoned CONTENTO COOK-OFF from a hook in the pantry and tied it on her petite frame. Visiting hours for the vineyard were over, and the employees had left for the day. The house was serene; empty, with only the sound of the birds in the ancient gnarled apple tree to disturb the profound quiet.

Andrea hummed as she rinsed the basil leaves and readied her food processor with the steel blade. She selected a bottle of olive oil from the pantry. The liquid inside was light colored, faintly tinged with green. She uncapped the bottle and inhaled its sweet aroma.

The oil, as well as the pine nuts she now pulled off a shelf, hailed from the property, the nuts gathered from two old trees that still produced remarkably well. Olive oil was a sideline for the vineyard that was becoming more and more profitable. Plans to expand the olive grove had been in the works for years, but they hinged on available land. With every square inch of the estate's acreage developed, there was simply no space to plant olive trees without sacrificing some of the precious vines.

Unless we buy more property.

That was the logical explanation, but so far none of the estate's abutters had wanted to part with any of their acreage. The family had looked to other locations in the valley, but nothing had proven worth the expense and aggravation. And then Carson Creek Estate & Winery had come up for sale, offering the seemingly perfect solution: more vines and an established olive grove, along with a picturesque farmhouse ready to be converted into a restaurant.

Andrea let the olive oil run in a slow dribble into the bowl while her food processor chopped the basil leaves and nuts. She grabbed a garlic bulb from the pantry, peeled it, and threw in several cloves. She ran the processor for a few seconds more, then tasted the bright green sauce. *Salt and pepper, and some parmesan,* she thought.

The ringing of her cell phone sliced through the tranquil afternoon. She wiped her hands on her apron and glanced at the screen.

"Hello, darling." She leaned against the granite countertop and listened for the sound of her husband Michael's rough voice.

"Andrea, I have terrible news." He paused, sounding tired, very tired. "There's been an accident at Carson Creek. It's Selena. Dan Stewart found her this morning. She's dead."

Andrea felt the silence of the house all around her. She drew in a quick breath and sank slowly onto the granite counter.

THREE

"Andrea, are you alright?"

No, she wanted to say. *No, I am not alright.* "What happened?"

"She was in her hot tub. She may have had a heart attack." He exhaled. "I'm with Tim and Christophe in the far field. We're all coming back to the house. Later on we'll head up there, see what we can do."

"Of course." She imagined the scene at Carson Creek Estate and shuddered. There would be family coming—Selena had at least two brothers—and maybe more relatives, plus friends from the valley dropping in to pay their respects. Everyone would be shocked at the tragedy. Selena had been well regarded, both for her business ethics and her kind personality, and liked by all who knew her.

"I'll go up there with you. I'll bring along some pasta for them to heat up."

His voice softened. "That would be nice."

The click of his mobile disconnecting signaled the end of the conversation. Andrea placed her phone on the granite countertop, stood thinking a moment, and then returned to her pesto.

———

Sophie Stewart, fourteen, flipped her long sandy brown hair off her face and picked up the pitcher of lemonade. With her other hand she grabbed a stack of plastic cups and headed toward the dining room at Carson Creek Estate & Winery.

"I'm going to put the drinks in here, on this table," she said, plunking down the pitcher and cups. She looked up at her father, standing with his back to the table, gazing silently out to the vineyard.

"Dad?" It was creepy, the way he was so still, like he hadn't even heard her. She walked behind him and rested a hand gently on his shoulder. He started and turned.

"Sophie Doo," he murmured. It was his pet name for her, something he'd coined because of her addiction to the Scooby Doo animated television show.

She scrutinized his face. He looked like crap—that was the truth, with big bags under his eyes as if he'd been crying for two days straight. "Can I get you something? Make you a sandwich?"

He shook his head and turned back to the window.

Sophie eyed the array of sliced deli meats and bread on the farmhouse table and decided to make him one anyway. She spread mustard on a finger roll, added ham, a slice of turkey, some lettuce and a piece of Swiss, and placed it on a napkin. "Here," she said, handing it to her father.

Dan Stewart took the sandwich and gave the ghost of a grin. "Just like your mom. She never listened to what I said either."

Sophie felt a pang in her heart as she watched him devour the sandwich. Not at the mention of her mother—she had been gone for a decade, and Sophie was long past the pain of her death. It hurt to see her father so sad.

She put her hands on her hips, resting them against the leather belt she'd gotten from her grandmother last Christmas. "What time did you say they'd be here?"

Dan glanced at his watch. "Around seven. Carlos waited for his brother to drive up from San Diego. The Contentos will head over once they're here."

Sophie nodded. She knew all this—he'd told her when she'd first arrived on the bus from school—but it was good to hear her father talking. "I'll go and check on Jasper." She turned to walk back to the kitchen but her father's hand on her shoulder stopped her.

"I'm sorry about this morning," he said. "I shouldn't have yelled at you like that."

She bit her lip. "Don't worry about it. I can't wear that skirt with the new dress code anyway."

His face softened. "Thanks for coming over to help."

"No problem." She gave him a quick hug, felt his strong arms hold her more tightly than usual. God, he was a wreck.

Released from his embrace, she walked back to the kitchen, hunting for Selena's black and white feline. He appeared without a sound from another room.

"There you are, kitty." She used a soothing voice and looked into Jasper's amber eyes. "Look, here's something yummy." She gave the cat a scrap of turkey, felt his pink tongue rough against her finger. Poor thing! Did he wonder where his owner was, why she hadn't fed him that morning? Sophie squatted to stroke his soft fur. The cat lifted his tail in sheer happiness.

It was so weird—weird and sad—to think that Selena Thompson was dead. What would happen to her father's job at the winery? He'd liked Selena, enough so that Sophie had sometimes wondered whether they were more than just friends. She rose from her haunches and watched the cat tiptoe out of the room. Selena was dead, and her father had been the unlucky one who'd found her. She shuddered. Slasher movies were one thing, but a real dead person—especially someone you worked with—that was another thing entirely.

She washed an oval platter and put it on the wooden drying rack. Her father had found her mother, too, all those years ago. She glanced back at the dining room. Two women; two dead bodies. What would Scooby Doo say?

———

Carlos Gomez had the same dark hair and eyes as his older brother ET, but there the similarity stopped. While ET was tall, with a courtly manner, his brother was compact and loquacious, with a face that revealed a shifting array of strong emotions. From the very cramped back seat of Darby's Karmann Ghia, Carlos let loose a torrent of emotion which ET interrupted only occasionally with soothing sounds.

"And then she had to put in the freakin' pool and hot tub," Carlos fumed. "Remember that, Rico? I told her not to do it. Those things are too much maintenance and they cost a fortune to heat. But Selena, she went ahead and did it anyway."

ET sighed. "She could afford it, Carlos. She wanted it."

"And look where it got her! A heart attack. *Dio*, she was only forty-four! How can that be?" Cries filled the small car and Darby glanced in the rear-view mirror. Poor Carlos lay across the small back seat, his head in his hands, sobbing.

She slid her gaze toward ET. He was ramrod straight, his eyes unblinking and focused on the road. These brothers were very different, that was clear. And Selena? What had her personality been like?

"I think this is the turnoff," Darby said, slowing her speed and putting on her left blinker.

Carlos managed to look up from his cramped position. "Yeah," he croaked, clearing his throat. "This is it. Ten miles to go." He blew his nose into a tissue. "Rico, did you hear from Auntie Teresa?"

"Yes, I spoke with her as we were driving and she arrives on Sunday. I called Dan at the winery and he booked rooms in Wyattville for her and the cousins. We thought it would be better than trying to cram everyone into the house."

"Yeah." Carlos sighed. "Guess you're right."

The brothers were silent as Darby steered her car over the twisting roads toward Carson Creek. Suddenly, it seemed they had entered the heart of wine country, with nothing but gentle hills planted with row upon row of vines as far as Darby could see. The countryside was glowing in the late September sun, the leaves of the trees lining the vineyards suffused in a buttery yellow color that lit up the road. She cruised around one corner and the vista opened up even more, revealing the valley and meandering Carson Creek cutting a blue swirl through it.

"That's Contento Vineyards," Carlos offered, pointing at a large estate-like property with many buildings. "That whole spread to the west. Old Vincenzo Contento started the place when he was just off the boat from Italy."

Darby slowed to admire the world-famous vineyard. "It's gorgeous. Who runs it now?"

"The founder's grandson, Michael Contento, and his children, right Rico?"

ET pulled his gaze away from the view. "Twenty-five years ago, Michael was a professor at Stanford," he murmured. "He taught nineteenth-century American fiction. It was obvious that he preferred academia to winemaking, but when his father died, he proved to be a dutiful son and came back to the valley."

"You took some of his courses, right?" Carlos sounded like the eager younger brother, in awe of his older sibling's accomplishments.

ET nodded. "Yes. I would have liked to take more."

Slowly Darby continued along the twisting country road, bordered on both sides with fields full of compact grape vines. A distinctive white sign with gold lettering announced Carson Creek Estate & Winery, and her passengers both sighed. "We're here," muttered Carlos.

She steered the car into the vineyard. The rows of grape vines were hypnotic, so incredibly straight that they seemed artificial. Beyond the sides of the fields stood several buildings—one a classic farmhouse with a small shingled barn, the other, a larger, new red building constructed to look like a barn. Darby saw a grove of some kind of trees to the right of the property, and, as she approached the house, glimpsed the fenced-in pool area bordered by a small cabana. She felt her stomach tighten. Undoubtedly this was the location of the hot tub as well.

Carlos and ET sat in silence as Darby parked the car. She respected their need to be quiet. How else could they possibly come to terms with the awful family tragedy unfolding on a sunny September day?

She grabbed their bags as they emerged from her car, and followed them to the door of the farmhouse. Before they could knock, the door was flung open and a lanky man in his forties greeted them.

"Thank God you're here," he said. "What a heck of a long ride." He reached out to clasp both brothers' hands, but ended up giving them both tight hugs. "I am so sorry," he said, his voice husky with emotion. The brothers nodded numbly.

ET cleared his throat. "Dan, this is my employer, Darby Farr. Darby, meet Dan Stewart. He was Selena's right-hand man."

Darby shook his hand. "I'm here as Enrique's friend, not his boss," she said. "It's nice to meet you."

"Likewise." Dan Stewart took the bags from Darby and led the way inside. "Sophie?" he called. A tall, lean girl with sandy brown hair and a close resemblance to Dan appeared around the corner. "Sophie, these are Selena's brothers, Carlos and Enrique."

She stretched out her hand. "I'm really sorry. I liked Selena a lot."

Again Carlos and ET nodded. Darby sensed it would not take much for them to lose control of their emotions. She gave the girl a small smile.

"Sophie, I'm Darby Farr. I work with Enrique in the southern part of the state."

"Really?" An arch of a beautiful eyebrow. "What do you do?"

"We sell real estate," Darby said.

Sophie and her father exchanged a quick look. Dan Stewart bent over and picked up the suitcases. "There are three bedrooms upstairs, in addition to Selena's. I've also booked several rooms in Wyattville. Do you want to go into town, or are you okay with staying here?"

"This is fine," Carlos said flatly.

Sophie led the way up the stairs with ET and Carlos in tow. Her father paused and turned toward Darby. "Where's your suitcase?" he asked, lifting a piece of the luggage.

"I have a few things in the car, but I'm not planning to stay."

"You mean to tell me you're going to turn around and drive back tonight?" Dan Stewart's look was incredulous. "It had to have taken you seven or eight hours! That's crazy."

"I only wanted to get ET—that's my nickname for Enrique— here safely," Darby explained. "He hates to fly, and I felt he was far too upset to drive. I figured I'd stop at a motel in a few hours."

"I see. There's an empty guest room up there. You wouldn't be any trouble."

"Thank you, but I'll only be in the way."

Dan Stewart gave her a searching look. "Actually, I don't think that will be the case." He glanced up the stairs, seemingly unsure as to whether to continue talking, and then turned back to Darby. "Selena was in the middle of something when she died. Her brothers don't know about it, but I'll tell them as soon as they're settled.

I can't speak for them, but I have a feeling they'll be wanting your help."

Darby met Dan Stewart's gaze. She guessed whatever Selena had been doing involved real estate, and wondered what kind of deal she'd set in motion. Was she attempting to acquire another property? Or sell part of the vineyard? Whatever the scenario, it meant more complications for the already overwhelmed Gomez brothers.

"If ET and Carlos want me to stay, I certainly will," she said.

He nodded. "Come on, I'll show you that guest room—just in case."

———

Andrea Contento strode up the hilly road toward Carson Creek, feeling the burn in her thigh muscles as she pushed up the incline. She stopped to catch her breath and an image flooded her mind.

Selena Thompson, her face flushed, panting along beside her at this very spot. When had it been? Five years ago? Andrea remembered her companion's thick, black braid swaying as they continued the climb up the hill. "Let's jump in the pool when we finish," Selena had suggested beneath breaths.

"You mean, *if* we finish," Andrea had gasped in a melodramatic tone.

"Oh, we'll make it, don't you worry." And they had, too, reached the crest of the hill, finished the walk, and then hit Carson Creek's pool. *We splashed around in the water like a couple of school girls. I borrowed one of Selena's suits—red with a white racing stripe—and she told me it looked so good I should keep it.*

Was it only five years ago? Andrea thought back. That was the summer Michael hired Christophe Barton to manage the vineyards with Tim. *Christophe took Dan's place when he went to work at Carson Creek for Selena.*

And the little minx never did apologize for hiring Dan away, Andrea thought. She just assumed it would be fine, that her new friend Andrea would let it go. *I did let it go. When it came to Selena, I let a lot of things go.*

Andrea kicked a small rock down the hillside and watched as it bounced off an old stump. Those months had been the real beginning of the two women's friendship. The long walks through the Ventano countryside, the sharing of recipes, the jokes and parties and glasses of wine. *Endless* glasses of wine.

Selena's purchase of the property the previous spring had been a welcome breath of fresh air for the valley. Andrea recalled the enthusiasm with which she'd tackled the aged farmhouse, renovating the structure from top to bottom. An interior designer by training, Selena had planned the property's new barn, installing an office, a pretty tasting room, and ample space for wine production. Dan had been her chief advisor, and together they had transformed the once derelict property into a charming little winery.

"It's in my blood," Selena had once explained about her passion for winemaking. "My grandfather worked in the vineyards outside of Ensenada, in the Guadalupe Valley. That's why I like wine so much, too."

Andrea had giggled, glad to have a friend who was so open, so fun.

But two years ago, things began to change. Selena grew more distant, keeping to herself up at Carson Creek and rarely returning phone calls. When Andrea bumped into her at the supermarket in St. Adina, Selena had seemed thinner and older with each encounter. Andrea, meanwhile, became consumed by the growing popularity of her husband's vineyard. Michael had finally been recognized for his contributions to the valley's wine industry, and with his designation of Winemaker of the Year had come a new celebrity for him and the vineyard. There were social engagements nearly every night, trips to France to promote the business, and a never-ending stream of celebrities and politicians to entertain on the vineyard grounds. *I didn't see much of Selena over the past few years. I tried, but she didn't seem to care anymore.*

And now friends and family were gathering at Selena Thompson's vineyard to mourn her passing. Michael and his son Tim were on the way over with a huge bowl of pasta with fresh pesto; Christophe Barton, Contento Family Vineyard's estate manager, had been dispatched to the airport to pick up Tim's twin Margo. Andrea, who needed to stretch her legs before facing the hordes, knew it was anyone's guess as to who else would show up at Carson Creek.

I wish we'd remained friends, Selena, Andrea Contento said under her breath. She sighed again and resumed her march up the hill.

———

"The vineyard was for sale?" Carlos Gomez was on the balls of his sandal-clad feet, hands upraised and eyes wide with disbelief. "You're telling me that Selena was trying to sell?" He shook his head, causing his black curls to bob wildly. "She loved this place. That's crazy."

Dan Stewart nodded. He glanced at ET who, as usual, was silent, his back straight and tall.

"She was selling it herself," Dan explained. "She decided a few months ago. She thought she could handle it alone and save some money in broker fees." He shot a look at Darby. "No offense."

"None taken," she said smoothly. Darby sat on a comfortable loveseat in the living room of Carson Creek's farmhouse, with ET seated nearby. Dan had opened up a bottle of the vineyard's Pinot Noir and they were sipping it slowly while waiting for the Contento family to arrive.

"Were there any offers on the property?" Darby set down her wineglass on the coffee table and looked at Dan Stewart, who nodded.

"Yes. As soon as word got out, there was interest. Michael Contento offered Selena what I imagine was a very fair price."

"How much?" Carlos demanded.

Dan shrugged. "I don't know the particulars."

"Was she going to sell to Michael Contento?"

"At first she planned to, and then ..." Dan paused. "There were other offers."

Carlos exhaled. "As in more than one?" He plunked down his wineglass, not noticing the small amount of red liquid that splashed onto the wood.

"That's right. An accountant from back east—her name is Vivian something. The second one's from a yoga expert with a TV show—Fritz Kohler. He wants to have a yoga retreat center here."

"And what are Vivian's plans?" Darby inquired.

"Selena said she wants to keep it just the way it is. She's looking for a lifestyle change, a quiet little place where she could retire."

Darby looked at ET, whose face wore an almost bemused expression. He caught her glance and gave a sheepish little grin.

"I can't help but think it is funny that in this market, my sister would have not one, but three offers on her property. She must have been some terrific salesperson."

"The property sells itself," Dan said, his voice tight.

Darby threw him a glance, surprised to see a look of longing cross his handsome features. *He wanted the property too*, she realized.

"So where does it stand now?" Carlos was finally sitting, although he looked ready to spring from his chair. "Who was the lucky one that Selena picked?"

Dan took a sip of wine and shrugged again. "I can honestly say that I don't know. She didn't tell me, and I didn't ask. I think she was prepared to call one of the buyers today."

Darby's mind went over the scenario. Multiple offers to purchase a breathtakingly beautiful vineyard, and then the untimely passing of the vineyard's owner. It was all so strange. She cleared her throat.

"Do you know if Selena had a will?"

The brothers glanced uncomfortably at each other and shook their heads.

"I found the contact information for her lawyer," Dan said. "I left a message at his office today."

"Thank you," murmured ET.

"In the meantime, what do we do about these offers on the property?" Carlos directed his question to Darby.

"I'd recommend doing nothing until you've had a chance to confirm the particulars of each offer as well as Selena's final wishes for the property," said Darby. "She may have mentioned something to her lawyer. It's too soon to do much more."

Carlos grimaced. "What if she already chose someone? Does her death negate the whole thing?"

Darby shook her head. "If she accepted one of the offers, chances are you will be obligated to carry out her wishes, but it won't be a quick sale."

"What do you mean?" Carlos asked. "Why not?"

"Under California law, the property will have to go through probate, and that's a long process. All of Selena's non-cash assets will need to be appraised by a probate referee, and that could take months."

ET spoke once more. "I don't understand. My sister loved Carson Creek. She poured her heart and soul, not to mention every penny, into this property. Why in the world would she have wanted to sell it?"

"I think I know why." Everyone turned to see Sophie Stewart, standing in the kitchen doorway, holding a tray full of plastic bottles with orange caps. Pointing at the prescription medicine, the teen drew on her training as a candy striper at Ventano Valley Community Hospital and stated in a clear, strong voice: "Selena Thompson was sick."

FOUR

Harrison Wainfield surveyed the St. Adina farmland with a critical eye. Twenty acres of prime grape-growing land, and only twenty minutes from town, but when he'd mentioned it to Margo Contento, she wouldn't even take a look. "Too far," she'd sniffed on the phone, and he'd known by her imperious tone that it was pointless to try and convince her otherwise. He gritted his teeth and gunned his Mercedes, sending small stones skittering in a plume below his tires.

The sienna-colored fields, now home to a dwindling herd of cows, whizzed by as the real estate agent sped up the hill leading away from the property. The Contento family had been his client for more than a decade, and the relationship was both a blessing and a curse. Sure, he'd made money buying and selling homes and land for them, but dealing with the various Contento personalities was not a walk in the park. Margo, with her mane of blonde hair and cover-girl looks, was a tigress. She and her father, Michael, were opinionated to the point where they barely listened to each other, never mind his wise advice. Tim, Margo's twin brother, came off as passive, but he could turn vicious in a heartbeat. And Andrea? To Harrison Wainfield, Michael Contento's wife equaled danger.

He pictured her pointed little face and sly smile and felt a longing that still, all these years later, made him hot with desire. His memories of the dark-haired brunette went back to the years before she'd married the much-older Michael, back when she was Andrea McDougal, paying off her college loans by being the twins' nanny.

Twenty-plus years ago. Could it really have been that long? Those were the days when the hills of Ventano Valley were still dotted with farms, when tourism was an industry that flourished someplace else. Restaurants back then catered to people who wanted dinner, not an "experience," and wine, if it was expensive, came from France.

He took a curve too sharply and felt a surge of adrenalin flood his veins. The key to satisfying the Contentos was Carson Creek. Michael was a fool not to have purchased the property years ago, back when Harrison had unrolled the surveys and spelled it all out. "Someday, you may want to expand Contento Family Vineyards," he'd predicted. "Getting this land now will give you that opportunity."

But Michael Contento had shut him right down, told him he didn't need any more property, and practically accused him of being a land pimp. *Idiot.*

That was weeks before Selena Thompson came out of nowhere to buy the acreage. Selena, who knew more about braiding her hair than she did about viticulture, and whose initial attempts at making wine were nothing short of ludicrous. She'd used words like "holistic, organic, biodynamic," and the wine makers of the valley had laughed behind her back. Harrison took a deep breath of the clean valley air as he zoomed past a recreational vehicle towing a tiny car. Selena had shown toughness in those early years, he had to give her that. Within months, she'd lured Dan Stewart from the Contentos and begun making wine in earnest. Gradually, the snickers turned to grudging admiration. And then, lo and behold, those ridiculous adjectives she'd tossed out came into fashion.

Rest in peace, Harrison Wainfield thought, swerving to avoid a red squirrel as his tires squealed in protest. Moments later he slowed the Mercedes, let his muscles relax, and stroked his strawberry-blonde goatee. What really mattered was that Carson Creek was once again available. The Contento family would get the extra land they wanted, thanks to him, and Andrea might be persuaded to show her gratitude.

He felt the familiar ache and smiled. It was practically a done deal.

———

Sophie Stewart brought a forkful of pesto-coated pasta to her lips. Delicious, but that generally was the case with anything that came out of the Contento's kitchen. She thought back longingly to when her father worked at Contento vineyards and a batch of freshly baked chocolate chip cookies would magically appear. They were to die for, Sophie remembered. Thick and yet soft, and absolutely chock full of milk chocolate morsels…

She chewed the bite of pasta and went for another scoop. Minutes earlier she'd seen annoyance on her father's face when she'd brought the tray of pills into the living room, but the Asian woman from San Diego with the funny name—Darby Farr—had quietly told her "Good job." And it had been a nice piece of detective work, finding all those prescription pills and knowing it meant Selena had some sort of serious illness. Her dad hadn't had any time to say anything, because the door was suddenly opened by the Contentos and a few people from town.

Sophie tucked her hair behind her ears, savoring the taste of the fresh basil and the perfect chewiness of the penne. Poor Selena had never cooked like this. Sophie remembered that she followed some kind of weird diet that meant all her food looked like—and probably tasted like—cardboard. Maybe that was because of all those medications. Despite the fact that Selena didn't make anything anywhere near as delicious as those chocolate chip cookies, Sophie knew her father had been much happier at Carson Creek than he had been when he'd worked at the Contento's vineyard. *Much* happier.

She bit her lip and thought about the question she could never seem to answer. Her father and Selena Thompson... had they been more than co-workers? Had they been lovers?

She squirmed at the thought.

It doesn't matter any more. Selena is gone.

Sophie took another bite of the pungent pasta and watched as her father crossed the living room to the kitchen. His cheeks were hollow, his head tilted down toward the polished wood floor. She chewed, swallowed, and gulped her fizzy water.

If Dad and Selena were lovers, it means he's not just sad but devastated. And it means that once more he's lost the woman he loved.

She wiped her mouth with a napkin, picked up her plate, and followed her father into the kitchen. He turned to face her, still holding his dish of uneaten food. On his face she read her answer. He was a man in mourning, a man with nothing left to lose.

———

"I'm glad there is a professional here to help Carlos and Enrique," commented the petite brunette as she held out her hand to Darby. She was in her forties and wore slim jeans and a pumpkin-colored blouse. "I'm from the neighboring vineyard. Andrea Contento."

Darby shook her hand. "I don't really know that I'm here to help them in any professional capacity. I drove ET—Enrique—up the coast because he's my friend. This was a huge shock to him, and to Carlos."

"To all of us." Andrea Contento gave a rueful look. "I'm absolutely stunned. I knew Selena didn't seem herself, and I'd heard rumors that she wasn't well, but I never suspected she was sick enough to die." She took a sip of her wine and frowned. "I wish I could have helped her. I'm going to miss her tremendously."

"What was wrong with Selena?"

"I don't know exactly. It seemed as if whatever it was, it made her very weak, that much I do know." She put down her wine glass. "A few years ago, she was the picture of health. We used to walk together just about every morning. Up the hills, down the hills, chatting all the while." Andrea Contento lowered her voice and grinned mischievously. "Selena knew the dirt on everyone in this town, and if she didn't she made something up. Believe me, we had some fascinating conversations."

"With Selena? Of course you did." A tall man with strawberry-blonde hair and a neatly trimmed goatee appeared beside Andrea

Contento. Darby watched as he placed a hand on her elbow. "I know you and Selena were good friends," he said softly. "I'm sorry."

Andrea nodded and tilted her head toward the man. "Meet your competition," she said to Darby. "This is Harrison Wainfield, one of our area's top real estate agents." She pursed her lips. "It's Darcy, isn't it?"

"Darby. Darby Farr."

Wainfield gave a little bow, holding her gaze as he did so. "Always a pleasure to meet a fellow realtor," he said. "Are you new in the area?"

"No, I work for Pacific Coast Realty, down in San Diego."

Harrison Wainfield's whole body melted into a more relaxed posture. "I see. What brings you to wine country?"

Darby explained that she worked with ET and had driven him up that afternoon. "I'm just here for the night," she said. "ET and his brother have a lot to work out."

Wainfield nodded. "I've already told Carlos that I'll be happy to help them deal with the sale of the property. I'll mention it to his brother, as well." He nodded in Andrea's direction. She'd moved to another group of people and had her arm entwined in an older man's. "The Contentos have wanted more acreage for quite some time now." His smile was wistful. "That's rather convenient, don't you think?"

Darby felt the pace of her heart quicken. It wasn't often that she disliked people on sight, but Harrison Wainfield was making the hairs on the back of her neck prickle. She watched as he fished in the pocket of his corduroy jacket, pulling out a glossy business card.

"Perhaps I'm making you uncomfortable, talking business at this kind of a gathering." He leaned toward her, and Darby smelled spearmint on his breath. "But in my thirty-odd years in real estate, I've found that absolutely any time is right for making deals."

He gave a smug smile and began weaving his way back through the small crowd and out the door. Darby shuddered and took another sip of her wine. No wonder Selena had chosen to sell the vineyard herself.

The gathering seemed a bizarre mixture of a cocktail party and a wake, a chance for people to express their shock over Selena's sudden death. Darby looked about for ET. She spotted him speaking with Andrea Contento and a tall, older man, and headed toward them.

ET made introductions, and Darby looked into the vigorous and tanned face of the famous winemaker, Michael Contento. He was tall and fit, his hazel eyes the color of the grape leaves Darby had glimpsed growing in the fields. He grasped her hand and shook it, and the strength of his grip was that of a man half his age, which Darby guessed to be in the mid-seventies.

"Damn shame about Selena," he said. "I can't believe she's gone."

"I wish I had known her," Darby confessed. "She must have had some very special qualities."

"Quite the accomplished grape grower, you know. She and Dan were putting out some fine wine. Her Pinots were getting a reputation in the state and beyond. Not to mention, she was a hell of a nice person."

ET nodded somberly. "Thank you, Professor Contento."

"Please, call me Michael. My teaching days are long gone—I'm lucky if I get a chance to read a whole book nowadays. This damn wine business keeps a man busy."

"Selena was busy as well, but always seemed to make time for fun," commented Andrea. She gave a tiny smile. "We had some great parties here and at the vineyard. Christmas—Halloween—you name it. Selena liked practical jokes, too. One year on April Fools' Day she made a special bottle of wine for Michael. Remember that, darling?"

He grinned. "Changed the label on one of my own bottles and brought it to dinner. I tasted it and couldn't believe how good the wine was. Little did I know I was drinking one of my own star Cabs."

"Cabernet Sauvignon," Andrea explained. "The label was something atrocious, like "Dwarf's Head" or something like that, with a horrible little drawing of a gnome sitting on a mushroom. You should have seen Michael's expression when he tasted the wine!" She laughed and then immediately became quiet. "That's what I will miss about her—that wonderful sense of humor."

The brief moment of lightheartedness evaporated as quickly as it had come. The Contentos hugged ET, murmured their sympathies, and moved away. Darby took another sip of her wine, deep in thought.

———

From the crest of a hill overlooking Carson Creek Estate & Winery, Vivian Allen focused her binoculars on the old farmhouse. It was nearly eight p.m., but cars were still arriving, carrying people who entered the spacious kitchen to pay their respects to Selena

Thompson's brothers. She directed the powerful lenses toward a window and waited. Catching a glimpse of one of them would be helpful, but it wasn't totally necessary. She pulled the photos from her jacket and scrutinized the images. The older one was Enrique; the younger, more fleshy-faced one, Carlos. She lingered on his photograph, committing his features to memory. *Carlos is a photographer from San Francisco*, she thought.

Vivian ran through her plan once more in her head. Wait for the rest of the visitors to leave, and then head down to the farmhouse and meet Carlos. If she could get him to listen to her strategy, she just might have a chance. *If…*

She shoved the binoculars back in the big pink shoulder bag that was draped over her shoulder. Timing was everything, and hopefully her time had come.

———

The man at the bar was drunk. Toby Bliss, owner of the Blissful Grape, glanced at the clock and then back at the stool where the guy was slumped, his massive head down flat on two enormously powerful arms. Only eight o'clock on a Friday night and the guy was out cold, his black hair sticking up at crazy angles from his shaggy head.

The door opened and a crowd of tourists entered, laughing and crowding toward a table in the corner. *Probably on their way back from a wine tasting party at one of the vineyards*, Toby thought. His experienced eye told him they were just boisterous enough to order several rounds with appetizers, and maybe dinner, too, but not inebriated enough to cause any trouble.

Unlike Mr. Universe, draped like a sack of potatoes over his bar. The guy seemed harmless, but Toby eyed his biceps with trepidation. He definitely lifted—a lot—and probably took enhancing drugs to boot. Toby took a step closer. A tattoo peeked from the guy's white tee shirt. It was some sort of a wheel from the looks of it, but that was as close as he wanted to get to those guns. He wiped down a section of the bar with a damp rag. The guy had downed tequila, straight, until he'd just laid down his head and passed out. From the sound of his snores, he'd be there awhile.

Toby looked around for Cecilia, who was turning out to be one of the worst waitresses on the planet. Figuring she was out back smoking a cigarette, he grabbed a few menus and a pad of paper and headed for the new arrivals, giving the man at the bar a wide berth. *The best course of action is to leave the big guy alone. Hopefully his wife—if he's got one—will realize he's missing and fetch him before too long.*

Toby approached the boisterous table and put on a big smile. "Hey folks," he said in what he thought was a Western twang. "Get you all something?"

———

Darby carried a platter of sliced turkey, ham, and cheese into the kitchen and placed them on the counter. ET was behind her, a basket of finger rolls in hand. She turned to him. With concern in her voice, she asked, "How are you holding up?"

He shook his head. "Not very well, I'm afraid. I feel like I will collapse any moment."

She nodded. The gathering had gone on much longer than she'd expected, with all kinds of people coming from neighboring towns to drop off food and pay their respects. They were beginning to leave, trickling out in small groups, and now only a few stragglers remained behind to help clean up. "Selena was certainly well loved," she said quietly.

"Yes." He looked around the kitchen. "Did I tell you about the holidays we spent here? When my mother was still alive, Carlos and I brought her for Christmas, and then another year for Easter. We had a wonderful time. Selena was a fabulous hostess, so happy to show off her winery and so proud of all she'd accomplished." He paused. "I am glad my mother got to see her like that."

Darby wondered why the family gatherings at Carson Creek had not continued, but she said nothing to her stricken friend. Instead she reached out and placed her hand on his. He gave a small, sad smile and walked heavily out of the kitchen.

Darby sighed. Would this have been any easier had Selena's brothers known she was sick? Why hadn't she confided in anyone from her family? *She wanted to keep her independence,* Darby thought. *I was the same way.*

She flashed back to Hurricane Harbor, Maine, the craggy island on which she'd been raised, and her decision as a teen to flee her hometown for California. It was not unlike what Selena Thompson had done, leaving her family to settle in a ramshackle Victorian in San Francisco. *Except Selena's family had been close-knit, and loving, and mine vanished in an afternoon, leaving me alone.* Perhaps Selena's ties, as well-meaning as they were, had been even harder to sever.

She looked up as Michael Contento entered the kitchen, a distinguished looking man by his side.

"Darby, this is Edward Martin, Selena's attorney." She looked up into the dark eyes of a handsome African American man wearing horn-rimmed glasses and a suit that showed off his athletic physique.

"I came as soon as I could," he said in a sonorous voice. "I'm absolutely shocked. Saddened, too. I really liked Selena."

"It's been a rough day for her brothers, but I know they'll want to meet you." She motioned for him to follow and threaded her way through the dining room and into the farmhouse's living room. ET was seated on an armchair, his brother beside him talking quietly to a neighbor.

She introduced the brothers to Attorney Edward Martin.

"I'm sorry to come so late," he said, "but I did bring a copy of your sister's will. Would you like to know the details now, or should we talk at some point over the weekend?"

Carlos leaned forward. "I'd like to hear it now."

ET shrugged, his face impassive.

Edward Martin opened a black binder. "It's very straightforward. She left everything to the two of you."

Carlos hung his head, muttering something softly under his breath.

"Enrique, your sister requested that you, as the eldest, serve as her Executor. In other words, you are legally empowered to make decisions concerning the disposal of her property. In terms of the vineyard, Selena met with me two months ago and we created a trust in which to hold the property. This means things can move along rather quickly, if that's what you both decide. Enrique, you were also named as the Successor Trustee. That title indicates that you are the point person for the trust." He paused. "I'll need to file some paperwork on Monday to make this appointment final, but that shouldn't be any problem." He looked from ET to Carlos, a kind look on his face. "You can call me anytime with questions. I just wanted to stop by and tell you how sorry I am."

The brothers nodded and Edward Martin handed ET the binder. "I'll see you both at the funeral. Again, my condolences."

Darby saw him to the door and nodded a goodbye. Back in the kitchen, she opened a drawer, found the plastic wrap, and stretched it over the deli meats, thinking about the attorney's words. Selena Thompson had lived life on her own terms, even as an ailing woman. Thank goodness she had possessed the foresight to draw up not only a will, but a trust. Darby knew from her experience that with a trust in place, ET and Carlos could conduct the sale of Carson Creek in a matter of weeks, if that was what they wanted.

A slight man with a smooth, shaved head and Michael Contento's handsome features entered the kitchen carrying a large tray of pesto-coated penne pasta. "May I?" He pointed at the plastic wrap and Darby tore off a generous sheet. Together they covered the platter and placed it in the refrigerator.

"Tim Contento," he said, pausing to lick pesto off his fingers before shaking her hand. His brown eyes were framed by thick brown lashes. "You came with Selena's brothers, right?"

"I'm Enrique's friend, Darby Farr. I think I met your mother and father earlier."

"Stepmother. Don't worry. You're not the only one who's made that mistake. Even though there are ten years between us, she looks incredibly youthful while I'm getting positively ancient." He grinned and his tanned face crinkled pleasantly. Just as quickly it clouded over in a frown. "Hey, I'm so sorry about Selena. She was a really great lady."

"So I understand. I didn't get the chance to meet her, but I know her brothers are devastated."

"As they should be. Such a sudden thing." He lowered his voice. "Carlos told me she hadn't been feeling well."

"Did she appear healthy to you?"

He frowned again and shook his head. "I'm not sure. I hadn't seen her around in awhile, and when I did she was moving slowly. But certainly none of us knew she was truly ill." He wiped his hands on a checkered towel and glanced at his watch. "Guess my sister isn't going to make it tonight. Why don't I get everyone else out of here so that people can get some sleep?"

Darby nodded. She felt weary, and could only imagine how Carlos and ET must feel. Not to mention Dan and his daughter, Sophie. "I think that's a good plan. Thanks for your help."

"That's what we do here in the valley," Tim said. "We help each other out." Moments later she heard him telling the remaining visitors that it was time to "let these folks get some rest."

When Darby reentered the living room, Carlos and ET had retreated upstairs. Only Dan Stewart remained in the room, standing and looking out a window into the darkness, his hands tucked into the pockets of his jeans. Darby gave a quick glance around the room for stray dishes or wine glasses, and spotted the slender figure of Sophie Stewart. She was in the adjoining dining room, leaning against the door frame, and watching her father intently. On her face Darby could see a mixture of tenderness and love. Without warning, Darby's eyes filled with tears and she backed slowly out of the room.

The farmhouse was still and silent under the dark California sky, the temperature lower now than it had been since the spring. Vivian Allen shivered in her thin denim jacket. She had walked a quarter mile in her strappy sandals up the hill to the estate, hoping to speak with Carlos Gomez, but now it looked as though that plan was on hold. She hugged her arms to her chest and swore softly. *I should have gone in earlier. But everyone stayed so long, and I didn't want to see that creep Wainfield ...*

She made an exasperated sound and turned to walk back down the hill to her car. Just then a swipe of fur against her ankle made her scream and stumble.

"What the ..." Vivian looked into the amber eyes of a cat as he turned his black and white body to rub once more against her calves. "Damn pest!" She wobbled on her sandals, making sweeping motions with her hands. "Shoo! Shoo! Go home!"

Jasper glared at her, narrowed his eyes, and leapt silently into the brush.

———

Back at the farmhouse, Darby Farr peered into the inky night. A cry had startled her and she'd gone to the closest window. Was it the shriek of a jay? Or something else? She shook off the unsettled feeling and reached for her smart phone. Time to respond to the list of e-mails she'd ignored all day long.

She responded to Helen Near's chatty message and Tina's engagement news as best she could, although she felt the need to tell them both about Selena's untimely death. Replying to the mysterious Kenji Miyazaki was far easier. She simply told the businessman from Genkei Pharmaceuticals that she had no wish to meet with him.

Several e-mails could be handled by Claudia Jones, and Darby forwarded them with a brief message explaining that she planned to drive home the following day.

ET and Carlos weren't the most communicative of siblings, but they'd need to overcome their different styles and manage their sister's affairs. *They'll have to figure it out*, Darby thought.

Feeling a vague sense of uneasiness, she climbed into the guest room's double bed. Hours later she fell into a troubled sleep.

———

"Closing time," announced Toby Bliss, prodding the still slumped figure at the bar. Once again he jabbed a finger into the guy's shoulder, noting how the white fabric of his tee shirt puckered and then released. "Come on, I'll get you a cab."

Slowly the man, whom Toby had started to think of as "The Incredible Hulk," raised a shaggy head. He wiped his mouth with the back of his hand, smearing drool across his cheek. "What's going on?"

"You're in a bar and you had a little too much to drink," Toby said, thinking this was surely the understatement of the year. "Time to go home."

The man turned his head slowly from side to side and tried to swallow. His eyes were dark and unfocused. Toby shoved a cup of black coffee in front of him. "Drink up," he said.

Obediently he took the cup and drained it in one gulp, again wiping his mouth with the back of his hand. "I've got a car out back."

"That may be true, but you're in no shape to drive." Toby picked up the phone. "Where you staying?"

"St. Adina. Little motel."

Toby thought a long moment. His girlfriend would kill him, but maybe she didn't need to know every single thing he did. "I'm going that way," he said. "I'll give you a ride, just as long as you don't get sick in my car."

The corners of The Incredible Hulk's mouth lifted in what was nearly a smile. "No worries." He reached behind him and Toby saw the circular tattoo—some sort of spoked wheel—on his bicep. The man plunked down a wallet thick with bills. "I owe you for those shots."

"Yeah, you're right about that." He collected the money and breathed a silent sigh of relief. *The guy can't be an ax murderer*, he reasoned. *There's no way he'd be paying off his bar tab.* He put the cash in the register and yelled to Cecilia to lock up. Turning to the Hulk he said simply, "Time to get out of here."

FIVE

DAN STEWART SWITCHED OFF a small television set positioned on the butcher-block counter in Selena's kitchen and pointed at the coffee pot. His red-rimmed eyes were already tired. "Good morning, Darby. Can I get you a cup?"

She nodded and took a seat at the kitchen table. "Thanks. It's Saturday, right? What are you doing here?"

"I thought I'd better come in and keep an eye on things." His voice caught.

"Where's Sophie?"

"I dropped her at a friend's house last night. She'll call when I need to pick her up."

"Have you seen ET or Carlos?"

He shook his head. "I'm sure they are exhausted. What about you? How did you sleep?"

"Not very well, I'm afraid. The room is very comfortable but . . ."

"This kind of thing isn't conducive to resting, I know." He took a seat at the table and rubbed his eyes. He wore a plaid cotton shirt, rolled up at the sleeves, and jeans. "I figure work is the best thing I can do right now. It's how I can help Selena the most, too." He looked down at his hands, struggling to compose his thoughts. After a minute he spoke again. "According to the report I just heard on television, we're in for some crazy weather. This cold front's gonna give way to a heat spike, believe it or not. That means we'll probably have to push up the harvest."

"The grapes?"

"That's right. I was planning on late next week at the earliest, but if the temperatures climb like they're predicting, it could be much sooner."

"How do you know?"

"Oh, an incredibly scientific test—I'm not sure you'd understand." He saw her look of surprise and grinned. "I taste them. Fortunately for me, grapes are my favorite fruit." The shuffle of feet made them both look up simultaneously. A rumpled Carlos Gomez pointed at the coffee pot and groaned.

"I think I drank too much of my sister's wine last night," he moaned. "The red stuff and I just don't agree. I'm more of a gin man, myself."

Dan handed him a cup of coffee. "Which did you drink? The Pinot?"

Carlos shrugged. "Maybe it's not the kind that mattered, but the amount." Lifting the coffee cup to his lips and taking a sip, he sighed. "Just what the doctor ordered."

"Speaking of doctors," began ET, declining coffee and pouring himself a glass of water, "Who was my sister's physician?" He was impeccably dressed, as usual, in pressed tan pants and a striped Oxford shirt. "I'd like to find out just how sick she was."

Dan nodded. "She saw Jenna Yang, a local internist with a very good reputation." He opened a drawer and pulled out a flowered appointment book. "I'm sure Selena would have her number in here." He flipped through a few pages and handed it to ET. "Top of the page."

ET studied the book. "She was supposed to see Dr. Yang on Monday," he muttered. He shook his head and looked at his brother. "Why didn't she tell us about her illness? I don't understand."

Carlos spread out his hands in a gesture of incomprehension. "Who knows? She was stubborn, that little sister of ours, and she didn't like us interfering."

"I'm not sure she told anyone." Dan Stewart poured more coffee into Darby's and Carlos' cups. "I could tell when Selena was in pain, because we worked together so closely, but she never wanted to talk about it. I think she did her best to hide her illness. Maybe she was afraid people would treat her differently. Even me."

Darby thought a moment. "I think she was right about that. I've spoken to women with chronic illness who have to keep their conditions a secret from their employers and clients. Theoretically discrimination is illegal, but we all know that kind of thing happens." She took a sip of coffee. "And think about the sale of the vineyard. As far as that's concerned, keeping quiet was also smart. Why give a buyer a negotiating advantage?"

"What do you mean?" Carlos asked, running a hand through his bushy hair. "Remember, my brain is fuzzy this morning."

"Darby means that if a buyer knew you were sick, they would use that as leverage against you and not offer as much for a property," said ET. He rinsed his glass and put it on a drying board. "I am going to speak with the priest later this morning and discuss Selena's mass. I guess we need to take a look at those three offers as well." His eyes sought Darby's. "I hate to ask for more assistance from you, Darby, but will you look at those with us?"

"Of course." She glanced at Carlos. "I know that Harrison Wainfield spoke to you as well, Carlos."

"Yeah. Seems like a nice enough guy. Said he'd be happy to list the vineyard for us if we wanted a fresh start."

The coffee pot slammed on the counter with such force that it rattled the glasses in the cabinet. "Sorry," Dan Stewart muttered. Darby watched as he struggled to get his emotions in check. "Here's the deal: Harrison Wainfield works for the Contentos. All he cares about is helping them acquire Carson Creek so he can collect a nice fat check."

Carlos raised his bushy eyebrows. "Oh." He glanced at Darby and ET. "And what's so bad about the Contentos getting the property? God knows they can pay for it, and they seem like decent people. Look at the way they came over with all that food."

"And they have offered their private chapel for Selena's funeral," ET murmured.

Dan licked his lips, considering his words. "Michael Contento is a very decent man. A good man." He paused. "I don't know if I can explain it. On the one hand, they'll take Carson Creek and make the wines famous, I know that. We're producing a damn good product here and with their marketing muscle, it could be on everyone's list of favorites in a few years." He sighed and shook his head. "Contento Family Vineyards is a corporate winery. I don't believe Selena would have wanted to see Carson Creek become just another of their labels."

He looked at the brothers with an earnest expression. "I'm not sure if you know how we worked here, how special this place is." He sighed. "In the vineyard, we have our own small crew and do all of our own tractor work and hand labor. Most vineyards—like Contento—have farm teams of a hundred people to do one operation, like leaf-pulling, and then do another operation with a whole different set of workers." His face was growing more animated. "But you don't build a vine-by-vine relationship like that, and that's what mattered to Selena. We walk the same rows every day, and we treat each vine individually." He looked down at his hands. "That's what makes Carson Creek different."

Darby regarded him quietly. "Dan, did you ever let Selena know that you wanted the property?"

He whipped his head around, clearly surprised. "That was out of the question. Whatever Selena was asking for Carson Creek, it's more than I've got saved."

"Did Selena know of your interest?"

He gave a harsh chuckle. "Did Selena know how I felt about this place? Is that what you're asking?" He sucked in a breath and then with great effort whispered, "Yeah, she knew."

The other three watched as he walked out of the room.

"Well, that explains a lot," said Carlos, hefting his body off the chair and heading toward the coffee machine. He poured the steaming beverage into his mug.

ET raised his eyebrows. "Such as?"

"Obviously he's angry that Selena wasn't going to hand over her property. He admits he couldn't afford it, but he thinks she should have just given it to him." He ran a hand through his unruly curls. "I'm not sure if he should continue working here."

ET shook his head. "Carlos, I disagree. It's evident that Dan loves this place. It's that love for the property that is speaking. I think we need to listen to what he says."

Carlos frowned and looked at Darby. "I know that my brother trusts your judgment. And after all, he is the executor of the will." She heard the sarcasm in his voice. "What do you think?"

Darby turned her almond eyes toward the younger Gomez brother. "I can see where you'd be concerned, Carlos, but it seems to me that Dan Stewart is totally committed to the vineyard and knows the operation here inside and out." She looked through the window, watching as Dan headed out to the fields, undoubtedly to test the ripeness of the grapes. "If you want to sell Carson Creek, the last thing you want to do is jeopardize the harvest, or lose Dan's expertise and passion. He's recognized as one of the top winemakers in the valley. Anyone purchasing this property would be lucky to have him."

"Okay, okay." Carlos rose from his chair. "I don't trust the guy, but I'll listen to you. Tell me, Rico, what do we do now?"

ET pointed at his sister's appointment book and Darby saw pain etched across his handsome face. "There is a private number listed for Dr. Yang. I'm going to call her."

"To find out exactly what Selena died from?" Carlos looked perplexed.

"Yes. Perhaps she also knows Selena's wishes." He looked at his brother. "We need to decide what happens to her body."

Carlos put his head in his hands. "*Dio*," he murmured, in a plaintive cry for help.

———

Dr. Jenna Yang's voice was crisp and clear. "Normally I won't discuss a patient's illness without their consent, but I do make exceptions. In this case I feel that you, as Selena's closest family members, are entitled to know about her condition." She paused and Darby waited, listening over the speakerphone with Carlos and ET. "Your sister was suffering from a slow paralysis brought on by Guillain-Barré syndrome, a condition in which the insulators around the body's nerves, the myelin sheaths, are destroyed by the immune system."

"Paralysis?" Carlos ran a hand through his hair. "But no one here even knew."

"She was determined to disguise her symptoms; nonetheless, it was becoming impossible for her to walk without pain. I suggested to her at our last visit that it was time she get a cane. I suspect that a wheelchair would not have been far behind."

"Would this disease have gone away? Would she have been able to walk again?" ET's normally resonant voice was shaky.

"It's difficult to say. Selena was such a fighter that I think she would have worked very hard to regain her mobility, although she probably would never have been pain-free."

ET gripped the table. "Is it common for patients with this syndrome to have heart attacks?"

Jenna Yang paused. They heard the sound of rustling paper. "I think we should speak in person. Could you come into my office in downtown St. Adina? I'm heading there in forty minutes to do some paperwork."

ET looked at his brother and then at Darby. "We'll be there," he said.

———

The winemaker was in the middle of one of the fields, row upon row of trellised vines flanking him. He looked up as Darby approached.

"Hey." Dan Stewart's sandy brown hair was disheveled and he had a sheepish look on his face. He shielded his eyes from the sun. "Sorry if I was a little abrupt back there."

"I can't imagine how you must be feeling," Darby said. "You and Selena worked very closely for several years."

"Five years. She was like a sister to me." He raised his face to the sun. "This was the kind of day she loved."

Darby fingered a cluster of grapes. They were glossy purple, and firm to the touch. "Have you always been in wine production?"

He nodded. "Growing up here, It was a natural choice. Before I worked for Selena, I was at Contento Family Vineyards."

"In the same capacity? As their winemaker?"

"Pretty much. Contento is a bigger operation, so there are many more fingers in the pie, so to speak. That's what attracted me to Carson Creek. Selena was passionate about doing a small-scale but excellent product, right from the beginning. She was uncompromising in how the grapes were raised and how the wine was made."

"What do you mean?"

"I mean she took the whole organic thing seriously. For her, it wasn't just a marketing term, it was a philosophy. Here at Carson Creek, we pay attention to soil depletion and erosion, water pollution, resistance to pests, and chemical dependence—things like that." He snapped off a cluster of deep purple grapes and handed them to Darby. "Go ahead, give them a taste."

She pulled off a grape and popped it in her mouth while Dan Stewart chuckled.

"That's how you taste grapes? Come on, I thought you were a Californian." He grabbed another bunch and held it before her. "This is how you taste them. Put a bunch in your mouth and then pull the stem." He demonstrated as purple juice dribbled onto his shirt. "See?"

Darby opened wide and put about half of the cluster in her mouth. She pulled the stem and bit down, while the wonderful sensation of crushed grapes filled her senses. She tasted juice, skins, and a rich velvety flavor that hinted of blackberries, cherries, and the rich California earth.

"Ummm…" She wiped her mouth with her hand and Dan laughed.

"Now you're talking. So what do you think? Are they ready to pick?"

"I don't have a clue, but I can tell you this: they are delicious. Pinot?"

"Correct. Pinot Noir grapes, the hardest to grow, but also, in my humble opinion, the best." Suddenly his mood grew somber and he swore softly under his breath. "It just keeps coming back to me—she's gone. Selena is gone. I can't believe she isn't going to celebrate this harvest after all she's been through."

Darby looked into his tanned face, saw the circles under his blue eyes.

"What do you mean? Her illness?"

Dan shook his head. "Maybe I was obtuse, but I didn't register that there was an illness—not a serious one, anyway. I can think back to times when she seemed wiped out, but I had no idea there was something so wrong."

"Then what did you mean?"

He looked confused.

"You said 'after all she's been through'—what did you mean by that?"

Dan tossed the grape stem into the field. "Strange things happened over the past few months. A string of bad coincidences—or, at least that's what we tried to tell ourselves."

"What kinds of coincidences, Dan?"

"I guess the first thing was a fungus in the barrels, which fortunately we caught before it ruined too much of the wine. Then, one of our batches of yeast was so bad it would have spoiled production. Thank God we managed to find out before we'd added it to the juice." He exhaled. "Was all this nasty luck? Maybe. But Selena wasn't so sure."

"What are you saying?" Darby felt her pulse quicken.

"She was concerned." He kicked the dirt with a work boot and sighed. "She started looking at security systems."

"For protection?"

Dan gave her a level gaze. "Selena believed that someone was trying to destroy Carson Creek."

———

Vivian Allen parked her rental car next to a beautifully restored Karmann Ghia with California plates and sauntered up to the door of the tasting room of Carson Creek Estate & Winery. "Hello?" she called out. "Anybody home?"

She opened the heavy oak door and stepped in. A curving bar dominated one part of the room; a small gift shop the other. "Hello?" she called out again.

Footsteps came from another part of the building and a door opened to reveal a stout man with curly black hair and bushy eyebrows. "I'm sorry—we aren't open," he said.

"Carlos?" Vivian's face broke into a big smile. "Are you Selena's brother Carlos?"

He nodded, puzzled.

"I'm Vivian, Vivian Allen," she announced, striding toward him and extending her hand. "Selena told me all about you! You're a photographer in San Francisco, right? She gave me your website and I'm dying to have a look. She went on and on about how talented you are." Vivian clasped her hands in front of her and beamed. "And I can't wait to tell Selena that her description of you was dead on."

Carlos put a hand through his hair and shook his head slowly. "Selena…is…" his breath caught. "She passed away on Thursday."

"What?" Vivian Allen gasped, leaning against the bar for support. "But I just spoke to her on Wednesday! How can that be? What happened?"

"We are not sure yet, but she may have had a heart attack. We are about to go and see her doctor."

"Oh my God," Vivian's head sunk in dismay. "Carlos I am so, so, sorry. Your sister was—well, we'd become very good friends. I know our friendship would have continued even after I'd purchased the vineyard."

He gave her a quick glance. "You were going to buy Carson Creek?"

"Yes, that's right. I'm sure you knew that it was for sale. Selena was lucky enough to receive several offers, but I was the fortunate one she'd chosen to be the new owner." She pulled some papers out of a voluminous pink pocketbook. "I'd be happy to show you…"

Carlos peered at the papers. "Maybe you'd better come into the farmhouse and meet my brother," he offered.

"Enrique? I'd like to see him, although I would have preferred to have done so under happier circumstances. I'm in shock, I really am. Selena was such a fabulous woman! With so much more living to do!" She followed Carlos out the oak door and down a curving path leading into the main house. "There's the pool," she said, pointing a graceful arm in the direction of the cabana. "And she loved soaking in that hot tub."

Carlos gave her a pained look but said nothing.

The pair entered the farmhouse living room where Enrique sat leafing through a file of papers. He stood up as his brother and Vivian approached.

"Rico, this is Ms. Allen. She's one of the bidders on the property."

ET regarded the tall redhead. "Please, sit down," he said.

Vivian draped her tall frame on a nearby couch and ran a hand through her tousled hair.

"I'm so sorry to be barging in here! I had no idea this had happened. I explained to your brother that Selena and I had become quite friendly. I'm going to miss her tremendously."

ET nodded. "Thank you for your kind words."

"Rico," Carlos interjected. "Selena was planning to sell Carson Creek to Ms. Allen. She has some documents…"

"Yes, they're right here." Vivian pulled a stack of white papers out of her pink pocketbook. "We spoke on Tuesday and agreed that my price was acceptable. I'm buying the vineyard right after the holidays."

ET looked sharply at his brother and then at the stack of papers. "You know that there were other offers..."

"Oh yes, in fact I told Selena from the beginning that I would do my best to match the highest one."

Carlos' head jerked upward. "You did?"

Vivian nodded. "Owning a vineyard has been my dream for years, and when I saw Carson Creek, I absolutely fell in love with it. I'm a financial analyst, but a few years ago I had a significant health scare." She gave a rueful smile. "Cancer. That was when I said to myself, 'Carpe diem!' and I started to look seriously for a property." She sighed. "Your sister and I often discussed the fragility of life. I think my personal story resonated with her. After all, she was fighting her own health battles."

ET gave a quick inhale. "She told you about her illness?"

"Not the nitty-gritty details." Her voice grew softer. "We discussed how difficult it was to tell other people—even people we loved—that we were sick." She looked down at her hands. "People treat you differently when they know you have a chronic illness. They mean well, but still—it's very difficult."

ET cleared his throat. "Carlos, would you mind going out to the vineyard and finding Darby? I would like her to meet Ms. Allen before we head to St. Adina."

Carlos nodded, rose, and headed out to the fields.

SIX

Darby's first impression of the tall woman with wavy auburn hair was that she looked vaguely familiar. Her second thought was that she was working very hard to assure ET and Carlos that she had been chosen as the purchaser for Carson Creek.

"I asked your sister whether Dan would be interested in staying on," she was saying as Darby entered, "and Selena thought that was a distinct possibility. I know that would be very helpful for us as we get going in this business."

"Us?" Darby inquired. "Do you have a partner?"

She shook her head emphatically. "It's just me and my cocker spaniel. He's such a good companion that I do think of us as a team. It's silly, I know, but the little guy has been my salvation." Vivian Allen gave a nervous giggle. "You must be Darby."

"Yes. May I take a look at your contract for the sale of Carson Creek?"

"Of course." Vivian handed her the papers and turned back to ET and Carlos. "Anyway, what do we need to do to finalize things?"

She stopped, slapped a hand over her mouth, and exclaimed, "Forgive me! Of course you have some arrangements to make, now that Selena has passed away."

"That's right." ET nodded gravely. "We need a little time, Ms. Allen, but we will look over these papers carefully and figure this thing out. Just give us a few days."

"Of course." She scooped up her pink pocketbook. "You can keep those—I have another set of copies. And my phone number is right here." She handed ET a card. "Please keep me posted."

Darby raised a finger as if to ask a question.

"One quick thing, Ms. Allen. Your offer to Selena Thompson isn't signed."

"Of course it is! My signature is everywhere."

"I mean, it isn't signed by Selena."

"Well, that's right, I guess. We agreed on the phone. I thought I'd bring the papers to her in person." She frowned. "I know she had every intention of signing."

There was an awkward silence as Vivian Allen left the room.

––––––––

"Your sister did not have a heart attack," stated Jenna Yang, steepling her hands together as she regarded Carlos and ET. She peered over blue-framed glasses at them, her angular face sharp-boned but pretty, in a severe kind of way. "I apologize for being blunt, but I've examined her body and conferred with the county coroner. The autopsy revealed no damage to the heart muscle." She paused, as if to let the words sink in. "Myocardial infarction was not the cause of death."

Darby Farr sat in the back of Jenna Yang's office in a brick building in downtown St. Adina, willing to give moral support but not wishing to intrude on the brothers' time with the physician. They had driven over together in Darby's Karmann Ghia as soon as Vivian Allen departed, hoping to glean more information about Selena's unexpected death. Now Darby watched as ET and Carlos absorbed this startling news, their faces a mixture of pain and confusion.

"If she did not have a heart attack, then how did my sister die?" ET's voice was barely more than a whisper.

Dr. Yang pursed her lips. "Her lungs were full of water, indicating drowning. I imagine that it happened quite peacefully. I believe she simply fainted and then slipped under the water."

"Fainted?"

The physician nodded. "Perhaps when she was getting out of the hot tub. Her blood pressure dropped as she stood, causing her to lose consciousness."

Carlos' hand slammed down on his chair's wooden armrest. "She should never have gotten that thing! I told her they were dangerous, that they breed diseases, but she wouldn't listen to me!"

"Hot tubs can be hazardous, Carlos," the doctor said gently, removing the blue frames from her face. "But your sister knew the risks. Keep in mind that warm water was also very therapeutic. It helped her cope with the pain when nothing else could." She rose and walked around her desk. Putting a hand on Carlos' shoulder, she said, "I knew your sister well. She was determined to live life to its fullest, illness or no illness. I very much admired Selena, and I will miss her tremendously."

The brothers rose from their seats. "*Gracias*," ET whispered to Dr. Yang. "Thank you for your kind words."

Darby waited a moment until the brothers were out of the office before asking her questions.

"Doctor, did Selena have low blood pressure?"

"No, quite the contrary. She suffered from hypertension. But the temperature of the water and the alcohol in the wine would have caused her blood vessels to dilate, decreasing her blood pressure."

"And that was enough to cause fainting?"

Dr. Yang sighed. "I'm afraid so."

———

The ride back to Carson Creek Estate & Winery was quiet. Darby let her eyes wander over the rows of vines, thinking about Selena's last moments in the hot tub. Hopefully it had been a peaceful death, a mere slipping from one reality to the next.

Dan Stewart met them at the door of the farmhouse with a red folder. "I think this is what you've been looking for," he said, handing the folder to ET. "I found it in Selena's desk in the office. I believe you'll discover three offers to purchase Carson Creek inside."

ET thanked him and motioned to Darby. Taking her out of earshot, he gave her a frank look. "Carlos and I talked. We'd like to sign a contract with you to handle the sale of the vineyard."

"You know I'm happy to help you, ET, but are you sure this is what you want? There are plenty of good realtors here."

"I know, but we want you." He paused. "Not only do I know firsthand what an exceptional agent you are, but I appreciate your kindness to my sister."

Darby looked puzzled. Had ET forgotten that she and Selena had never met?

She waited while he continued.

"A few months ago, I asked you for fifty thousand dollars, and you did not inquire as to why I needed it." He took a few seconds to compose his thoughts. "Darby, that money was for Selena." He looked heavenward, as if for answers, and continued. "Perhaps I should have asked her why she needed such a large sum, but I didn't want to pry. Now I have the chance to pay you back through the sale of this property. Choosing you as the broker means Carlos and I can give you something for helping my sister."

Darby nodded. "I see." She looked over the rows of vines and then back at her friend. "It's a gorgeous property, ET, and you must know I'd love to sell it. Let me think about the logistics before I say yes."

"Fair enough. I for one would like to wait on all this until after Selena's mass, but Carlos is of a different mind. Will you join us to look over the contents of the folder?"

"Of course. Depending on what we find, you may not even need a broker for Carson Creek."

"Perhaps not." He sighed. "I have one last favor to ask of you." He glanced down at his well-manicured hands. "Will you stay until Selena's service on Monday? You've been so helpful to me. I don't think I could sort through all this without you, and you're one of the few people Carlos will listen to."

Darby sensed that ET liked having her as a buffer for his hot-tempered brother, and she did not mind playing the role. As an only child, Darby was intrigued by siblings and their relationships, however rocky.

Darby squeezed her assistant's shoulder. "I'm happy to stay, ET." She pictured her suitcase's contents. The few casual items of clothing she had grabbed before leaving Mission Beach were hardly adequate for a funeral service. *I may need to make a quick shopping trip,* she thought. A little voice inside added: *There are worse things in the world.*

———

"Who the heck is this Fritz Kohler, outside of being buyer number three?" Carlos waved one of the offers in the air, a puzzled expression on his fleshy face. He lifted a glossy brochure advertising a series of workout DVDs and frowned. "And how in the world can he be a yoga instructor? He's immense! He looks more like a boxer than some guy who can twist himself into a pretzel."

"His discipline is called power yoga," corrected ET. "It's a blend of yoga, body sculpting, plyometrics..."

"Plyo-what? Oh never mind!" Carlos tossed the papers on an empty pressed-back chair. "I don't get it. All three offers are unsigned, and all are for the same amount. Nine million dollars. It's as if she told them the price and they matched it."

"That may indeed be what happened," Darby said. "Selena knew what she wanted to get when she sold, and she wasn't taking any less."

"Could she have gotten more?" Carlos twirled a pencil, deep in thought.

"Perhaps. We don't know how much she played the three buyers off against one another. The question is, are any of them willing to pay any price?"

"I think you will find that the answer is yes, at least where one of the buyers is concerned." The smooth voice of Harrison Wainfield slid through the room like butter. "I knocked, but no one answered." He glided across the floor of the dining room and gave a tight little smile. "Forgive me for intruding. I was in the area and thought I'd stop by." He glanced at the offers spread out on the table. "It certainly seems my timing is impeccable."

"You've got that right." Carlos stood and shook the realtor's hand. "We've got three offers here, all the same price. For some reason, my sister selected one of them, but who knows why."

ET shot his brother a warning look. "Carlos, we need to discuss this privately first."

Carlos barked out a laugh. "I know you, Rico. You'll discuss it to death. There's nothing to talk about, anyway. Selena picked Vivian. This place is already sold, right?"

Like a shot, ET sprang from his chair and confronted his brother. "Listen to me, Carlos. We have a sister to bury. Selling her real estate is hardly our first priority." He turned to Harrison Wainfield. "I ask you to leave us now, so that we can talk privately."

"Of course." He spread his hands in an understanding gesture. "Anything I can do to help, please call."

Darby rose as well. "I'll be outside," she murmured. She met ET's anguished eyes and gave a small nod, hoping he knew that she believed he was right.

———

Harrison Wainfield lingered outside the door of the winery. "Tough situation," he commented, unwrapping a piece of gum and popping it into his mouth. The scent of spearmint wafted on the late morning air. "What did Carlos mean when he said Selena picked Vivian?" He frowned. "You've got to wonder whether the poor thing was in her right mind, making such important decisions. One could argue that she wasn't mentally capable."

Darby remained silent, fighting the urge to punch Harrison Wainfield in his pompous nose.

He continued, blissfully unaware of her strong feelings. "Between you and me, the Contentos will pay just about anything to get this vineyard, and they've got the resources to do it." He frowned, fishing in his pocket. "Did I give you my business card?"

"I don't need it."

His eyebrows shot up in surprise.

"The Gomez brothers have asked me to handle the sale of Carson Creek. We'll be working out the details of Selena's estate, and then contacting the buyers. You might want to advise the Contentos to make their best offer at that time." She whirled and left Harrison Wainfield standing in the dust, his business card in his hand.

———

Dan Stewart was standing by a battered yellow tractor in the old barn. Darby took one look at his wild expression and her anger at Harrison Wainfield melted away.

"What's up?" The post-and-beam structure smelled of hay mingled with lavender. "You look homicidal."

"That's because I am, and it all has to do with that daughter of mine. I tell you, Darby, raising teenagers is murder." He held up a bottle of wine. "I found this in here, hidden over in the corner. I went and picked up Sophie and asked her point blank if she put it there. She did!"

Darby couldn't help but smile. "At least she's got good taste, right? She's sticking with the Carson Creek label."

Dan managed a weak grin. "It's one of our best pinots, to tell you the truth. Selena's pride and joy." He frowned. "The other day Sophie tried to wear this ridiculously short skirt to school, and now this. These are the times I absolutely hate being a single parent."

"I imagine it's tough, for both you and Sophie."

"Yeah." He sighed. "When Natalie died, I decided to put all my energy into raising our daughter. And that's what I've done. There hasn't been time for much else, between running vineyards and keeping an eye on her." He looked at the bottle of wine again. "I'm starting to think that I did it all wrong. Maybe I should have concentrated on finding her a mother instead."

Darby watched him leave the old barn, the bottle gripped in one hand. Dan Stewart had his hands full with the harvest, Selena's death, and an impending sale. Now he had to worry about underage drinking as well.

She turned to leave, her eyes falling on an old scythe leaning against the barn wall. It was a beautiful hand-crafted tool, with a wooden handle smooth from years of use.

Her gaze swept the floor of the barn, noticing a small piece of paper just a few feet from the scythe. Curious, she knelt and picked it up. It was a crumpled receipt from a store. Darby scrutinized the address. *Save-All Pharmacy, St. Adina, California*, she read. She shrugged and, without bothering to study it further, put it in her pocket.

The air outside the barn felt fresh and clean against Darby's face. Wishing to give ET and Carlos some space, she found herself wandering into the fields among the straight rows of vines. She marveled that the russet earth and dry air were able to produce such bounty. *It's so different from Maine*, she thought, remembering the lush greens, tall pines, and dark brown soil of the island on which she'd been raised.

At the far edge of one field was a small shelter, barely more than a lean-to, and Darby marched toward it. She was about to continue past the structure when she heard a sighing sound.

Startled, she peered inside the shelter.

Sophie Stewart was sitting on the wooden floor, her chin on her denim-covered knees.

"Hey, you okay?" Darby spoke quietly.

The girl looked up and nodded. "I'm just sitting here a minute."

Darby regarded the lean-to with curiosity. "What is this place?"

"A little picnic spot for the guys who work in the fields. You know, so they can eat their lunch out of the sun."

"Oh." Darby paused. She guessed that she knew why Sophie was here. "Your dad's pretty upset, huh?"

"I'm the one who should be upset," Sophie said indignantly. "He picks me up at my friend's house, practically explodes when we get in the car, and then he doesn't even listen to me. I told him I didn't drink that wine. The bottle was already empty."

"Then why did you take it?"

"Because it was the last thing she was drinking!"

"Who? Selena?"

The teen nodded sullenly. "It sounds stupid, really stupid—but I thought he might want the bottle, for a kind of keepsake."

"Your dad jumped to conclusions."

She nodded emphatically. "Totally! As if I'd be drinking Carson Creek Pinot Noir!" She made an exasperated sound and rolled her eyes. "He's always doing that. Like he thinks I'm some major loser or something."

"I know he doesn't think that. It's just that he's worried about you."

"Yeah, well I'm the one who should be worried! He's in total denial about his feelings for Selena, and now she's gone, and it's like the death of my mom all over again." She put her head on her knees once more.

Darby's heart ached for the girl. "Your dad will be okay. Why don't you tell him that you're concerned? I think he'd really like to communicate more with you."

She looked up, seemed to consider Darby's words, and then rolled her eyes once more.

"Give me a break. The last thing he wants to talk about with me is his love life."

"What about telling him why you took the bottle? Wouldn't that be a start?"

"Maybe." She rose to her feet and wiped the back of her jeans with her hand. "I'm going to go for a walk. If you see my dad, please tell him I'll be back at the house in a little while." She managed a tiny grin. "Thanks, Darby."

———

Dan Stewart shook his head in amazement when Darby told him about the wine bottle. "Sophie has this idea that Selena and I were lovers." He sighed.

"Were you?"

He looked at her sharply before answering. "You can be kind of nosy, you know that?" He shrugged. "Sophie may have picked up on some of Selena's vibes."

"What do you mean?"

He raised his eyes upward as if avoiding her gaze. "I mean that Selena wanted to be more than friends."

"I see. But you didn't feel that way?"

"I liked her, respected her, and enjoyed her company. But I didn't want to take it any further, and I certainly didn't want to get married." His ran a hand through his hair. "She knew how much I loved this place, so she suggested that we tie the knot even if I wasn't in love with her. She said that way, if anything happened to her, I'd inherit the property."

"When did she suggest that?"

"In the spring, before she decided to get serious about selling. I told her that I couldn't do that, because it wouldn't be honest. No matter how much I want Carson Creek, I can't live a lie."

Darby nodded. "Why don't you talk about this with Sophie? I think she'd appreciate knowing how you feel."

"I will." He gave a rueful grin. "Thanks for the advice."

"Out of curiosity, where is that bottle?"

"On my desk. I was about to put it in the recycling bin." He gave her a strange look. "Why would you want it?"

She shrugged. "I don't know. Just a funny feeling, that's all."

Once inside the large red building, Darby told herself there was nothing special about the bottle on Dan's desk. It bore the Carson Creek Estate & Winery label—a lovely watercolor of the property with a soft sunset behind it—and was made from heavy, dark colored glass. As Darby lifted it, she noticed a few tablespoons or so of liquid remained on the bottom. She pulled out the stopper, a cork with a glass ball on the top, and sniffed it. The odor was what she recalled from the glass of Carson Creek Pinot she'd enjoyed the night before.

Curious, Darby tilted the bottle gently and put a small amount of the ruby red liquid on her finger. She licked it with her tongue and let her taste buds go to work.

Blackberry, cherry, with a licorice finish...and something else. The flavor was of a bold pinot noir mixed with something odd.

Darby replaced the stopper in the bottle. She carried it back to the house, determined to ask Dan about the wine's strange taste. She found him in the kitchen, handing a set of keys to Carlos.

"These are for Selena's truck," he told him. "It's the blue Subaru. I just filled it with gas, so you're all set."

"Thanks." Carlos nodded in Darby's direction, his eyes bearing dark circles. "See you later."

Darby was about to question Dan when ET entered, carrying Selena's folders in one hand; and two coffee mugs in another. "I'm afraid my brother needs a little break," he said, as the squeal of tires marked Carlos' departure. "He wants to go for a drive in the country, clear his head."

"I can certainly understand that," Darby said. "It's an awful lot to absorb at once."

"Indeed." He placed the folders on the kitchen table. "Sometimes I think that if Carlos and Selena had been closer, this wouldn't be so painful."

"They weren't close?"

"Not really. Carlos tried, but my sister kept her distance."

"Do you think that was because of her illness?"

ET looked thoughtful. "No, she was always that way. Her independence didn't bother me as much as it did my brother. Carlos couldn't understand that she needed to break ties with us." He frowned and put his hands on his hips. "Darby, we would like you to offer the property to the buyers next week, as soon as my sister's mass is behind us."

She nodded. "Fine. Assuming we get the go-ahead from Edward Martin, I'll have it ready to go on Tuesday. I'll need to figure out who can show the vineyard in my absence, but that shouldn't be too difficult. I'll interview a few agents as soon as possible."

"Actually, that is something Carlos and I discussed. Would you consider staying here for just a few days more? Choosing one of the three buyers doesn't seem like it will take long." He gave her a hopeful look. "I know it is asking a lot, but Carlos and I cannot stay. Our plans are to depart as soon as possible following Selena's funeral. It is just too painful for us."

Darby thought quickly. She could do most of her work from Carson Creek, thanks to her smart phone. New listings—including her neighbor Doug Henderson's home—could be shown by Claudia, and ET would be back in the office by Tuesday, providing assistance.

Darby thought back to Eric Sanchez, the speeding ticket, and her vow to slow down her hectic life. Here was a chance to do that as well as help a friend.

"I can stay for a few days if that's what you'd like," Darby assured him. "I agree that it seems this will be a quick deal to put together." She paused. "Do we have a time for Selena's service on Monday?"

Dan Stewart spoke up. He'd been stirring something in a bowl on the counter, and now he quietly interjected.

"Late morning at the Contento vineyards, as long as ET and Carlos think that's appropriate. Margo has already begun working out the details."

"Margo?" ET looked puzzled.

"She's Tim Contento's sister. Handles quite a bit of the corporate stuff for Contento Family Vineyards, and travels around the world promoting the wines. She thinks Selena's funeral could draw quite a crowd, and wants to be prepared."

"Oh." ET looked exhausted. He held his forehead with a hand.

"I think what Dan is saying is that the Contentos will take care of the arrangements," Darby said gently. "They were Selena's friends and neighbors, as well as fellow vintners. They want to help."

"That's right. You'll see, it will be beautiful. Margo wants to talk to you as soon as possible and get your and Carlos' input. Her number is right here."

ET nodded. "I see." He took the piece of paper from Dan and glanced at the message. "I will call her, but first, perhaps I will go and lie down. I did not sleep very well last night."

Darby and Dan watched him head out of the kitchen.

"Poor guy," Dan said, shaking his head. "It just doesn't get any easier."

"No, but it's wonderful that the Contentos are willing to host Selena's service. Of course, they are also interested in purchasing this property. Do you think that's part of their generosity?"

Dan reached up in a cabinet for a bag of sugar and measured out a cup. "I could be cynical and say yes, but the truth is, it's just the way people are around here. We work together—celebrating each other's successes and commiserating over the bad stuff. We trust each other. I know they want this property but they are doing this because it's the right thing to do."

She considered his explanation. "I'm starting to understand what a close-knit community this is. It's really pretty special."

"Definitely. Now you see why it was so important to Selena that she choose the right person to run Carson Creek. It's more than just the transfer of a deed. There's the whole fabric of the valley to consider." He pushed the bowl aside and turned to face Darby. "By the way, I had a quick chat with Sophie while I drove her home. I think it helped." He gave her a puzzled look. "What are you doing with that empty bottle?"

Darby had nearly forgotten that she was clutching it. "I'm curious as to why the wine inside has a funny taste."

"What do you mean? That's our best pinot."

"I'm no expert, but I tasted a tiny bit. It has a strange afternote."

Dan motioned for her to hand him the bottle. He poured a few drops onto a tablespoon and dipped his finger in. After tasting the wine on his finger he frowned. "You're right. My guess is that Selena didn't notice. Her senses were off, although she certainly didn't complain about it much."

Darby put the bottle on the counter. "Let's hang on to this, Dan. I'd like to find out why this wine doesn't taste the way it should."

"You and me both," he muttered.

SEVEN

VIVIAN ALLEN POWDERED HER nose in the rental car's rearview mirror. *Not bad for someone who'd had a very late night,* she thought. A small blue pickup truck pulled into the diner's parking lot, and Vivian resisted the urge to swivel around for a better look. She watched as Carlos Gomez climbed down from the cab and walked quickly across the tar. *Right on time.* He glanced over his shoulder but did not spot Vivian.

She checked her lipstick and applied another swipe. *Let him wait a few minutes, get a little anxious. Let him worry that perhaps I changed my mind.*

Another car, a small blue hybrid with advertising on the side, pulled in and a well-built man wearing dark sunglasses emerged. He strode toward the diner with purposeful steps. *Busy place,* thought Vivian. The newcomer reminded Vivian of someone, but the tall redhead could not place him. She shrugged and looked at her cell phone. If this little rendezvous went well, she'd have just enough time to make it to the concert pre-show at the polo grounds.

She grabbed her pink purse. *Turn on the charm,* she thought.

———

"So did that wine turn? Is that why it has an off taste?" Darby was spooning apples onto a bottom crust as Dan Stewart rolled out the top.

"Not in a matter of a few days."

Darby wiped her hands on a dishtowel. "Do you think it was bad when Selena uncorked it, but she drank it anyway?"

"Nope. We would have discovered other inferior bottles if that were true."

Dan cut the top crust into strips and began creating a lattice pattern over the mounded apples. "That about does it." He gestured toward the oven. "Want to open that for me?"

Darby complied. It was early afternoon, but already Dan had a delicious dinner ready for the house guests, so that they could have an early night without going out.

He turned to face her, taking off a white butcher's apron as he did so. "I've got the timer set on that. Just put it on the counter to cool. The chicken and salad are all set, so you can spend the afternoon relaxing." He hung up the apron. "I'm wiped out. I imagine the three of you are as well."

"Carlos and ET are exhausted. This has taken such a toll on them emotionally. I'm okay, but I appreciate you going to all this trouble so that we can have a relaxing night. This kind of thing can't be in your job description."

"No problem." He placed his hands on his hips. "Think I'll head out; see what that teenager of mine has got planned for Saturday night. Good night, Darby. Thanks for your help with Sophie."

"She's a great girl. My pleasure."

Darby heard the noise of Dan's jeep as it crawled down the hill. *He's such a good guy,* she thought. *No wonder Selena was attracted to him.* Her eyes fell on the bottle of Pinot Noir. Selena had been drinking it just before she died. Why did it have an aftertaste? It was almost as if something had been added.

Stop it, she admonished herself, shaking her head. *You're becoming one of those people imagining conspiracies at every turn.*

Darby set the table in the dining room and glanced at her watch. As far as she knew, ET was still sleeping; Carlos still cruising among the valley's many hills. Both of the brothers were dealing with their grief in very different ways.

The ring of the phone cut through her reverie, and she hastened to answer it before it disturbed ET.

"Darby?" An English accent, slightly hesitant. Her heart began to pound as she recognized the caller's resonant voice.

"Miles? Where are you?"

"I'm in California. San Francisco, to be exact. I called your office and the secretary told me what happened to ET's sister. I'm so sorry. She gave me this number." He paused. "It's wonderful to hear your voice."

"I can't believe it's you. When did you leave Afghanistan?"

"Beginning of the week. It all came about so suddenly, I didn't have time to tell you."

"I understand. I'm so glad you're safe."

"As safe as one can be riding these old wooden contraptions up some of the steepest hills in the world."

She smiled, imagining the tall reporter clinging to one of San Francisco's famous trolleys.

"What are your plans?"

"I'm hoping to come and see you." He paused, and Darby felt as if a pit in her stomach opened wide. "I'd like to drive up to Ventano tomorrow. It's been two months since we've seen each other. I can be there by ten."

Darby held her breath as her emotions flashed from desire to dread and back again. She wanted to see him, and yet the idea was somehow petrifying. This wasn't the best time for a visit, and yet, when would be the best time? *Admit it, you're chicken.* Finally she took a breath and spoke.

"I'll see you in the morning, Miles. Drive safely."

———

Carlos, ET, and Darby were quiet as they ate the dinner Dan had prepared, each lost in his or her own thoughts. Darby wasn't sure what the Gomez brothers were thinking, but she knew that her mind was flooded with images of Miles Porter, the journalist for the *Financial Times* she'd met only a few months before.

Miles had appeared on the island of Hurricane Harbor while Darby was dealing with the death of her aunt, and Darby could not deny that she'd felt an instant attraction to the tall Brit with the shock of dark hair and rugged face. When he'd left only a week after their initial meeting to serve as a journalist embedded in an Army unit in Afghanistan, she'd swallowed her disappointment and communicated several times with him via Skype. She'd often wondered whether the feelings she'd felt for him were genuine, or whether she'd imagined it all. Now, it seemed, she'd have the opportunity to answer her question.

"You are deep in thought, Darby," Carlos commented, helping himself to a hefty portion of roast chicken. "What's up?"

She debated telling him about the bottle of wine, but decided it was too strange an item with which to burden Carlos and ET. "A friend is arriving for a short visit tomorrow—someone I haven't seen in awhile. He's been in Afghanistan."

"Miles Porter?" ET's voice was smooth.

"Yes." She felt herself blushing and quickly took a sip of wine to try and hide it. "I'm sure it will just be a quick hello."

ET gave a little smile but said nothing.

Carlos cleared his throat. "I was thinking quite a bit while I was out driving around. I think we should sell this property to that woman who came by—Vivian, the one who had cancer. After all, she and Selena had a verbal agreement."

ET nodded. "That has been troubling me as well, Carlos. I cannot bear to think that we would not uphold our sister's wishes, if indeed those were her wishes."

Darby passed the chicken to ET who speared another slice. "Do you still want me to offer Carson Creek to all the buyers, or just contact Vivian for a private sale?"

"Private sale," said Carlos. "Why go through the whole rest of it?"

ET motioned for Carlos to pass the salad and took a second helping. "I disagree with you, brother. I would like to see what the other buyers feel about the property now that Selena has passed.

Perhaps there will be additional interest as well. I don't want to count on Vivian Allen, although she may be the one we choose."

"Seems to me like a big waste of time." Carlos stabbed a forkful of chicken and held it, ready to chew. "If we already know we want Vivian to have the vineyard."

"I see your point. But I do not want to leave any stone unturned." ET rose from the table, his shoulders uncharacteristically stooped. "I must head upstairs. Although I rested this afternoon, I am still very tired. Tomorrow we will meet with the Contentos to see what we need to do for Selena's service. I hope I have the energy to do that." With a sad smile, he left the room.

Darby turned from ET to Carlos, watching as he chewed his chicken with what seemed like furious speed. Suddenly he slammed down his fork. "I am so sick and tired of his slow, plodding pace! I've got things to do back in the city and he wants to drag his feet every second of the way. Vivian is here, she wants the property, and all we have to do is have her sign. Bingo! We're done. But no, Rico's gotta go through the whole damn process, just for the hell of it. I can't stand it."

Darby remained quiet, listening to Carlos' rant. She understood how infuriating it could be to accommodate differing operating styles. She herself could lose patience with people who analyzed every single step of a process before ever taking action. But Carlos' annoyance at his brother seemed to be misplaced. *He's tired, and he's grieving,* she reminded herself as she watched Carlos attack the rest of his food. *Everyone grieves differently.*

"I'll do my best to make sure this goes as smoothly and quickly as possible, Carlos. I know how difficult this is for you."

He looked up and Darby was surprised to see his eyes filled with tears. "I loved my little sister. We fought a heck of a lot, but she always saw the best in me."

Darby rose and put a hand on his shoulder. Carlos nodded, rose from the table, and gathered his plate and silverware. Nodding toward the kitchen, he said quietly, "I need some time alone. I'll take care of the dishes."

Darby nodded and headed out of the dining room, leaving Carlos clearing the plates.

————

The polo grounds were jammed with cars, and Vivian Allen began to think that coming had been a mistake. Parking her rental car as close as she could to the stage, the tall redhead began trudging across the trampled grass toward the entrance. What possessed all of these people to pay so much money to come to these things? She looked around to try and gauge the demographic. Teenagers with torn jeans and the requisite piercings, young couples holding hands as they wove their way through the parked cars, and older fans carrying lawn chairs and coolers. A mixture of ages, thought Vivian, a testament to pop star Veronica's ability to captivate any and all with her quirky songs and energetic shows.

Vivian ducked as a neon green Frisbee careened through the air, narrowly missing her left temple. She hugged her pink pocketbook more tightly as the throngs grew even larger. Swept up in the crowd, she was carried by the current of ticketholders headed toward the gate.

Muscular security guards stood watch, peering into backpacks and coolers for alcohol. Vivian opened her purse and the guard waved her on. She presented her ticket to another burly man and began looking for her seat.

In Darby's dream, she was in a war-torn city, creeping through a maze of bombed-out buildings. She entered an empty room in which the ceiling had been blown away to expose blue sky. Chunks of plaster littered the floor and in the distance she heard a baby crying. She was searching for something, someone . . .

Trying not to make a sound, Darby crept around the room, her heart thudding with fear. A pile of rags lay in the corner, and she kicked at it with her toe. To her horror, it began to move . . .

She woke with a rush at the sound of a heavy door slamming shut.

Eleven-thirty. Who was coming to the vineyard at this hour? She rose and looked out her bedroom window.

Dan Stewart's jeep was parked in the middle of the drive. She glanced toward the fields and saw him running, a solitary figure in the pale moonglow.

Darby threw a sweatshirt over her nightgown and pulled on a pair of jeans. Shoving on her sneakers, she moved rapidly down the stairs, out the door, and into the driveway, then beyond, to the neat rows of vines.

The vineyards were bathed in moonlight and the air was sharp and brisk. The temperature had dropped a few degrees more and Darby saw silvery frost on the leaves of the grapes.

Dan was in the middle of the field.

"What's going on?" she cried.

His face was wild. "Someone's cut the sprinkler lines. We're going to lose the grapes."

"Cut the lines?"

"Yes. The sprayer system—it provides frost protection." He turned to Darby, his face grim. "Every line that I've seen has been sliced open. This is sabotage. Selena was right—someone is trying to destroy Carson Creek."

The gravity of Dan's words hit Darby like a slap. "I'll get Carlos and ET," she yelled, beginning to run toward the house.

"Hurry!" Dan implored. "Tell them if we don't save these grapes tonight, they won't have a vineyard to sell!"

Seconds later, Darby bounded up the stairs to the guest bedrooms. The brothers were groggy, but shook themselves awake once they understood the seriousness of the situation.

Dan met them in the barn and handed them rolls of duct tape. "We're going to try a patch job first. If repairing the lines doesn't work, we'll have to drape fabric over the vines." He told them where to locate the hoses that carried the water, and how to check for damage. "As long as we can fix the system enough so that it sprays the plants soon, we have a fighting chance."

"You think this was done deliberately?" ET's face was haggard in the moonlight.

"You can bet your life on it," Dan said. "And don't ask me to guess who's to blame. What we need to do now is try to save those grapes."

Darby took her roll of tape and headed off into the vines. She followed the snaking lines of the sprayer system until she found a break. The ends were severed neatly, without any ragged edges, and Darby quickly ripped off a piece of tape and secured them together. Then she continued down the row.

As soon as the team finished one field, Dan turned on the sprinkler system to see if it worked. When water sprayed out over the vines, the small group cheered. "Okay," Dan commanded. "Now we have to finish the other two fields."

It was nearly three in the morning when the exhausted Gomez brothers and Darby climbed into their beds, the roar of Dan's truck as he headed home echoing in their ears. He'd been cautiously optimistic about the health of the fruit. "I think we caught it just in time," he muttered.

"How did you know to come here?" Darby asked.

"I didn't. Something woke me up and I couldn't sleep. And then I had a strange feeling that I needed to drive over. As soon as I arrived, I saw that the sprayers weren't on." He sighed. "Hopefully we'll harvest in a day or two. I can't wait to get those little suckers off the vines."

———

Five hours later, the morning sun filtering through the windows woke Darby, who yawned, dressed, and headed down to the kitchen. She inhaled the rich aroma of coffee as Dan Stewart handed her a mug full.

"Yesterday you were here to work, last night you saved the grapes, and now it's Sunday and you're back. Pretty heavy schedule, Dan."

"I'm always here when there are major emergencies to deal with." He pointed at a box on the counter. "Homemade donuts and muffins from the bakery in Wyattville," he said. "Sophie picked out quite a selection. Help yourself."

Darby chose a maple-glazed donut and sat down at the kitchen table. "How do the grapes look?"

"I'm pretty hopeful. They taste fine and the vines themselves look healthy. I think we dodged another bullet."

"You're convinced these incidents are related? The fungus, the yeast, and now someone cutting the lines?"

"Absolutely." He frowned. "I don't want to believe it, but I have to."

"What happened with the security system? Why didn't Selena install it?"

"I don't know. She looked into it, but never finalized the contract with the company. Now that I know about her health issues, I wonder if she had more pressing expenses."

"Morning." It was Carlos, rubbing his eyes as he staggered into the kitchen. "That was some little field trip last night. I feel like I ran a million miles."

"Coffee?" Dan held up a cup and Carlos nodded.

"Have we seen my brother yet?"

Darby shook her head. "I hope he'll keep sleeping for a bit. He looked so tired."

Carlos took the cup of coffee. "Thanks." He spied the box of pastries and pulled out two muffins. "I'm starving. This farming life sure gives you an appetite."

Dan chuckled. "Selena once told me that you're a photographer, right Carlos?"

"You got it. I take portraits, mainly."

"Where's your studio?"

"Downtown San Francisco, over by Coit Tower. I'm in a great spot."

Darby finished her donut and took a swig of coffee. "Do you exhibit there as well?"

Carlos nodded. "I do. I'm in a few galleries, too. There's one in St. Adina that carries my work. In fact, I found out yesterday that they sold two of my portraits."

"That's wonderful news." It was great to see Carlos occupied with something other than his sister's death, but nevertheless Darby felt the need to change the subject. Selena's service was only a day away, and the Contentos had called with a few requests.

"Speaking of photos, Margo Contento called. She's setting up for tomorrow and looking for a few photos of Selena."

"I've got one I can get printed," Carlos said. "I'll take care of it today."

Dan pointed a finger up into the air. "There's an album in the attic crammed full of photos. I could ask Sophie to go through it and pick out some good ones, and then she could show you and ET?"

Carlos nodded. "That sounds good." He rose from the table. "All of you are so kind." His voice caught. "My sister was lucky."

Dan and Darby watched as Carlos left the room.

———

Darby laced up her sneakers following breakfast and went for a short run. She then showered, dressed in a pair of black pants and a tee shirt, and drafted a listing agreement for Carlos and ET to review. The two brothers had gone to meet Margo at Contento Family

Vineyards, and Dan had driven home with his daughter. Darby was alone with her laptop in the dining room.

A knock on the door made her suddenly shaky. She rose and opened it wide.

Miles Porter. The change in his appearance was striking, and at first Darby did not know what to say. Gone was his thick shock of dark hair: he now had a trim, military style cut that accentuated the rugged lines of his face and brought out the deep hazel color of his eyes. He smiled, and she felt a rush of familiarity, along with an emotion she could not quite name. He looked different—rougher, wilder, and more masculine—but he was still Miles.

"Hello." She reached out and hugged him, recognizing the tweedy jacket he'd worn back in Maine. He smelled faintly of bayberry, a clean, soapy scent she liked. "I'm so glad you're back safely."

His eyes twinkled above the chiseled cheeks.

"I was hoping you'd say that. May I come in?"

"Of course. How about some coffee? Or tea?"

"You know me—an Englishman to the core. Tea would be lovely."

Darby rummaged in Selena's cabinet. "Earl Grey?"

"Perfect." Darby could feel his eyes on her as she stretched for the tea. A moment later, he placed a hand on the small of her back and her spine literally tingled.

"You're more beautiful than when I saw you in Maine," he said, his voice husky. "How can that be?"

She felt her face growing warmer. Slowly she unwrapped the tea bag and placed it in a mug. "I think it's because you've spent nearly two months in a tent. Anyone would look good."

He grinned. "You've got a point there." She poured water, handed him the mug, and suggested that they sit in the living room.

"What a great old house," Miles commented as they walked through the dining room. "And the scenery outside—just outstanding. I've never been to this part of California, and I must say, it is breathtakingly beautiful."

Darby nodded. "You can see why ET's sister Selena loved this place." She paused. "Tomorrow is her funeral service. ET and his brother are starting to come to terms with it, but it's been very difficult."

"I can only imagine. Did they know the extent of her illness?"

"No. They didn't even know she was sick. Her doctor said it's not uncommon for people with a chronic disease—especially working women—to hide their symptoms. They are often at risk for discrimination if they show any kind of weakness."

"I know. I remember reading a story about that very thing, and the statistics were overwhelming. Poor Selena. She felt she had to go it on her own, is that it?"

"Yes." Darby was silent a moment, just taking in his presence, surprised at how happy she was to have him sitting two feet away. "You look well, Miles."

"No worse for wear?" His eyes crinkled as he smiled, and Darby thought she could see a few more lines etched in his tanned skin.

"No." She gave a smile. "I even like your buzz cut."

He ran a hand over his head. "I did it to blend in with the troops," he admitted. "Not only that, I'm saving a bundle on shampoo."

"I bet!" she laughed. "Hurry up and finish that tea and I'll take you out to the vineyards. There's a little mystery I'd like your help in solving."

"Brilliant." He took a gulp of the hot tea and grinned. "Always happy to be your Dr. Watson."

———

Harrison Wainfield parked his Mercedes in the farthest corner of the small parking lot and hurried across the tar toward the restaurant. Remy's was the most popular place in the valley for Sunday brunch, and last-minute reservations were practically impossible. Luckily Wainfield counted the chef owner, Alexander Remington, as one of his clients, and was assured of a table at a moment's notice. He pulled open the heavy door and entered the building. Light, bright, and spare, the space embodied the new aesthetic for dining, an almost Asian feeling of clean lines and uncluttered décor. He nodded to the maitre d' who gave the ghost of a smile.

"Mr. Wainfield, come this way."

He followed the man to a corner table and sat down. "My guest will be arriving shortly. You'll probably recognize him—Fritz Kohler?"

The man nodded. "The fitness expert. I'll show him to your table. Would you like something to drink in the meantime?"

"Bloody Mary with Absolut Citron."

"Very good."

Wainfield gazed out the window at the shops and restaurants of St. Adina. The city was started as an agricultural center back in the early 1800s, but was now a tourist destination, thanks to its location smack in the center of California wine country. Upscale eateries and luxurious lodging places now coexisted with dozens of wineries, and yet St. Adina still retained a certain charm. Wainfield had watched property values peak two years ago, but even with a slight decline since then, it was not an inexpensive place to live or run a business.

But Fritz Kohler didn't need to worry about that. Wainfield had done an extensive background check on the man, as he did with all his clients, and knew that Kohler's assets were considerable. The guy was a self-made fitness entrepreneur, first starting a bicycling company that grew from a small, California-based outfit to a worldwide phenomenon in less than a decade. When Kohler sold Off the Beaten Track Biking two years ago, he'd retained a hefty salary as a consultant, and turned his attention to the growing popularity of yoga. Sensing that the time was ripe for a new, more aerobic style of the ancient meditative discipline, Kohler created a variant he called "Power Yoga," a practice that included pumped-up poses and adrenaline-charged routines. In much the same way that kickboxing and Zumba had captured the exercise-hungry population's imagination and pocketbooks, Power Yoga— thanks to a public relations campaign that included print, television, the Internet, and a series of workouts—had become the next fitness craze, and Kohler, its multimillion dollar guru.

And now the ripped yogi wanted a vineyard.

Harrison Wainfield pursed his lips. Certainly Kohler wasn't the first celebrity to become attracted to the cult of wine. Wainfield's clientele included a film producer and supermodel, both now happily tending their vineyards here in the valley. Why were celebrities so taken with the vineyard lifestyle? Wainfield's personal theory was that owning a winery gave them something they couldn't otherwise access: membership in the elite community of wine producers. Wainfield knew (although not firsthand, having never so much as picked a grape) that many people found working in a vineyard, tending a fermentation, and blending wine to be rewarding. And, of course, there was the drinking of the final product with friends.

Rumor had it that the pop star Veronica, whose show at the polo grounds the night before had sold out in a matter of minutes, was looking for a vineyard. She fell into another category of wine-grower wannabees: those who were too well known or too wealthy to go around in public safely. People like that needed something fun to do, and a vineyard seemed to be the answer. He pictured Veronica, who wore some kind of big wings when she sang that "Heaven Bent" song, and wished he could get a part of that action. Supposedly the megastar had phoned Ann Johnson in Wyattville a couple of weeks earlier.

Harrison Wainfield grimaced. Ann Johnson! The skinny bitch couldn't sell a vineyard if her life depended on it. Give her a raised ranch or a bungalow and she could manage the deal, but a vineyard? *I should have been the one to get that call! I'm the one best suited to deal with the rich and famous.*

He exhaled and heard the clearing of a throat. His Bloody Mary had arrived, and none too soon.

———

Darby lifted one of the sprayer lines and showed Miles Porter where it had been sliced.

He took the tubing in his hands and gave a low whistle. "Not quite what you'd call a mean-spirited prank. Given the other incidents you mentioned, I'd concur that this is industrial sabotage."

He rose from his haunches and surveyed the fields. "I did a story for the *Financial Times* on a farm in Australia where seven million seedlings were poisoned. The saboteur pumped a lethal dose of herbicide into the irrigation system. In one night, the bulk of North Queensland's next season of fruit and vegetable crops was destroyed, an estimated twenty-three million dollar loss. It was devastating for the farm and the workers involved, but also for the consumers who had to pay a higher price for vegetables."

Darby shuddered. "Was the perpetrator caught?"

"Eventually. A hefty reward brought in lots of tips, and the police arrested a local farmer for the crime. Seems his motive was to decrease supply so that his crops would fetch more money."

"I guess that could be the case here. If Carson Creek's grapes are destroyed, other wines from the region might benefit." She paused. "That casts suspicion on dozens of local vineyards."

"Nasty business," Miles said, wiping his hands on his khaki pants. "You have to wonder, why just Carson Creek? Unless this kind of thing is happening at other vineyards and no one is speaking up."

"I suppose it's up to Carlos and ET to decide whether they will report this," Darby mused, thinking that with an impending sale, negative press would not be helpful.

Miles' touch on her cheek interrupted her thoughts. "Sorry to cut short our investigation, but it's time for me to whisk you off to the big city for lunch."

Darby smiled. Miles adored expensive restaurants with daring menus, and wine country was studded with several she knew he'd enjoy. "I remember your taste in upscale restaurants, Miles. There's one in St. Adina that's supposed to be fabulous, but I don't know if we'll be able to get a table."

"I do hope you're speaking of Remy's?"

She nodded, enjoying the playful look that softened Miles Porter's chiseled visage. "That's it."

"Off we go, then, to dine at Remy's." He clasped her hand and gave a boyish grin. "I've already spoken to them and they'd love to have a famous journalist and his exotic companion for lunch. Our table awaits us—one of the many professional perks I'm determined to enjoy."

———

Harrison Wainfield insisted on paying the bill for brunch, grateful that his muscle-bound companion had eaten little more than a garden salad. Overall, he felt the meeting had gone well. Fritz Kohler was cordial, with a real desire to own Carson Creek Estate & Winery and a hefty checkbook to back up his desire. All seemed straightforward, and yet, Wainfield got the distinct impression that the man was holding something back. Every word he'd uttered seemed rehearsed, as if he was on guard.

"What are my chances of getting the property?" Kohler had asked, not in a demanding way, but in a measured, careful tone.

"Fair. You're up against the Contento family, and they are formidable competition. As you know, their vineyard abuts Carson Creek and they have long had a wish—" here he spoke delicately— "to acquire more land." He took a final gulp of his Bloody Mary, wanting another but deciding against it. Kohler had sipped only mineral water.

"There is another interested party, a woman from back East, but she's nothing to worry about." After hearing Carlos Gomez's comment that Selena had chosen Vivian Allen, Wainfield had conducted a little research, and discovered Allen was a former financial planner with limited funds. His records showed that she had actually called his office several weeks earlier, asking about Carson Creek, but had balked at his terms, the same ones he was about to lay out for Kohler.

"If you want me to work for you, I charge a retainer of five percent. I'll get you the property, and when you settle, my fee comes out of my commission."

"And what about the fact that you also represent the Contentos?"

Wainfield tried to hide his surprise. *How did he know that?*

"I've worked with the Contentos in the past, and yes, I made some initial inquiries for them regarding Carson Creek." He paused and looked Kohler in the eye. "I work for whoever will pay me, but I have no formal agreement with them at this time." He didn't add that he had spoken to Michael Contento hours before and been stonewalled.

For Wainfield, the terse discussion was the last straw. He was sick and tired of Contento's bullying manner, his constant references to Wainfield's enormous commissions every time a property transferred ownership. Even Andrea's considerable charm couldn't soften the bitterness he felt from years of being treated like dirt.

Selena Thompson's death hadn't played out the way he'd imagined. Wainfield had fully expected her brothers to hire him to sell the vineyard, and was flabbergasted to meet the young Asian realtor from Pacific Coast and learn that she would be handling the sale. What the hell did Darby Farr know about wine country, or selling a vineyard? Might as well hire Ann Johnson! At least she lived in the valley.

His dismay was short lived when he snuck into Selena's office and managed to get his hands on Carson Creek's multiple offers. Looking them over, he'd realized that Fritz Kohler was the horse to back. He gave a smug smile. One way or another, he was going to profit from the sale of Carson Creek Estate & Winery. Thanks to this brunch, it appeared his plan had worked perfectly.

Kohler rose and flexed his biceps, a gesture that seemed almost unconscious. "Shall I meet you at your office to sign something?"

"We can head over there right now if you'd like."

The big man nodded, and for a second, Wainfield thought he glimpsed something simmering behind the brown eyes. Anger? Sadness? He couldn't be sure, and truthfully, didn't give a damn.

Wainfield steered his charge toward the door. "Follow me. I'm in the black Mercedes parked over in the corner."

Kohler nodded again and headed for a hybrid sedan emblazoned with "Power Yoga" on either side. Harrison frowned. *How tacky,* he thought.

He crossed the lot toward his car as a red Karmann Ghia turned into the restaurant. Behind the wheel was Darby Farr, and beside her a military-looking man Harrison had never seen.

He narrowed his eyes as he unlocked his Mercedes. She was trouble, he could tell. One of these young agents who thought she knew everything there was to know about selling property. He slid into his seat, welcoming the softness of the leather, and peered into his rear-view mirror. Darby Farr and the stranger were out of the car and strolling toward the restaurant.

Fritz Kohler wanted Carson Creek and Fritz Kohler was going to get it, it was as simple as that. Wainfield started the engine and crept slowly toward his new client's car. Darby Farr would be a fool to get in the way. *And if she does, I'll simply deal with her.*

He signaled and Fritz Kohler began to follow.

EIGHT

"Butternut squash ravioli," mused Miles. "Either that or the braised rabbit. What do you think?"

"How about both?" Darby grinned as she peered over her menu at Miles. "I promise to try a few bites."

"Terrific. And we'll need one of the local wines to go along with that." The waiter materialized and Darby asked for Remy's signature salad of greens, pear, walnut, and locally produced blue cheese. Miles ordered the rabbit with a side of ravioli, as well as a bottle of Chardonnay from Contento Family Vineyards.

"Selena's wine isn't on the list, is it?" Miles asked.

"No. I think she sold mainly to wine club customers and people who stopped at the vineyard. For a small winery such as Carson Creek, doing business that way makes sense, and can really be quite lucrative."

He buttered a whole grain roll and took a bite. "It certainly seems like she had this business figured out. Why did she want to sell? Was it totally her health issues?"

Darby shrugged. "Dan says it was all getting too much for her. Running a business is fine when things are going well, but when they aren't…"

"Such as the sabotage…"

"That's right. It's a whole different story." She paused. "Money is another factor. A few months ago, I lent ET some funds which he in turn gave to his sister. I'm not sure why Selena needed it—perhaps it was just the continued progress of her disease."

"Guillain Barré syndrome is devastating," Miles said softly. "It's not a disease that can be underestimated." He leaned back as the bottle of wine arrived, perused the label, and nodded. The waiter uncorked the bottle and poured a small amount in Miles' glass.

"I think I'll have the lady do the honors," he said. "I'm new to this whole Ventano Valley scene and she's been here a few days."

Darby smiled and took the glass. She swirled the buttery yellow liquid and then inhaled the scent of pears and apples. She took a sip and let it linger a moment. "Delicious," she announced. Miles grinned happily.

Once their meals arrived and they'd begun eating, Darby asked Miles about his time in Afghanistan. "It must have been incredibly difficult to live in a war zone," she said. "I can't imagine the things you saw."

"I wouldn't want you to. Some of the things—they were the very stuff of nightmares." He looked down at his plate and then back up again. "But I saw acts of kindness as well. Soldiers helping mothers with children, young girls giving bunches of wild flowers to men in uniform—little things that meant so much because of where we were. I witnessed the tenderness of families, even in the harshest of circumstances." His eyes took on a haunted look. "But it was very difficult, all the same."

"Are you finished with that assignment?"

He nodded. "Yes. I find myself at a bit of a crossroads." He met her eyes. "I'm not sure what the future holds."

Darby took a sip of wine. She wasn't sure either. She liked Miles, but were her feelings stronger than that? She had so many balls in the air—her career in Southern California, her obligations to real estate offices in Maine and Florida, and the unresolved mystery of her grandfather's involvement in World War II atrocities in China. The buzz of her vibrating smart phone interrupted the silence.

"Miles, I am so sorry." She took the phone out of her purse and glanced at the number. "It's my office—I'd better take it." She answered the phone.

Claudia Jones, the new agent hired to assist Darby, explained that an offer on Doug Henderson's bungalow had come in that morning.

"You're kidding!" Darby exclaimed. "You just listed it on Friday."

"I know," the sales agent chuckled. "I showed it to a cute young couple that same day, and they are totally smitten." She paused. "I'm trying to get in touch with Doug to let him know, but his cell doesn't answer, and the gift shop's number is disconnected."

Darby frowned. "How odd. What about e-mail?"

"Doesn't seem that he's looking at it. What should I do, Boss?"

"Scan the offer and send it to me, along with all of Doug's contact information—anything you've got. I'll deal with it from here." She thanked Claudia and hung up.

"Doug is my next-door neighbor in Mission Beach," she told Miles as she stabbed a forkful of salad. "He decided to go to Hawaii and live with a woman he met over the Internet."

"Isn't it amazing that so many people are connecting with these on-line dating services?" He grinned. "And to think that you and I met the old-fashioned way—pure chance."

Darby smiled, remembering the rush of feelings that accompanied her first encounter with Miles Porter. "Here's the catch: Doug had never met Rhonda in person."

"What? He flew to the islands for a blind date?"

Darby nodded. "I advised him not to list his house but he was adamant. Now someone's come along to buy it, and my agent at the office can't find him." She frowned. "I hope he's okay."

"The number one rule with Internet dating is to take things slowly," Miles intoned. "Chatting on-line makes couples feel that they've known each other forever, creating a false sense of foundation. It's easy to move too quickly and then the results can be heartbreaking."

Darby raised her eyebrows and Miles laughed.

"Remember, I'm an investigative journalist! There are very few things I haven't written about." His pushed his plate to the side. "Your friend Doug is probably fine. He's holed up in some little love nest with Donna—"

"Rhonda!" Darby laughed.

"Okay, Rhonda, and they are blissfully unaware that the rest of the world even exists. That's the kind of place I'd like to take you one of these days, if I can ever get you to stop working."

Darby looked at him with a playful smile. "Hey, I'm not the one who just came back from a war."

"Fair enough." His tone turned sober. "When you get Doug's information, I'll be happy to see what I can ferret out."

Darby felt a rush of gratitude. It was wonderful to have a friend like Miles. Why would she want to ruin this friendship by letting their relationship head in a more amorous direction?

She watched the muscles in his forearms as he reached for the wine and poured them both a little more. Once again she caught a whiff of bayberry, light yet pungent, his signature scent. He looked at her and smiled, and she wanted to reach out and stroke the planes of his face, knowing they would feel like sculpted marble. She exhaled and took a sip of the Chardonnay, wondering if her face betrayed her emotions. *Uh oh*, she thought. *I am in deep trouble.*

———

Carlos and ET were both cordial to Miles, but their thoughts were clearly on their sister's funeral service. ET seemed especially distracted, and Darby asked what she could do to help.

"I hate to impose, but I wonder if you might go to the Contentos and finalize a few details with Margo. She has everything arranged, and yet—" He spread his hands. "I am not sure I like the space where the reception will be held. The little chapel is beautiful, but the caves—" He sighed. "I hate to say anything, because they have been so kind."

"I'm happy to go and speak with her," Darby assured him. "I'll head over with Miles right now."

The journalist nodded. "I'll take my own car and depart from there." He shook hands with ET and Carlos. "I'm very sorry for your loss," he said.

The brothers nodded sadly as they left.

Margo Contento was tall, blonde, and energetic, with a ready smile and warm demeanor. Dressed in gray wool slacks and a gray cashmere sleeveless sweater, she met Miles and Darby in the tasting room of Contento Vineyards, a spacious room with large windows overlooking the fields and hills. She grabbed a soft pink shawl from a chair and motioned for them to follow.

"I'm glad to see you have jackets. We're headed to the caves, and it's a little chilly down there."

Miles glanced at Darby. "I hope you know I'm afraid of bats," he whispered, giving her arm a quick squeeze.

Darby's skin tingled. Whether it was from the chilly air or Miles' touch, she wasn't sure. It was still unseasonably cold, and as she hugged her jean jacket more tightly around her slender frame, she wondered whether the frost protection system would be operable tonight.

Margo led the way through a garden blooming with fall perennials and into a building housing the working part of the vineyard. "The entrance to the caves is from the tank room," she said, leading them into a spotlessly clean room with stainless tanks lining the walls. "When we crush the grapes, the juice is gravity-fed into these fermentation tanks. Once the wine has fermented, we transfer it into oak barrels to age." She stopped before two thick metal doors and turned to face Miles and Darby.

"Ready?" She pulled open the doors. "Welcome to the Contento Caves. Come on in."

Darby and Miles followed Margo into a long, arched hallway lined with oak barrels. Contrary to the image conjured up by the word "cave," the space was light, bright, and clean, constructed of bricks in the manner of a gothic church.

"Impressive," Miles said. "Not at all what I was expecting."

"Thank you," Margo said. "This is the main cave. There are two additional caves, but this is the one we use for functions." They came to what appeared to be the end of the corridor, but was in fact a huge, elaborate room, dominated by a banquet table under a crystal chandelier that twinkled with the fire of hundreds of crystals. In one corner stood a grand piano, in another, an oak lectern.

"We host private parties here, conduct tours, and age our wine as well." She smiled. "It's a terrific event space. I have to give my great grandfather Vincenzo credit. He was the one who came up with the idea."

"But these caves are new, right?" asked Darby.

"Three years old. I was on a trip to Europe when I met one of the world's leading builders of wine caves. I brought him back here to convince my father that we needed to create these." She waved her hands wide. "The bricks are reclaimed from an Italian villa that had to be demolished, and the chandelier comes from a castle near Vienna. We wanted to make the caves look timeless, as if they had always been here." She paused. "Old Vincenzo Contento did the same thing, back in his day." She grinned. "I like to call the original one our 'starter' cave."

"Does it still exist?" asked Miles.

She nodded. "Not for long. It's in the basement of the old barn, and water has eroded some of the walls. I'm afraid it's become a safety hazard." She put her hand against one of the brick walls. "It wasn't quite as well constructed as all this, but then again, it probably cost a tiny fraction of what this project cost."

She looked around the space and then back at Darby. "If ET and Carlos aren't happy with using the caves, we can certainly take over the tasting room. I felt this would be more private, but I'm not sure they shared my sentiments."

"I think it is a lovely space, but perhaps the tasting room would be more in line with what they have in mind," Darby said tactfully.

"Then that's what we'll do," Margo said, glancing at her watch. "Please excuse me. I've got to go and meet with somebody about flowers for tomorrow." She gave Darby a little smile. "Please assure Carlos and ET that everything will be beautiful. I loved Selena—we all did."

Darby and Miles exited the caves behind Margo, then lingered looking over the hillside.

"Those caves are incredible," Darby said. "I've never seen anything like them in this country. I felt like I was in Italy or France, under one of the great cathedrals."

"I agree. I wonder why your friend ET doesn't share our sentiments?"

"I think I know why. He has mild claustrophobia, so being in a space without windows doesn't sit well. I imagine the Contento's tasting area with the wall to ceiling glass made him feel much better."

"One does get the sense one is underground," mused Miles. He seemed to be thinking about something else, and a moment later he continued, "There must have been quite a bit of press when those caves were constructed. I wonder if that's why the Contento name rings some sort of bell with me."

"Possibly. Their wine has been winning lots of awards—that could be it as well."

"Yes." He turned to face Darby. "Well, my sweet, I hate to say this, but it's probably time for me to push off. You have duties with Carlos and ET, and I should let you get to it." He paused. "Remember, you're to send me that information on your neighbor, Doug. I'm happy to have a look at it this afternoon, when I get back to San Francisco."

"That would be great. It's not like him to be non-communicative, and I'll admit that I'm worried." She looked up at Miles' face. Concern and compassion showed there, and she blushed. "I'm sorry. I feel like I'm giving you all these things to do, when you just came back from a war." She made her tone lighter. "When will I see you again? I think it's my turn to buy you a meal."

He grinned. "I like the sound of that. I'm at your disposal, madam, depending on whether you're here or back in Mission Beach. I have a friend in San Francisco and I can stay at her flat for as long as I like." He grinned again. "She's an old Brit, a buddy of my mother's, a surrogate auntie if you will. Absolutely spoils me quite rotten when I visit. If you need me, I'm only an hour or so away."

"Great." She gave him a hug as he climbed into his rental car.

"I'll call you tonight," he promised.

She nodded, and he pulled away.

———

"Who are you?"

The question was French accented, and asked in such a penetrating manner that Darby was startled.

"I'm Darby Farr, a friend of Selena Thompson's brother." She had walked the few steps to her car when a man had materialized from one of the production buildings and hurried over. With one hand over her eyes to block the glare of the sun, she examined her inquisitor. He was short, with dark hair just beginning to gray, dark eyes, and full, red lips which he now pursed. "I'm staying at Carson Creek."

"I see. Who was that man with you, if you don't mind my asking?"

As a matter of fact, I do mind you asking. "A friend." She placed the key for her Karmann Ghia between two fingers, a self-defense move she performed almost unconsciously. "And you are … ?"

"Christophe Barton." He said it beautifully, and Darby nearly smiled. She had always loved the sound of the French language, so musical and lilting. It reminded her of her mother's pronunciation of the various Julia Child recipes she'd prepared for the family when Darby was a child. *Potage Velouté aux Champignons. L'Omelette Brouillée. Pommes Normande en Belle Vue.* The list went on and on.

She relaxed her grip on the key.

"You're the winemaker for this vineyard, right?"

"Estate manager," he corrected. "I am also a winemaker, but here among the Contento family my duties are, shall we say, more varied." He looked toward the driveway, noticing something that caused him to swear under his breath. "*Alors.* I must go. *Soyez prudent*, Darby Farr." He whirled and walked rapidly away from Darby, back toward the production building.

She shrugged and turned to her car. *Soyez prudent.* Darby knew enough French to recall that the phrase meant "Be careful." She climbed into the roadster. As a farewell, it was an odd thing to say.

A huge tour bus rumbled by her car as she began easing out of Contento Vineyards. A figure along the roadside waved, motioning for her to stop.

"Hello, Darby," Andrea Conteno panted. "I was going to call you. I'm just back from my walk, so forgive me if I huff and puff. Everything go okay with Margo?"

Darby nodded. "She seems to have thought of everything."

Andrea chuckled. "Margo's a master organizer, that's for sure. Even when she was small, she would boss Tim around, telling him what games they could play, that sort of thing." She gave a fond smile. "She was an adorable little girl. Very protective of her brother."

"You've known the Contento family for quite some time, haven't you?"

She nodded. "Whew! I'm still catching my breath." She inhaled and exhaled. "That's better. I came to work here right after I finished college. Guess I was, what, twenty-two at the time? The kids were eleven or twelve. I took care of them for a summer, and then my whole world changed."

"How so?"

"I fell head-over-heels in love with Michael." She looked wistfully at the hills and back at Darby. "I fell for him, and his whole life." She spread her hands. "This place, the kids, the whole shebang. We married the next year, and I became Tim and Margo's stepmother."

"You were young to take on so much responsibility," Darby commented.

"You think so? It was what I wanted, and I've never regretted a day of it." She gave Darby a frank look. "I'll be straight with you; I like to get what I want."

"Does that include Carson Creek?"

She brushed her hair back from her eyes. "Yes, it does. I love that property, and I've always imagined it a part of all this. I begged Michael to purchase it years ago, when it was first for sale, before Selena came on the scene. But Michael can be stubborn, and it doesn't help that he can't stand Harrison. At any rate, he said no, and Selena showed up and bought it. Lo and behold, she and I became friends."

Her eyes met Darby's. "The day before she died, Selena called and told me she'd made a decision. She said she would sell Carson Creek to us for nine and half million dollars. She said she'd initially decided on another buyer, but that deal was off. Her terms were simple. All she wanted was for us to keep the Carson Creek label intact, and let Dan have free rein." Andrea wore a wistful look. "I was overjoyed. I told her that she could continue to live at Carson Creek and asked our lawyer to look into setting up a life estate. It would have been ideal. Selena would stay in the farmhouse and she and Dan could keep on making wine as if nothing had changed."

"Was Selena interested in that idea?"

"Oh yes. She recognized that it would have worked out perfectly for her." Andrea sighed. "Michael and I can't believe that she's gone, and I miss her tremendously. But now it's my duty to convince her brothers to carry out her wishes. She wanted us to have the property. Meanwhile, I will do what I can to help celebrate Selena's shining but all-too-brief life."

She wiped quickly at her eyes. "Excuse me, Darby. I'm going to go see how things look in the chapel. I'll see you tomorrow." She paused and offered a small smile. "Cool car."

Darby thanked her and began the drive back to Carson Creek.

Carlos was outside smoking a cigarette when Darby drove up the drive to Carson Creek. He saw her and quickly stubbed it out, his face sheepish.

"Damn things. I quit for five years, and now they are all I can think about." He swore under his breath, apologized, and then lowered his voice. "Rico's a mess. He's all nervous about those caves at the Contento place."

"I know. It's all straightened out—the reception will be in the tasting room instead. Shall I tell him?"

"That would be great. Think I'll drive into town and get some of those nicotine patches, see if I can take my drugs that way." His eyes darted back and forth. "Darby, I don't think I can stay here much longer. I'm going crazy. I'm planning to rent a car and drive back to the city following Selena's funeral."

Darby nodded. "I understand. Perhaps we can sit down tonight and have one more talk about the sale of Carson Creek."

"What's there to say? I vote we sell it to Vivian. She's the one my sister wanted."

"Andrea Contento says Selena called her the day before she died and said she'd chosen Contento Vineyards as the buyer."

He snorted. "Ha! She's just saying that because she wants it."

"Couldn't Vivian be doing the same thing?"

He colored. "Not likely." Once more his eyes darted back and forth. "I'll tell you one thing: Vivian has got serious money behind her. I'm talking seriously *big* money."

Darby raised her eyebrows. "How so?"

"She has a close family member who wants in on the vineyard, and this person is loaded." He gave a smile of satisfaction. "As in mega-rich."

"Why does that make her a better buyer than the Contentos?"

"It's not just the money, it's her story. She had cancer, you know?"

Darby told herself to stop asking questions of Carlos, who was obviously an emotional wreck, but she could not help herself. "Carlos, is something in it for you?"

His face darkened. "What the hell? Why in the world would you ask me that?"

"I've been at this business long enough to recognize when someone is hiding something." She looked him in the eye. "What did Vivian promise you?"

Carlos balled his hands into fists. "You should stay out of this," he glowered. "Maybe you should go back to Mission Beach and leave us alone."

Darby felt her heart race as she watched Carlos jump into Selena's truck and career down the driveway.

"Where's Carlos going?" ET asked, emerging from the farmhouse to the front stoop. The sound of squealing tires reverberated for several seconds.

"Into town," Darby said, still pondering Carlos' reaction. Why had he become so upset, so quickly? "I'm afraid he's angry at me." She turned to ET. "Are you sure you want me to help you with this sale? There are plenty of brokers here who could do a fine job. I'm happy to interview them."

ET's handsome face was troubled. "I trust you. Tell me, what happened?"

"We were discussing Vivian Allen. I think I may have crossed the line, but I feel like there is some reason why he's determined that she should be the buyer."

ET exhaled. "I share your sentiments, and I know my brother. There is something he is not telling us."

The two entered the kitchen, both pondering Carlos' strange actions. In the hallway, a door slammed and Dan Stewart strode into the kitchen. "Sorry to interrupt, but I thought you'd like to know that I was just with the local cops. They came by to take a look at the damage to the lines."

"What did they say?" asked ET.

"They called it vandalism," Dan explained "They said it was probably a couple of kids."

"Vandalism? Did you tell them about the prior damage?"

"I did," said Dan. "Of course, they said I should have reported those incidents at the time." He shrugged. "Maybe I am making too much of it."

Darby shook her head. "I don't think so. But at least it's on record now, in the event something else happens."

ET shuddered. "What more could they do? They nearly ruined the entire grape harvest."

Dan's face was dark. "Believe me, if someone is trying to destroy Carson Creek, there are plenty more pranks they could pull." He sucked in a breath. "Sorry for the doom and gloom. The good news is, the police will keep this quiet."

"Good. What about the spray system? Will it function tonight?" Darby noticed the dark circles under Dan's eyes. The poor man was working around the clock to single-handedly run the vineyard.

Dan nodded. "Yes. It should be fine. The day after tomorrow we'll begin harvesting. The crews will arrive following Selena's funeral and we'll get started." His eyes met ET's. "I believe Selena's spirit will be with us in the fields."

ET nodded and left the kitchen, his face numb with grief.

NINE

Sophie Stewart flipped the channels on the television, but nothing was catching her eye. Sunday afternoon, and she was bored. Very bored. A pile of homework was staring her in the face, but she wasn't ready to tackle history, math, or vocabulary. She'd taken a walk down the road and back, hoping her father's jeep would come around the bend, but she knew he was grocery shopping on his way home from Carson Creek, and would probably be awhile longer. She turned off the television.

She closed her eyes and pictured the tray of orange-capped pills she'd found in Selena Thompson's bathroom. Why was it that Selena's death would not leave her mind? Something about the way her father had found the body, and the way he had also found her mother, ten years earlier—something about the two tragedies had captured her imagination in what even she admitted was a macabre way. How horrible, to discover two bodies! Most people probably went their entire lives without seeing even one dead person, never mind stumbling across two.

She thought back to what she knew of her mother's death. Very little, really. Her mom had some sort of illness and had died when she was four. The only memory she could recall was of a trip they had taken to an apple orchard. She remembered her mother hoisting her up high so she could pick a perfect red apple, then laughing and smiling as she took a greedy bite.

That must have been before she got sick, Sophie thought.

She realized she had no idea how her mother had died. She couldn't ask her father, not now, when he was dealing with so much. With sudden conviction she grabbed her cell phone. Grammy Kinney would know, and she wouldn't mince words.

———

ET was alone in the kitchen when Darby reentered the house.

"Dr. Yang just phoned," he said slowly.

Darby shivered involuntarily. *Now what?*

"She did a routine check of my sister's blood." He swallowed. "I'm not sure what this means, but Selena had an elevated amount of one of her drugs in her system. Beta blockers."

Darby's heart seemed to skip a beat. Beta blockers were given to lower high blood pressure. Would ingesting too many have made sitting in the hot tub deadly? "Did Dr. Yang know why Selena had this elevated level?"

"No." He turned an exhausted face toward her. "Do you think this could have contributed to her death?"

"I'm not a doctor, ET, but I do know that beta blockers and hot tubs are a dangerous combination. Both lower blood pressure to the point where a person can become unconscious." She made her voice gentle. "Something caused your sister to slip underwater and drown. This could be the explanation."

"But why would she have taken more than her prescribed dosage?" His voice was full of uncomprehending pain.

Darby gave him a hug. "I don't know." Her mind flashed to an unthinkable question that she could not quite bring herself to voice: *Had Selena Thompson been so ill that she'd taken an overdose of beta blockers deliberately? Or,* she thought, as a darker, more insidious question formed in her brain, *had someone else given Selena the increased dose?*

———

"Tell me again how you are related to Selena?" Detective Nardone, a petite woman with jet black hair streaked with gray and worn shoulder-length, sounded skeptical and bored. She raised her eyebrows and waited for Darby's explanation.

"I'm no relation. One of her brothers is my friend, and I drove him up from San Diego." She paused. "I know it sounds odd, but I'm wondering if perhaps Selena Thompson's death was not an accident."

The detective's eyes narrowed. She picked up a pen. "Go on."

"Her physician, Jenna Yang, said that there were elevated levels of a beta-blocking drug in Selena's bloodstream. Now, Selena took beta blockers for her hypertension, and I did a little research. An elevated level could have caused her to become unconscious. I can't help but wonder whether this overdose was accidental or deliberate, and if it was deliberate, could someone besides Selena herself have caused it."

"You're talking murder." She tapped the pen on the desk. "But how?"

Darby held up a plastic bag with the Pinot Noir wine bottle. "It was Selena's habit to have a glass of wine while she soaked in the hot tub."

"Yes. A glass was found in the water alongside her body."

"This was the only open bottle in Selena's kitchen." She handed the bag to Detective Nardone. "There's something wrong with the taste."

"How do you know?"

"Well, I'm no expert, but I put a small amount on my finger and tried it, as did Dan Stewart, the vineyard's winemaker."

"And you both thought it tasted odd?"

Darby nodded. She felt sure the detective would dismiss her musings as ridiculous, but to her surprise the petite black-haired officer considered her words, scrutinizing the bottle through the plastic bag. "I'll have the liquid analyzed today. Fingerprints are probably out of the question, but if need be, we can try that, too." She tapped the pen against her lips. "Are you aware that we were at Carson Creek just a few hours ago?" She glanced at a notebook on the corner of her desk. "Vandalism of the vineyard's spray system."

"Yes. I believe Dan Stewart told you there were other incidences?"

"Correct." Detective Nardone's eyes flashed. "So we may have a poisoned wine ingested by the victim while in the hot tub. Have I got it right?"

Darby nodded. Did Detective Nardone actually believe her suspicions, or was she merely being tactful?

The detective rose from her desk. "Thank you for coming in. We may have something here."

Darby tried to conceal her surprise but the detective was too quick.

"No need to look surprised, Ms. Farr." Her eyebrows were arched, her face bemused. "I'm a homicide detective, have been for nearly twenty years." She held up the plastic bag and cocked her head. "This is the kind of stuff I live for."

———

On the way back to Carson Creek, Darby stopped at a little clothing boutique in Wyattville. Other than the black slacks she was wearing, she had nothing suitable for Selena's funeral the following day. She flipped through the racks of skirts and dresses, finally finding a simple black linen shirtdress. It was more casual than Darby preferred, but under the circumstances, it would have to do.

Moments later, she paid for the dress, a few pairs of underwear, and some stockings. As she exited the boutique, she caught a glimpse of dark-haired Christophe Barton disappearing into the adjacent hardware store.

———

Back at Carson Creek, Darby had barely emerged from her Karmann Ghia when ET burst through the farmhouse door. "A detective is coming over," he panted. "I've called Carlos and he's on his way."

The sound of tires crunching on the pebbled drive signaled his brother's arrival in Selena's Subaru truck. "What is it? Has the family arrived?"

"They called and are nearly here," ET explained. "This is something else. A detective from the police station is on the way to speak with us."

Carlos looked from ET to Darby. "About the cut sprinkler lines?"

ET shrugged. "I do not know."

"I just came from the station," Darby said. "I told the detective about the elevated levels of beta blockers in your sister's system. I thought it was important that the police know that."

"But why?" Carlos frowned. "I hate dealing with police. They are always so obnoxious, throwing their weight around and trying to intimidate." He scowled as an unmarked police car rounded the bend and parked. "You watch, the guy will get out with his sunglasses on. It's all about the power trip."

Detective Nardone emerged from the car, her trim form in tailored lightweight wool pants and a short jacket. She walked toward them and shook hands with ET and Carlos.

"I'm Detective Nancy Nardone," she said. "Sorry to trouble you on a Sunday. May I go inside?"

"Wait a minute, wait a minute." Carlos ran a hand through his bushy dark hair. "We've got our sister's funeral, our family coming into town ..." ET gave him a sharp look, but Carlos continued. "We don't have time to talk about the sprinkler lines ..."

She raised a hand, cutting him off midsentence. "This isn't about the sprinkler lines, sir. I'm here to talk about your sister's death."

"What do you mean?" ET's voice had a dangerous edge to it.

"The bottle of wine your sister was drinking the day she died," began Detective Nardone, looking into his face, and then shifting her gaze back toward Carlos. "I just ran some tests on the contents of that bottle and found high amounts of metoprolol."

ET raised his hands in disbelief. "Metoprolol?"

"It's a common beta blocker, possibly the same one your sister was taking as prescribed by her physician." She pursed her lips. "This chemical was finely ground and added to the wine in the bottle, and I'm betting that happened without Selena's knowledge."

"Detective, what are you saying?" Carlos looked like he was on the verge of tears.

Her voice was hard. "I'm saying that your sister may have been murdered."

———

After showing Detective Nardone where the bottle had been located, ET and Carlos announced they were leaving to meet various relatives and have dinner with them in Wyattville.

"Don't bring anyone back here," Nancy Nardone warned. "This house is now a potential crime scene."

They nodded numbly. Minutes later Darby heard them start the truck's engine and drive away.

"Tell me again about the bottle," Detective Nardone ordered. "Where exactly did you first see it?"

Darby pointed to a spot on the counter.

"Do you remember anyone touching it the night Selena died? When you were gathered in here?"

Darby shook her head. "I remember noticing it there because it was empty. I thought it was odd that an empty bottle with a stopper in it was sitting on the counter."

"Did you notice that it was empty before or after people came?"

"I noticed it as soon as I came into the kitchen."

"Who was here at that time?"

"Dan Stewart, and his daughter, Sophie." She realized the detective was trying to determine if anyone else had compromised the bottle or its contents in the time between Selena's pouring the fatal glass and Sophie's removal of the bottle from the kitchen.

"I'll need to speak with Dan and Sophie," said Detective Nardone. She glanced at a chunky watch with a black band on her forearm. "I think I'll head to their house right now. I'm also sending up an evidence guy. We're several days too late, but who knows."

Darby followed the detective to the front door. "Tomorrow is Selena's funeral. It's too bad this all came out now."

Detective Nardone's voice was brisk. "That's not the way I look at it. I wish you'd tasted the damn wine the minute you walked in the door."

She said goodnight and Darby watched her drive down the road.

———

Sophie Stewart opened the door and allowed Detective Nancy Nardone to enter. "I'll get my dad," she offered, wondering if a gun was concealed beneath the woman's fitted jacket.

Dan Stewart heard their voices and came out of the kitchen, wiping his hands on a dish towel. He shook hands with the detective and motioned for her to sit down. Sophie took a seat as well. She was waiting for a friend's mom to pick her up for the movies, but this little interview with a real live detective would give her a great story to tell the other kids.

"I'm sorry to bother you at this hour of the night," Detective Nardone began. She was perched on the edge of a faded, slip covered chair, her posture incredibly straight. "I'm here because some evidence has come to light that impacts Selena Thompson's death, and I need to ask you both a few questions."

Dan nodded. "Sure. How can we help?"

Detective Nardone turned her attention to him. "You were the one who found Selena Thompson's body. I want you to think back to that morning. Was there anything out of the ordinary at Carson Creek?"

Dan ran through the sequence of events in his mind. The realization that there was no coffee, followed by the awareness of Selena's absence. The annoying behavior of the cat, along with the discovery of his "accident" in Selena's bedroom…

"Jasper," he said. "I realized that Jasper had been closed up in the house."

"Jasper?"

"He's Selena's cat," Sophie interjected. "And he's an outdoor cat. He comes in to visit, but he likes to live outside."

Dan nodded. "The cat had been closed inside and was anxious to get fed and go out." He grimaced. "I cleaned up a little accident he'd had in Selena's bedroom."

The detective thought a moment. "Okay, what else?"

Dan recalled his dash to the office, his search of the pool, and then the spotting of the striped towel. He shuddered.

"What is it?" Nancy Nardone was watching him intently.

"I was remembering seeing her body," he whispered. "The tip of her braid was floating up at the surface."

"Did you see anything else?"

He shook his head. "I don't think so."

She nodded. "Now let's talk about that night, when people were coming over to pay their respects, and Selena's brothers arrived. Sophie, you were helping your dad in the farmhouse, right?"

She nodded. "I set out the drinks and sandwich stuff in the dining room."

"Good. Now, when you were in the kitchen, did you see a bottle of wine on the counter?"

"I saw an empty one."

"Tell me about it."

"It was on the counter with nothing except just maybe a tiny, tiny, bit of wine inside. It had a green glass ball on the top, attached to a cork."

"Excellent. Now that was the same bottle you took to the barn?"

She nodded, looking sheepish. "I didn't know it would turn out to be important."

"I know." The detective gave a little smile. "When did you take it?"

"While people were talking. I brought it into the barn and hid it in a corner."

"How did you know it was the bottle of wine Selena had been drinking?"

"It was the only bottle in her whole kitchen."

Dan cleared his throat. "Selena only drank a glass of wine a day. She always had a bottle on the counter with a decorative stopper stuck inside. She just didn't drink that much."

"Okay." The detective rose. "Thank you both."

She headed to the door and stopped, her hand on the jamb. "Since I'm here, let me ask you both one more thing. Would you describe for me your activities on Thursday afternoon?"

Sophie swallowed. This was the alibi question! She thought a moment before answering. "I stayed after school to work on a math project and Dad picked me up." She added, "Around four thirty, I think."

Detective Nardone nodded. Sophie watched as she turned her hawk-like gaze to her father.

"I was here at home," he explained. "I left work at one o'clock or so to take care of some projects. Selena gave me the afternoon off, said she was going to relax and take it easy. She knew that any day we'd be picking the grapes and I'd be working overtime."

"I see. What kind of projects did you work on?"

"Fall chores around here, basically."

"When you left Carson Creek at one o'clock, did you pass anyone on the road?"

Dan shook his head. "No." He snapped his fingers. "Wait a minute, I did pass a car. It was a compact car, blue, I think."

"Did you see the driver?"

"No. But there was some sort of writing on the side."

"Advertising?"

He nodded. Detective Nardone scribbled on a small pad of paper. She put the pencil to her lips as if deep in thought. "Mr. Stewart, can you think of anyone who wanted to harm Selena Thompson?"

There was a silence. "She told me once about an abusive man in her past, but to my knowledge he hadn't contacted her in years."

Detective Nardone nodded. "Her ex-husband perhaps?"

"Maybe. There were the incidents of sabotage at the vineyard as well."

"Yes, so you told us." She turned her attention to the teen. "What about you, Sophie? You spent a fair amount of time at Carson Creek. If you think of anything that might help our investigation, please give me a call."

Sophie nodded. To her surprise, Detective Nardone handed both her and her father a business card.

Her father's face was somber as the door closed behind Detective Nardone.

"You might have seen the murderer in that blue car," Sophie said.

He let out a long sigh. "Who would want to murder Selena?" he asked. "She didn't have any enemies."

A horn honked outside and Sophie gave her father a quick kiss. "Off to the movies." She gave him a determined look. "I think you'll remember more about that car if you try. Just give it time."

———

Darby was tearing lettuce into bite-sized pieces when a knock on the door broke the silence.

"Ms. Farr? I'm Roger Sherman, a technician from the police department." He flashed identification and gave a small smile. "Sorry to disturb you. May I come in?"

She opened the door and allowed the slight man to enter. He was carrying a bag which he placed on the floor and began to open. "I've been asked to gather any evidence from the property, focusing on the kitchen and pool area. Do you mind showing me where the bottle was located?"

Darby pointed to the spot and the technician began removing items from his bag. "It's a long shot, to try and lift fingerprints so many days after the incident, but Detective Nardone suggested that I try." She watched as he took a large flashlight out of his bag and examined the counter surface with its powerful beam. He then moved to the sink and faucets.

"It's too late here," he shrugged. "Thursday, Friday, Saturday, Sunday...plus you had some sort of party here the day she was found?"

"I wouldn't call it a party. People were stopping by to see Selena's brothers, and dropping off food." She thought back. There had been streams of people coming through the kitchen. "What about other areas of the house?"

"I'm going to examine the pool area right now. Maybe I'll have better luck there."

"May I come along?"

He grinned. "I'll warn you, it isn't very exciting, but sure."

Darby grabbed her jacket and followed Roger Sherman outside and to the pool area. The air was taking on a chill and she thrust her hands into her pockets. A slip of paper met her fingers and she drew it out, puzzled.

It was the receipt that she'd found on the floor of the old barn. She took a look at it, and the hairs on the back of her neck began to prickle.

"Mr. Sherman, I may have something for you."

He turned to her with a surprised look as she held up the paper. "I found this on Friday, on the floor in the barn. I picked it up and saw that it was a receipt from a drug store in St. Adina. I stuck it in my pocket and it has been there ever since."

Roger Sherman opened his bag and pulled out a pair of long tweezers. Gently he pinched the scrap of paper between them and peered at it carefully. "My luck may have just changed," he said. He looked back at Darby. "Please, Ms. Farr. Show me exactly where you found this."

————

Miles Porter whistled softly under his breath. "I can't believe it. Somebody murdered Selena Thompson?"

"It certainly looks that way." Darby had made herself a light salad and was sitting in the dining room of the farmhouse, talking with Miles on the phone. The evidence technician had left fifteen minutes earlier, taking with him the receipt.

"Someone who knew she was taking that medication—beta blockers—and knew her routine." He paused. "Anyone spring to mind?"

"No. She seems to have been universally well-liked—at least that's what everyone says. Of course, there are those incidences of sabotage at the vineyard. They could be related to her death."

"You mean that someone was trying to destroy both Selena and her vineyard."

"Could be. There's the multiple offer, too. The Contento family, Vivian Allen, and this third buyer, Fritz Kohler—perhaps one of those parties killed Selena."

"But why? How would eliminating Selena help their chances of getting the vineyard?"

"Maybe they figured they'd have a better chance with her heirs. Or maybe they knew they weren't getting the property, and they killed her because they were angry."

"Poisoning someone is a pretty deliberate act," Miles commented. "Not one of those 'fits of passion' kinds of killings. This was done by someone who knew how Selena spent her day."

"Half the people in the valley seem to know she relaxed in the hot tub with a glass of wine."

"That's because they're all doing the same thing. It's a California ritual, like drinking tea in merry old England," Miles chuckled softly. "Sorry, had to inject at least a little levity. Seems all we ever talk about is murder."

"You're right. What about my friend Doug? I had to tell the party interested in his house that I was having trouble contacting him. I didn't say that he'd disappeared off the face of the earth."

"It seems that where he's living has very poor cell phone reception, and the land line number is not connected, so that could be part of our problem," explained Miles. "I tried calling Rhonda's place of business, Beachside Gifts, but no luck there. Finally I called the local police. It seems Rhonda's gift shop has been vacant for years."

Darby swallowed. "This woman's pulling some kind of scam on Doug, I just know it."

"I could ask the authorities to keep an eye out for him. They could go to Rhonda's house and ask to speak with Doug." Darby pictured her friend's reaction when a pair of burly looking Hawaiian cops showed up one night. What if Doug was fine? Maybe Rhonda had begun a new business someplace else. *Maybe I am overreacting.*

She thought back to what she knew of her friend's schedule. "He arrived on Friday. It's only been two days." She let out a long breath. "Let's wait a bit. Thank you, Miles."

"At your service." There was a pause. "When are ET and Carlos coming back? I don't like the idea of your being alone."

"I'm not alone, I have Jasper." Darby reached out and stroked the cat, who gave a silent wink of thanks.

"Seriously. With all that has happened there—"

"It's bound to be quiet. What more can happen?" Later, Darby thought back to those words, stunned at how wrong she had been.

TEN

CARLOS AND ET CAME back to the winery in better spirits than they had been in days. "It was so good to see our cousins," Carlos said with feeling, leaning over the dining room table as he spoke. "Growing up in Ensenada we were such a close family, going for picnics every Sunday, and celebrating the holidays with huge family gatherings at Aunt Teresa's house in Guadalupe. They made me remember those good times with Selena."

ET nodded. "The stories we were telling! I felt as if I were a kid again and getting into trouble with my cousin Juan." He smiled, and Darby could not help but smile as well, trying to imagine the very proper ET as a mischievous little boy.

"We have invited them to see the winery tomorrow morning," Carlos said. "ET and I will get some pastries from the bakery in St. Adina and show them around."

"Do you think that's a good idea?" Darby asked. "Detective Nardone said we should treat the house as a crime scene."

Carlos lowered his voice. "They do not know about what happened, and we won't take them in the house."

Darby glanced at ET. "We did not tell them about the wine," he said. "They think Selena's death was accidental." ET sighed and sat down at the table. "I am having a hard time believing our sister was deliberately poisoned, and yet I know she would not have taken an overdose willingly. She was too much of a fighter." Looking down at his well-manicured hands, he continued softly, "Carlos and I need to have some space from all of this. We think we will leave tomorrow afternoon and go to his place in San Francisco. I will stay there the night, and take the bus to San Diego the next day."

"I understand," Darby said. The discovery that Selena's death had not been accidental—that someone had actually doctored her wine—had aged both the brothers. The new and sinister development had changed the whole atmosphere at Carson Creek. It was now a place of suspicion and fear. ·

Darby glanced at her empty plate and decided to change the subject. "Are you hungry, or did you have something to eat with your family?"

"We are fine," ET assured her. "There is never a shortage of food with Aunt Teresa around." He smiled. "Selena was always a slender girl, and kind of a picky eater when she was young. Teresa would give her a hard time about not eating enough, but Selena always ate just what she wanted and when she wanted." He stroked his chin and regarded Carlos. "That sister of ours could be very stubborn."

Carlos nodded. "She was one of those kinds of people who made up their mind and that was it, you know?" He frowned.

"That's one of the reasons why I think Vivian Allen should get Carson Creek. Selena chose her. We need to honor her wishes."

"What is your other reason?" Darby asked quietly. She pushed her salad plate to the side and met Carlos' glowering gaze.

"It is personal."

ET raised an eyebrow. "I should think that if you have personal reasons for choosing someone to purchase our sister's property, you would at least do me the courtesy of sharing that reason."

Carlos let out an exasperated sound and placed both hands on the table. "This is not the time."

"What?" ET was on his feet, his face incredulous. "Then when is the time? Once we are both back in our lives and Darby is here trying to help sell Selena's home? Give me a break, Carlos. You know something about Vivian Allen, and it is time you tell us. Now." His dark eyes burned into his brother's face. Finally Carlos gave a small shrug.

"I told you that Vivian had a backer for the property—someone with very deep pockets."

ET glanced at Darby and nodded. "Yes."

"This person has offered me a job as her personal photographer. It's huge." He looked into his brother's face, his eyes hopeful. "It would mean an incredible salary, as well as the chance to travel on her tours…"

"Tours? Just who is this mysterious backer?"

Carlos gave a quick grin. "You are not going to believe it. Vivian's sister is one of the richest women in the world." He paused. "Her sister is Veronica."

"The pop star?" ET looked confused. "The one who wears the leather shorts and fishnet stockings?"

"That's her. She wants to invest in a vineyard and Vivian wants to run it. They looked at a few other places, but Carson Creek is Vivian's favorite."

Darby thought back to their meeting with Vivian. *I asked her if she had a partner. Why did she lie?*

ET drew in a breath. "Carlos, if this position is something you want, I am happy to see you get it. But if Vivian is tying it to the sale of our sister's property, that sounds suspicious to me."

The color rose in Carlos' cheeks. "I knew you would see it that way! Any time something good comes my way, you try to find a way to stop it. Is it so hard to believe that Veronica wants me because I'm talented? Because my photographs really speak to her? Is that such a crazy idea?"

"No, no," ET soothed. "I know of your vision and I am sure Vivian and her sister do as well."

Carlos seemed somewhat mollified. "Thanks." He turned to Darby. "Can we even sell the place now that there is a murder investigation? Will any of them want to buy it?"

"You bring up a good point, Carlos. I don't know the answer. Certainly I will need to disclose that there is an ongoing investigation. It may indeed influence some of the interested parties."

"I guess we'll just have to see," Carlos said. He sighed and looked at ET. "You're right about Veronica. If she wants me, she can make me an offer whether she gets Carson Creek or not." He ran his fingers through an unruly mass of curls. "I'm going upstairs and see if I can get some sleep. Tomorrow will be a long day."

ET nodded and rose from the table. "I shall head upstairs as well. Good night Darby. I hope you will get some rest, too."

Darby took her plate into the kitchen, her eyes lingering on the spot where she remembered seeing the wine bottle. What had happened on the day of Selena's death? Had someone come to the vineyard deliberately to add the ground beta blockers to the bottle, knowing that Selena would have a glass of wine while sitting in the hot tub? Had someone deliberately poisoned her? Who? And why?

Could it have been the same person who was sabotaging the vineyard? Was murder their final, terrifying act?

She took a stenographer's pad out of Selena's kitchen drawer and sat down at the dining room table. There had been three instances when damage occurred at the vineyard, two that happened prior to Selena's death, and one that happened following it. Was Selena's murder just another form of damage? Or had the perpetrator of the sabotage not cared that she was dead, or known that she'd been murdered?

Could the sabotage and the murder be unrelated? Did Selena's death even have to do with Carson Creek? Selena had been married, many years earlier, to a man whose last name was Thompson. Surely ET would know about his ex-brother-in-law…

Darby rose and crept quietly up the stairs. Beneath ET's door was the feeble glow of a light. She knocked gently and he came to the door, wearing a stylish pair of pin-striped cotton pajamas. "What is it, my friend?" he whispered.

"Who was Selena's ex-husband? Do you know where he lives?"

ET thought a moment. "His name was Rick Thompson, and he came from the Bay area, but I do not know where he is now. I don't think Selena kept any contact with him." His eyes looked concerned. "Why do you ask? Do you think he could be connected to all this?"

"I don't know." She touched his arm lightly. "I wish I could figure this out for you."

"I know you do, Darby, but I don't want you to think this is your problem to solve. The police will handle any investigation. You just help me sell the vineyard."

"I will," she promised, backing away. "Good night."

"Good night," he said, and closed the door.

Back in the kitchen, Darby returned the pad of paper to the drawer and sighed. Perhaps Selena's ex-husband was a lead—it was worth exploring, anyway—but more than likely it was a dead end. And the scrap of paper on the old barn floor could easily have fallen from Selena's or Dan Stewart's pocket. Chances were, it, too, meant nothing.

Discouraged, Darby turned off lights and locked the kitchen door. A brush of fur against her leg was momentarily frightening, until she remembered Jasper and his urge to spend the nocturnal hours outside on the prowl.

She unlocked the door and opened it. The cat leapt out and into the gathering night.

Jasper had spent the night of Selena's murder inside the house. Had Selena let him in when she poured her wine and donned her swimsuit? Or was it more likely the murderer had closed Jasper in the house at some point?

If only Jasper could relay what he had seen.

―――――

In the middle of a dream in which she was packing box after box of her neighbor Doug Henderson's possessions, a loud sound startled Darby Farr awake. She lay still for a moment, wondering what she had heard, and then rose and went to the window. The night was inky black, with clouds obscuring the moon, and at first Darby saw nothing. She hurried to the other window overlooking the old barn and red winery building. What she glimpsed made her gasp.

Bright orange flames leapt from Carson Creek's tasting room, the tongues of fire a startling contrast to the night sky. Darby fumbled on the night stand for her phone. She dialed 911 and gave the dispatcher the vineyard's location. She then grabbed a sweatshirt and pulled it on over her nightgown.

"ET, Carlos, get up," she yelled, knocking on their bedroom doors. A groggy Carlos, his hair sticking up at odd angles, met her with a confused expression. "What is it?"

"The red barn building is on fire. I've called the fire department. Let's hope they get here as quickly as possible."

ET appeared in the hallway. "My God," he breathed. "What can we do?"

Darby's thoughts were racing. "Selena's office was in that building. Maybe we can save some of Carson Creek's data from going up in flames."

She grabbed her jeans and pulled them on along with her running sneakers. Together with the Gomez brothers, she rushed down the stairs and into the chilly September night.

To Darby's dismay she saw that the flames now covered the whole corner of the building. The fire was spreading, and fast.

"Hurry," she yelled. "I think we can still get into the office."

They ran across the parking lot and to the burning building. Thick smoke billowed from the flames, lighting the sky with an unnatural glow. The roar of the fire's growing intensity filled their ears. "I don't know if this is safe," ET yelled above the noise. "It isn't worth one of us getting injured."

Carlos gave him a grim look. "Selena worked her butt off for this place," he shouted back. "I'm going in and getting her computer at least." He dashed into the building, with Darby close behind.

Smoke filled the room, making visibility virtually impossible. Her eyes stinging, Darby moved blindly toward where she remembered Selena's desk. She spotted what looked to be a stack of files and grabbed them. Coughing and feeling as if she could no longer breathe, she stumbled for the door.

Carlos was beside her, clutching what appeared to be a laptop. His eyes were streaming with tears from the smoke.

"Where is Rico?" Carlos yelled. "Did he go in there?"

Darby looked toward the door. She hadn't seen ET, but in the smoke-filled office it was impossible to see anything. "I don't know," she cried. "I thought he stayed out here."

A sick sensation filled her stomach as she watched Carlos lunge toward the building. As he was about to enter, the crouched figure of ET emerged from the smoke. Carlos reached for him and pulled him across the lawn toward Darby.

"I don't know what I grabbed, but at least it is something," ET said, dropping several binders to the ground in exhaustion. The high-pitched whine of sirens filled the night. "At last," he cried.

Moments later two fire engines roared up the road and pulled to a stop before the building. Men jumped from the truck and began pointing hoses at the fire. Water shot from the hoses and Darby felt a glimmer of hope. Maybe the firefighters were not too late.

A tall man wearing yellow turnout gear and a firefighter's helmet appeared beside Darby. "I'm the Captain here," he yelled above the din. "Anyone inside?"

"No," Carlos yelled. "It is just the three of us staying at the property."

The Captain nodded. "Good. Let me get this under control, and I'll be back to ask a few questions," he yelled.

Just then the voice of one of the men rose above the fire's roar. "Captain Montera," he cried. "Come over here, sir! We've got some-one! We've got a body!"

———

Andrea Contento woke to the sound of sirens. She shook her head, trying to understand what she was hearing, and realized with dread the wailing meant a fire. She looked at the figure of her sleeping husband beside her. "Michael," she whispered, tugging at his shoul-der. "Something's wrong."

"What?" He was a deep sleeper, difficult to rouse, and she knew it would take a few moments before he was lucid.

"Listen. Those fire engine sirens are close."

"Carson Creek." He was awake now, out of bed and yanking on a pair of jeans and a shirt. "I'm going over there."

"Do you think you should?"

He gave her a sharp look. "What is that supposed to mean?"

"It's just that I'm worried about you."

"What? For God's sake, Andrea, what are you talking about?"

"Your heart! You know you should be taking it easy."

He shook his head, irritated. "Let's discuss this another time, shall we? I'm going to see what the hell is going on."

"Don't go alone, Michael. Tim stayed over last night. Take him with you."

"Listen, I'll go alone if I want to go alone. It's not like he's going to be much help."

"Please."

Michael Contento yanked open the bedroom door. "Tell him to meet me at the truck."

Andrea grabbed her robe and knocked on the door where Tim was sleeping. When he opened it, she explained what little they knew and asked if he would accompany his father to Carson Creek.

"I don't want him going alone," Andrea said.

Tim rubbed his eyes and nodded. "Yeah, I'm on it."

She shut his door and headed downstairs to make coffee. It was going to be a very long day.

————

From where Darby stood, huddled on the grass with ET and Carlos, the corpse found in the tasting portion of the building appeared to be burned beyond recognition. *Please don't let it be Dan,* she silently chanted, even though the voice of reason kept repeating inside her head, "Who else could it be?"

An ambulance had arrived and the paramedics were already loading the body into the vehicle. ET and Carlos were silent, watching as the uniformed emergency medical technicians slammed shut the doors and prepared to drive to the hospital.

No one said a word as the ambulance crawled away from the scene of the fire. *No need to hurry,* thought Darby. *It isn't life or death...*

A large truck with "Contento Family Vineyards" emblazoned on the sides pulled up beside them. Doors opened and Darby recognized Michael Contento and his son, Tim.

"What's going on?" Michael thundered. "Who is going to the hospital?"

ET explained the discovery of the body, his voice a monotone. "We do not know who it is," he said dully.

"Christ. It's not Dan Stewart, is it?" Michael had voiced their worst fear.

Tim Contento exhaled and regarded the building. Most of the blaze was out and it looked as if the firefighters had been able to save a good portion of the building. "What happened?"

"An explosion," Darby explained. "It woke me up." Her cell phone rang and Darby yanked it out of her pocket. She glanced at the screen. *Sophie Stewart.*

Her heart sank. With shaking hands, she answered the phone.

"Is my dad there?" Sophie asked.

Darby felt as if she would faint. *She is looking for her father,* she thought. *He was the one in the building. That is his body in the ambulance, on the way to the hospital. How can I ever tell this girl that he was killed in the explosion?* She swallowed. "Sophie, your dad—"

"He told me to tell you he's on his way." She yawned. "Now I'm going back to bed."

"What?" Darby was gripping her phone so tightly she thought it would snap in half. "What did you say?"

"My dad just took off in the jeep and told me to tell you he's coming to the vineyard. He got a call from his friend Jake on the fire department." She yawned again. "'Night. I'll see you tomorrow."

Darby hung up and looked at the men beside her. "That was Sophie Stewart," she explained. "Dan is on his way over. He's safe."

A collective sigh of relief rose from the crowd. Michael Contento sent his eyes skyward. "Thank God," he breathed.

Tim Contento rubbed his smooth head. "So if it wasn't Dan in there, then who was it? And what were they doing snooping around?"

No one answered as Captain Montera approached them and nodded to the new arrivals. "Mr. Contento, Tim," he said gruffly.

Michael Contento clapped him on the back. "Good to see you," the older man barked. "You and your men have done a fine job containing this fire."

"Thank you," the captain said. "The sprinkler system helped, and we were lucky to get the call so soon after the explosion occurred."

"So then it was an explosion, eh?" Michael Contento looked back toward the building. "Gas leak?"

The Captain shook his head. "No. I almost wish it was a gas leak. This was arson." He grimaced. "There will be an investigation, but I'd say we're dealing with a pipe bomb."

"What?" Tim Contento's voice was incredulous. "Who in the world would set off something like that?"

"Whoever it was that we carried out of there on a stretcher," the captain said, his voice grim. "The police are on the way, but I'll bet my rubber boots that our Kentucky fried corpse was the bomber." Darby saw the captain's eyes sweep over her and saw them soften in the murky light. "You folks need to get on up to the house where it's warmer," he said, motioning to the group. "Go ahead. Detective Nardone is on her way."

Darby nodded, and turned toward the house. Taking her first step, she was surprised to realize that her whole body was shaking.

ELEVEN

THE BEEPING OF HER phone woke Vivian Allen and she swore. *Why don't I ever turn the damn thing off,* she thought. She groped in the dark for the light switch. Chances were it was her sister, calling as she sometimes did after a show, wanting to tell her which celebrity went off the wagon, or how many encores she'd done after the ballad "Heaven Bent." She sighed, put on some reading glasses, and scrutinized the phone.

She had an unread text message. *All that noise for a stupid little message?* She made a vow to take the phone into her provider and get the alarm silenced for good. *A message! Give me a break.*

Yawning, she found the text, noting it had been sent an hour or so earlier. *Our plan is in motion,* it read.

Vivian's puzzlement turned to dread as she looked at the sender's number. *When will he leave me alone?*

———

Darby heard tires on the driveway and looked out to see Dan Stewart's battered jeep, followed by an unmarked sedan she recognized as belonging to Detective Nardone. She saw them greet each other and watched as Dan shook his head, pointing toward the red barn building. He was still talking as they entered the farmhouse.

"Whoever did this is the guy responsible for the other things, right?"

Detective Nardone shrugged. "It's possible. We're waiting for a positive ID on the body."

Dan glanced over at Darby. "An exciting Sunday night at Carson Creek," he said. "I can't believe somebody tried to blow up the place." He ran a hand through his graying hair and reached for the coffee pot. "I'm making another pot if you're interested, Detective."

She nodded. "Find me when it's ready." Detective Nardone turned her gaze to Darby. "I understand you were the one who heard the explosion. Tell me about it."

"Just a loud boom that woke me up," Darby said. "I got ET and Carlos and we headed over to the building. We went into the office…"

"Wait a minute. You entered the burning building?" Dan stood with the coffee pot in hand, the water faucet running in the background.

"We went into the side that wasn't on fire." She looked back at the detective. "We wanted to save what we could."

"And what did you get?"

"Selena's laptop, a few files, and some ledgers. The smoke was too thick for us to make a second trip."

The detective nodded. "I'll let Captain Montera tell you how dangerous it is to enter any burning building, whether you see flames shooting out or not. Meanwhile, let's talk about this intruder. Did you see any sign of him or her?"

"Nothing. We had no idea anyone was in the building." Darby wondered if she should raise her suspicions concerning Selena's first husband and decided to go for it. "Detective Nardone, did you by any chance contact a man named Rick Thompson, Selena's former husband?"

Her eyes narrowed. "Why do you ask?"

"I was wondering whether he would be considered a suspect."

Detective Nardone nodded. "The answer is yes. Rick Thompson dealt drugs, served time for petty theft—the whole lot. He was at the top of our list until we discovered his alibi." She waited and added dryly, "He died in a car crash three years ago." She tossed her chin toward Dan. "Let me know when that coffee is ready."

———

Andrea Contento heard the door slam and roused herself from a deep sleep. She flung an arm to the other side of the bed, expecting to encounter her husband's sleeping form, but his side of the king-sized mattress was empty. Then she remembered the sirens. He'd left in the middle of the night with Tim and she'd dragged herself down to the kitchen to make coffee. *I thought I'd wait up for them.* Instead she'd staggered back up the stairs, exhausted, and fallen back asleep.

She glanced at her bedside clock. Barely five a.m. on Monday morning.

She groaned and swung her legs over the side of the bed. There was still so much to do in preparation for Selena's funeral, plus planning for several major events at the winery occurring during harvest, as well as the harvest itself to supervise, and yet she felt as if she was running on empty. She slid on a satin robe. Caffeine would help; it always did.

She slipped quietly down the stairs and into the kitchen, expecting to see Michael at the picture window, surveying the vines. His absence meant that he was probably in his office, looking over paperwork or reading a few of his favorite wine blogs. She shrugged and poured herself a strong cup of coffee. Let him have his quiet time. He'd be back in the kitchen for a refill soon enough.

Andrea added cream to her stoneware mug and went over the day's schedule. The mass was at 11 a.m., followed by a light lunch served in the tasting room. Margo had set up the luncheon, consulting only briefly with her stepmother regarding the menu, but Andrea didn't care. Contento Family Vineyards ran smoothly because each of the key family members had clearly defined roles to which they tried to adhere. Michael insisted on it, saying frequently that it was the only way to run and grow a successful family business, and for the most part, he'd been right.

The sound of her husband's footsteps interrupted her reverie. He headed straight for the coffee pot, poured coffee into a stainless steel travel cup and nodded in her direction. "Those sirens we heard at Carson Creek? Somebody set off a bomb in their tasting room."

"A bomb? Was anyone hurt?"

"Whoever set it off was killed in the blast."

She felt a sinking sensation in her stomach. *Please don't let it be Christophe*, she prayed, and yet even as she thought the words, she knew with certainty he had perished.

"It's Barton," she said flatly. "It's got to be."

Michael Contento gave her a long, steady, look. "How can you be so sure?"

She paused. How much should she tell him, this aging vintner who believed in the world's goodness, and seemed to see nothing of its savage underbelly? How much could he take, at this stage of his life? And yet it was strange that he hadn't questioned her assertion of Barton; only asked how she could be sure. *Perhaps I am underestimating you*, she thought, knowing it would not be the first time.

"Chris was obsessed with Carson Creek," she finally said. "I guess I'm not surprised that he would try to destroy it."

TWELVE

THE FUNERAL OF SELENA Thompson was by turns a somber Roman Catholic Mass and a celebration of her creative, determined personality. Darby listened as several Gomez cousins read passages of Scripture and parts of poems, their grief coming to the forefront as they tried unsuccessfully to choke back tears. Carlos stood by ET's side as he read a short statement they had written together, barely keeping his emotions in check as he thanked family and friends for coming, and gave his sincere appreciation to the Contentos for their help.

Darby had never seen a space so crowded. The little chapel was filled and overflowing with mourners—some of whom Darby recognized from the first night at Selena's home, and others whom she surmised to be family relatives. She was surprised to see a large, powerfully built man in a beautifully tailored navy suit whom she recognized from fitness magazines as Fritz Kohler. She was watching him exit the chapel when there was a tap on her arm.

"Who's he?" Detective Nardone looked more petite than usual in a black sheath dress and black flats. Her gaze, however, was just as penetrating.

"A potential buyer for Selena's property, Fritz Kohler." Darby realized she had heard nothing from the man regarding the sale. Perhaps he was no longer interested in purchasing the vineyard, particularly now that the production area had been destroyed.

"Hmmmm." Nardone narrowed her eyes. "Seems odd that he would show up. What about the accountant? She here, too?"

Darby shook her head. "I don't think so." The chapel's occupants had started filing out, heading to the tasting room, leaving only a handful of Gomez cousins speaking quietly with Carlos and ET. "Any word on the identification of the body from last night?" Darby asked.

Detective Nardone nodded, her dark eyes shrewd. "Christophe Barton, Estate Manager at Contento Family Vineyards." She frowned. "It's public knowledge now."

Darby watched as Margo Contento carried a large bouquet of flowers toward the back of the chapel. So the odd man she'd met in the Contento's parking lot had been the saboteur. "Any idea why?"

The detective shook her head. She jerked her head in the direction of the tasting room. "I'll see you over there. Got some things to check on first."

Darby approached Margo and asked if she needed a hand. Margo accepted Darby's offer of help with a grateful smile, asking her to bring the portrait of Selena from the chapel to the tasting room.

The portrait was at the front of the chapel where ET and Carlos stood talking. Darby lifted the large framed, studio image of a smiling Selena and began carrying it to the back of the room.

"I remember the day I took that," Carlos said, coming alongside her. "Selena still owned the house in Haight-Ashbury, and I'd just moved to the city. We'd taken a walk over to Coit Tower and admired the Bay. Coming back we stopped at a little coffee shop by Levi Square for scones and eggs. We had a wonderful talk about our childhood, about the things we remembered from growing up, and then …" His voice trailed off. He looked away, visibly upset.

"And then what?" Darby kept her voice gentle, but she sensed that whatever Carlos had been about to say was important.

He swung his head back, the black curls bobbing emphatically. "And then I saw the bruises."

"On Selena?"

He nodded. His teeth were clenched and she could see that the memory of that day still angered him. "She pulled the sleeves of her blouse down, but it was too late. I'd seen the purple and black marks, mottled bruises, the kind that come from hands squeezing flesh so hard that the blood vessels rupture."

"My God. What did she say?"

"She said they were nothing, tried to change the subject, but I demanded to know who was hurting her. At first I was convinced it was her ex-husband, Rick Thompson. A lowlife if I ever saw one. But she said no, that she hadn't seen him in years. 'Who's doing this then?' I yelled. 'Who's hurting you?'

"Finally she told me it was a guy she'd been dating, someone she knew from cycling. I asked for his name—I wanted to kill him! But she wouldn't tell me. All she said was that she'd ended the relationship. 'I'm totally done with him,' is what she said. That's when I first heard of her plans to buy the vineyard. She was so excited about that, I forgot my anger. I had to share in her joy."

He gazed down at the photograph he had taken of his sister and tried to smile. "We went back to my studio, and I took this portrait. I never again questioned her about those bruises, but I believed she'd left that man for good." He frowned. "I hope that was truly the case." He turned and walked out of the chapel, leaving Darby clutching Selena's portrait, deep in thought.

Darby found Margo Contento ushering people into the tasting room. She handed her the portrait and Margo mouthed her thanks. Darby watched as she brought it to a table in the corner where a sort of shrine to Selena had been set up. Along with the large studio photograph were smaller, informal shots of Selena, some taken when she was a child.

Darby hung back from joining the mingling mourners in the tasting room. Very few—if any—of the assembled people knew the circumstances of Selena's death. ET and Carlos had begged Detective Nardone to keep the news quiet until after the service, and it appeared to Darby that she'd complied with their request. As a result, none of the visiting family, and few of the locals, knew that Selena's cause of death was under investigation, although Darby knew they were discussing the vineyard explosion.

To Darby, the residue in the bottom of the wine bottle clearly indicated foul play. Had Selena intended to kill herself, she would have ingested the medicine in her glass, or taken the extra pills by hand. Jasper's overnight confinement was also strange. From what Dan and Sophie Stewart had said, Selena would not have closed the cat indoors. It made much more sense that he had followed someone into the house at the time of his mistress' death.

Darby looked over the assembled mourners, more convinced than ever that Selena Thompson's life had been taken from her. Could a past relationship with an abusive man be the answer to the mystery of her murder? If so, who was that man?

———

Vivian Allen did not know what to do, an unusual predicament for the frenetic redhead. Somehow word had leaked out that she had a partner interested in the purchase of Carson Creek, and that partner was none other than her mega-rich, mega-famous baby sister Veronica. She took another look at what passed for the area's local paper, her nose wrinkled in disgust. A front-page story headlined "Ventano Bent?" mentioned the pop star's interest in acquiring a vineyard, and quoted real estate broker Harrison Wainfield as predicting someone like Veronica could ruin the special character of the valley.

She tossed the *Wyattville Tribune* on the floor. Harrison Wainfield was an idiot; she'd known that the first time she'd spoken to the man. She thought back to the call she'd made to his agency and the questions she'd asked regarding property in wine country. The smug bastard had ridiculed her motives for wanting a vineyard, and had insisted on a hefty retainer just to provide information. She'd told him to take a hike and hung up.

Now Vivian Allen smirked. Regardless of his comments to the newspaper, Wainfield was undoubtedly sorry that he'd missed out on working with the super-famous Veronica. *You should have played nice,* she thought.

The comments of the regular residents of the Ventano Valley were more troubling. *They ought to welcome a celebrity of Veronica's status to their sleepy little hamlets!* Of course her purchase of Carson Creek Estate & Winery would impact the valley, but in the best way possible. Veronica's fame would draw even more tourists to the mom-and-pop vineyards that dotted the hillsides. She'd give money to local charities, grace some fundraising events with her effervescent presence. She'd draw attention to the humble life of the vineyard owner, maybe even star in a movie about the business.

Vivian's daydreams were cut short by the ring of her phone. She glanced at the display, afraid of what she would see. A sigh of relief escaped her lips. *Carlos Gomez.* Perhaps he was ready to accept her offer and become one of Veronica's on-location photographers. Vivian hadn't yet discussed the arrangement with her sister, but there was plenty of time for that once the vineyard was secured. Getting the property was the essential thing.

Vivian plopped down on the bed in her hotel suite, put on a hopeful smile, and answered her phone.

———

Darby saw the solitary figure of Michael Contento standing outside of the tasting room. His back was to her and he was gazing out over the vineyards.

"What an incredible view you have here," she commented, hating to break his reverie but wanting very much to talk with the wine scion.

Still watching the fields, he nodded. "Yes, it's nothing short of spectacular. On a clear day you can even see the Wyatt River off toward St. Adina." He gave a small smile. "I've been coming to this very spot for close to forty years now. Ever since I realized I was going to be at the helm of this vineyard."

"It hadn't been your original plan, I understand."

He turned to meet her eyes. "That's correct. I was in academia, and totally happy with the path I'd taken. But plans change. My brother David was the one who loved this place from boyhood. He went off to the Vietnam War as an officer and became a statistic—one of the unlucky guys who didn't come back." He gave a thoughtful look as if remembering the story for the first time. "I hoped that my father would find someone else to take over, but he made it clear it was my duty. And so, when the time came, I left the world of literature and became a farmer." He gave a small smile. "Whenever I've been tempted to feel sorry for myself, I take a walk across that ridge." He pointed off to the distance where the roof of a building was just visible.

"That's Carson Creek Estate, isn't it?"

"Yes. Only a small bit of the grounds are visible from here, but along the property line it's another story." He made a sweeping gesture with his arm. "This view never fails to convince me that I'm one lucky professor."

They stood in silence for a moment before Michael Contento asked, "Do you believe in luck, Darby?"

She thought of her parents, perishing on a sailboat in the middle of a Maine bay. *My father had asked me to come on that sail, but I declined.* Was that luck? If so, was it good or bad? In escaping the fate of John and Jada Farr, Darby had been forced to live with the pain of their loss and her guilt at surviving.

"No," she said. "I don't believe in luck."

"I don't either. And yet look what has befallen our neighboring vineyard: a string of incidents that most people would term 'bad luck.' First Selena's death, and now this explosion in that new building." He gritted his teeth. "I remember when she had the damn thing built. She was so proud of her tasting room, those offices, and her production area! Who could have done something like that?"

Darby glanced down, wondering if she should tell Michael Contento what she'd heard only minutes before.

"Detective Nardone has released the identity of the body." She hesitated. "This will doubtless be a shock, but it's Christophe Barton."

He turned a somber face to her. "So I'd heard. I can't for the life of me understand it. Barton was kind of an odd, quiet guy, but to blow up someone's business? It just doesn't make sense. My wife claims he was obsessed with the place, ever since Selena turned him down for that position." He frowned. "But dammit, that was five years ago! Why would anyone hold a grudge for that long?" He looked back over the fields. "I suppose we never really know what is going on deep in other people's minds."

Darby looked out over the Contento family's property. The native landscape gave way to row after row of perfectly straight vines, bordered by low hills in the background. Christophe Barton had been in charge of this paradise, and yet at the same time, he'd plotted against Carson Creek, first tampering with the yeast and the barrels, and then cutting the sprinkler lines. Blowing up the tasting room was his final act of terrorism, one in which he'd lost his own life as well. But what about Selena's death? Darby knew from Detective Nardone that Barton was now the number one suspect.

"Tell me about what happened when Selena chose Dan Stewart as winemaker instead of Barton."

Michael Contento thought a moment. "Everyone knew Barton was furious. He assumed he had the position because of his credentials—extensive training in the vineyards of Burgundy, stellar recommendations from several wineries here—so it came as a total surprise when she passed him over. Carson Creek would have been the next logical step for him, a place where he could really make his mark. But I guess Selena didn't see it that way."

"Why didn't she choose Barton?"

"I don't think she ever liked the man. Christophe could be very blunt, and he had a tremendous amount of arrogance. In many ways he was the total opposite of Dan."

He shook his head. "I'll confess that I was hoping Selena would hire Chris Barton. I certainly never dreamt she'd lure Dan away! I thought he was happy here. But that's the way things go."

"You must have been annoyed, to say the least."

"I was extremely disappointed. After all, Dan's an incredible winemaker—very gifted—and I hated to lose him, but I understood."

"Did you ever see any evidence that Barton was capable of these acts of terrorism?"

"Never. Like I said, he was quiet. Obviously he was resentful at first, but all that was five years ago! Forgive and forget is my motto." He sighed. "Could that man's anger toward Selena have been festering all that time? Or did something new prompt him to act this year?" He grimaced. "Thank goodness Selena's death was from natural causes."

Darby bit her lip, wondering if she should confide in Michael Contento. He was a good source of information, and she wanted to know what he thought.

"Selena didn't die a natural death," she said quietly. "She was poisoned."

The look he gave her was one of pure surprise.

"Poisoned? That can't be."

"The wine she drank had an overdose of her blood pressure medication. It caused her to lose consciousness in the hot tub and drown."

"She must have caused her own overdose! Apparently she was not a well woman."

"The police think she was deliberately poisoned."

Michael Contento put a hand up to his chin and Darby noticed it was shaking. "Ridiculous," he muttered. "Totally ridiculous."

"I'm sorry to give you this news," Darby stammered. "I thought that you should know."

Slowly a change came over his face. The shocked look hardened into a snarl and his eyes became brittle. He took a step toward her, his eyes narrow.

"Who do you think you are, throwing out your theories as if you actually knew something? We all loved Selena. Not even Barton would have harmed a hair on her head." He gave a harsh laugh. "For once that idiot Wainfield is correct—you have no right butting into our business. Go back to Southern California, Darby Farr, and leave us to grieve for our dead."

Michael Contento turned abruptly and stormed back to the vineyard's kitchen entrance. Darby heard the door close with a bang. Her heart was beating hard from the confrontation but she forced herself to analyze the scene objectively.

Clearly the news that Selena's death was intentional had taken the older man by surprise. Darby had witnessed his shock become rage, and then felt his anger directed at a convenient scapegoat—her. She knew with certainty that behind his tirade lurked fear.

Who are you really angry at, Michael? What is it that you are afraid of?

———

Detective Nardone raised an eyebrow as Darby approached the tasting room and the crowd of mourners. "I think I saw some sparks flying between you and Michael Contento," she commented drily. "What was that all about?"

Darby glanced around and saw that they were alone. "I told him about Selena and the beta blockers. He was surprised and then very angry at me."

"Listen, Darby, I can tell you are one of those frustrated amateur detectives and I don't doubt that your instincts for this kind of work are very good, but—and this is a big but—this is my investigation and you need to let me handle it." She pursed her lips. "That said, it's often very useful to have someone in the field who is not law enforcement, someone who can do the kinds of things we can't do, say the kinds of things we'd get our hands slapped for." She tilted her chin at Darby. "I'm going to be looking for your cooperation on that score."

Darby nodded. "I'm sorry if I jumped the gun with Michael. The timing seemed right..."

"Timing is everything, I agree. Now describe for me again his reaction. Shocked, and then extremely pissed off?"

"Yes, but mingled with something else—apprehension, fear. I got the impression that telling him about the metoprolol triggered something."

"He thinks he has an idea of who might have poisoned that girl, and ten to one he doesn't believe it was Barton."

"And what do you think, Detective? Did Christophe Barton poison Selena? Was she just another link in his chain of terror against Carson Creek?"

"Nah, I don't think so. It doesn't fit what we now know of Barton's profile. Barton liked to do showy things, crimes involving action. He saw himself as a French *saboteur*. Poisoning? It's too passive for him." She thought a moment. "Now, he may have been teaming up with someone else, and that person poisoned Selena while he handled the planning of the explosion." She put her hands on her hips. "He strikes me as a lone wolf kind of guy, but just to be sure, I'll get someone analyzing his computer and phone records."

Darby saw Carlos across the room in a conversation with a cousin and remembered his story about Selena's bruises. She told Detective Nardone about the possibility of an abusive boyfriend in the victim's past.

"That's a good lead. Selena's body was bruised on her abdomen, but that looked to have been from a fall." She paused. "We could find some of the people she lived with in San Francisco, discover who this guy was."

"I can ask Carlos if he remembers any of her friends. Perhaps Dan would know as well." They were quiet a moment as a staff person passed them with a tray of sliced avocados and miniature quesadillas. Detective Nardone motioned for the waiter to stop and then chose one from his tray.

She took a bite, chewed, and then nodded. "Good."

Darby wasn't sure if the detective was commenting on the quesadilla or the case. She waited.

"Dan Stewart mentioned seeing a car pass him on the road to Carson Creek on Thursday—blue, with writing on the side. I noticed the big yoga guy drives a hybrid car, blue, with advertising. If you get the chance, put on your Nancy Drew hat and find out why he's here. He may want to purchase Carson Creek but it's odd to show up at the dead seller's funeral service, don't you think?" She finished the quesadilla and pulled a pair of sunglasses from the pocket of her jacket. Darby noted with surprise that they were Chanel.

Suddenly Detective Nardone seemed all business. "Questioning on this case will start this afternoon. I'll talk to Dan Stewart again, meet with the Contentos, question the yoga guy, and have a little chat with Vivian Allen. If you hear anything else that could be pertinent to this investigation, give me a call." She pulled a business card out of her jacket pocket and handed it to Darby. "Watch your back. This is a murder investigation. We're dealing with someone who thinks killing is a way to solve problems."

Darby nodded and watched Detective Nardone walk away. A sudden breeze blew up from the valley, ruffling the tablecloths laden with trays of food. Darby shivered. The wind and the weight of the detective's words gave her goose bumps. She crossed her arms for warmth and headed into the room.

———

Toby Bliss took a bite of smoked salmon and chewed thoughtfully. There it was again, the circular tattoo on the big beefy guy he'd driven home from his bar. A wheel, with spokes—possibly for a motorcycle club, he thought. So the guy had known Selena Thompson. He must have been a friend of hers from before her days in the valley, because Bliss knew everyone, and this guy was not a local.

He gave a little wave to Margo Contento, who nodded back from across the room. She was stunning: tall, blonde, and with a kind of energy that seemed to light up the room. Too bad she had to work for such a prick, he thought. Michael Contento was one smug son of a gun, never satisfied with anything, from a dry martini to the charity 5K held at Toby's bar. He shook his head and popped another piece of salmon into his mouth. Even now, the guy was giving his daughter a hard time, pointing a finger in sharp little bursts, a hand on his hip. Toby could read his body language from across the room. Michael Contento was not happy.

Margo seemed to be explaining something to him and her furtive looks indicated that she did not want to make a scene. Her father, however, had those big Italian emotions that you couldn't tamp down if you tried. Toby watched as he threw his head back in a dramatic fashion and then stormed out of the tasting room. Margo waited a moment, looking for all the world like an abandoned little girl.

Toby looked around. No one else seemed to have noticed the father-daughter fracas. They were busy talking and eating the food coming from the Contento kitchen. He shrugged. Hopefully Margo wouldn't have to wait too long until her father headed for the big vineyard in the sky. After all, the guy was ancient and looking more so all the time. He helped himself to one last piece of salmon. *That funeral will be one to remember,* he thought. It wasn't too early to come up with a special commemorative Contento drink—maybe tee shirts, too. Smiling, Toby Bliss sauntered to a new table to sample more food.

————

"Excuse me, but aren't you Mr. Kohler?" Darby offered her hand to the big man who was balancing a glass of sparkling water and a tray laden with protein-rich foods.

He nodded. "Yes, and I believe you are the broker for Carson Creek Estate & Winery. Darby Farr?"

"That's right. I'm hoping that we can discuss your offer on the property when the time is right." She looked down at her hands. She'd criticized Harrison Wainfield for talking business at inappropriate times, now here she was doing the exact same thing. "I didn't introduce myself for that reason, however. I wondered if you knew Selena Thompson personally."

He made a thoughtful sound and gave a small nod. "I've known Selena for many years. We were friends in San Francisco before she moved here, and I hoped to stay in touch following her departure, but it didn't work out that way."

"Why not?"

He looked off to the side as if considering whether to answer. "I'd like to say something trite like, 'Times change,' but that wouldn't be the truth. The fact is, I treated Leni badly and although I wanted to make amends, she didn't want anything to do with me." He exhaled, his face weary. He put down his plate of food as if no longer hungry.

"Where did the purchase of Selena's vineyard come in?"

"I found out she needed funds and I thought I could help her by purchasing the property. I still feel as if that's the case. Her soul will rest easy knowing it is well cared for."

"I've heard that you plan to run one of your yoga retreat centers at Carson Creek. Would that have made Selena's soul rest easy?"

"Oooh—your words have got quite an edge, you know that?" He narrowed his eyes. "Leni approved of my centers. She was excited about the fusion of Carson Creek's gorgeous setting and the meditative practice of yoga. So excited, in fact, that she told me I was the winning offer."

"She told you this before she died?"

"I went up there in the early afternoon on Thursday. Selena was happy to see me, and we agreed to finalize the details this week."

"I see." She looked into his eyes but they betrayed nothing. "I'm sorry for the loss of your friend, Mr. Kohler," she said.

"Thank you." He gave a brief nod. "Please excuse me."

Darby watched as Fritz Kohler moved through the mourners and ducked out of the tasting room.

———

Sophie Stewart smoothed her black skirt and surveyed the groups of people embracing and saying goodbye. Funny how the day had been a mixture of sad and happy: sad when people spoke about Selena's short life, but happy when they remembered little stories about her and her brothers or described her accomplishments as a valley businesswoman. She watched Carlos and ET as they hugged and shook hands with people heading out of the Contento's tasting room. Both of them looked as if they needed to take long naps.

Her father approached her and his whole body appeared weary as well. "Let me take you home, Sophie Doo," he said softly, ruffling her hair the way he always did. A mischievous twinkle came into his eye. "Or would you rather go back to school? It is Monday, after all."

She looked up at him quickly to make sure he was kidding. "If I go back now I'll just have gym. I might as well keep you company."

He smiled. "I could use some company today." He looked around the room, nodding toward Carlos and Enrico. "Let's go back to Carson Creek with them and say goodbye."

Sophie nodded. "What about Jasper?"

Dan Stewart thought a moment. "Darby will be there for a few more days. I guess we can think about taking him home with us after that, although he really loves the vineyard."

Sophie grabbed her jacket and followed her father out of the tasting room. He told the Gomez brothers that he'd meet them at Carson Creek for their departure.

"That's crazy," Carlos said. "You've done so much already. Go home with Sophie and rest. Tomorrow will be a long day, right?"

Dan nodded. "We'll start picking the grapes at dawn."

"Take a break with your daughter, then."

ET smiled at his brother in agreement. "Carlos is right, Dan. You have earned some time to relax. The property will be in good hands with you in charge, and Darby will be there to manage the sale."

Dan Stewart shook hands. Sophie hugged Carlos, and then ET, trying not to notice both of the brothers' tears.

———

Darby was in her Karmann Ghia, ready to drive back to Carson Creek, when Detective Nardone hurried up to the car. "Do you remember giving a slip of paper to one of my crime scene technicians?"

She thought back and recalled the cash register tape she'd found crumpled on the floor of the old barn. "Yes. What's up?"

"It comes from a pharmacy in St. Adina and is date stamped 4:15 p.m. on Thursday, the day Selena was killed. One of my officers watched the store's video camera to see who might have stopped in. Guess who he spotted at the counter? Mr. Yoga Man, Fritz Kohler."

"So he dropped that receipt in the barn sometime after 4:15," Darby said.

"That's right."

"I asked him if he saw Selena before she died and he told me they spoke on Thursday afternoon. In fact, he claims that Selena had chosen him as Carson Creek's new owner."

"What is this, some strange version of a real estate game show or something?" Detective Nardone snorted. "That timing backs up what Dan said about seeing a blue car with writing passing him when he left at one." She paused. "You know what I think? I think Fritz Kohler went up there at one, had a talk with Selena that did not go well, left Carson Creek, and headed to the drug store."

Darby felt a chill come over her. "Detective, any idea what he purchased?"

She nodded, her face grim. "Mr. Kohler filled a prescription," she said. "For one of the most common beta blockers, metoprolol."

THIRTEEN

It was a relief to see Carlos and ET Gomez drive away from Carson Creek. Only minutes before, Darby had watched them climb into the rental car, their eyes sunken and their expressions grim, and head down the driveway, two men who were drained, mentally and physically, from the days of dealing with Selena's funeral preparations, as well as the vineyard. Encounters with their family members, everyone from Aunt Teresa to the smallest Gomez cousin, had rejuvenated them, and yet Darby sensed the visits had siphoned off whatever remaining energy ET and Carlos possessed.

It wasn't just the brothers' health that Darby considered.

As the inquiry surrounding their sister's death developed into a full-fledged murder investigation, the presence of Carlos and ET made it difficult for the realtor to sift through the facts of the case. Had Fritz Kohler confronted Selena in the old barn and then poisoned her? Did Christophe Barton somehow fit in? As she prepared to sit down at Carson Creek's table and review what she knew, her cell phone rang with the signature sound she had given to Miles Porter: a cavalry charge. She smiled and answered it.

"Been thinking about you." His voice was warm and welcoming. "How did Selena's funeral go?"

"Everything was lovely and I believe Carlos and ET were pleased. They left a few minutes ago to head to San Francisco, and I've got the place to myself."

"I don't much like the sound of that, not with a murderer on the loose. You haven't had any more excitement, have you?"

Darby bit her lip. "A little."

"What happened?"

She could hear the concern in his voice as she told Miles about the explosion. He gave a low whistle.

"So it was a chap from Contento who was doing the industrial sabotage? Their wine grower?"

"Estate manager was his official title. It's not clear whether or not he was acting alone."

"What's the damage to Carson Creek?"

"The red barn building is pretty much destroyed. Dan's found another winery to handle production for this year. It will be up to Carlos and ET whether the facility is rebuilt."

"How will that affect a sale of the property?"

"It's not a good thing, that's for sure. Neither is a murder investigation." She told Miles about her conversation with Detective Nardone. "Fritz Kohler, one of the buyers for Carson Creek, went to a drugstore in St. Adina at four fifteen on Thursday, the day Selena was killed. He purchased the same medicine found in the wine bottle."

"So he might have killed her? What's his motive?"

"He told me that she'd picked him as Carson Creek's new owner. Perhaps that wasn't the case at all. Perhaps Selena told him he wasn't getting the property."

"The crime of passion scenario, am I right?"

"Could be. Here's another thing: they knew each other before she moved to the valley. He admitted that it wasn't all smooth sailing between them, and Carlos told me about seeing bruises on Selena's arms when she was dating someone in San Francisco."

"Kohler is the one who owned the cycling company, right? Off the Beaten Track Biking?"

"That's right. They are headquartered in San Francisco, I think."

"Yes. Believe it or not, I've seen their offices. I'll pop down there and see what I can dig up on Kohler." He paused. "Speaking of digging up, do you remember that I thought I'd seen the Contento family in the news?"

Darby felt her interest piquing. "Yes?"

"A few years back there was a scandal involving the sale of wine futures with several people in the valley. One of the names that popped up was 'Contento.'"

Now it was Darby's turn to be surprised. "Who, exactly?"

"The son of the great winemaker himself, Tim. He wasn't charged with anything, but some of the people named were fined."

"Interesting. I'm not quite sure I understand the whole wine futures concept. Is it like the commodities market? People bet on future grape yields?"

"Not exactly. Immature wine is purchased with the hopes that when it matures it will be worth more than what one paid. Trust me, I could give you a wonderful explanation over dinner. What do you say to my jumping in my car and heading north?"

Just when I think it can't get any more complicated, it does, she thought. She picked up her pencil and made a small doodle. "Sure. I'll work on a reservation right now."

"Already done."

Darby had to smile. "You are pretty sure of yourself, aren't you Mr. Porter?" Her tone grew more somber. "What about Doug? Any news from Hawaii?"

"Nothing. You must be worried that you'll lose the buyer for his house."

"I could care less about his buyer, Miles. I'm worried about him. I'm going to call the police in Honolulu and find out how to reach law enforcement in Sunset Beach. It's been three days with no word. I think it's time to let someone know."

Now Miles' voice was somber. "Do what you think you need to do," he said. "Calling the authorities may be premature, but you've got pretty darn good instincts." He paused. "I hope we find out he's just off to Maui for the weekend, or sleeping off a hangover. I'll tell you one thing: Doug's damn lucky to have you for a friend." He cleared his throat. "I'll see you by five," he said.

———

Vivian Allen read the text message from her sister with growing alarm. *Vineyard losing charm. Thinking orphanage in Africa.* An orphanage? As in little children with bulging bellies? Vivian Allen groaned and tossed her phone on the hotel bed where it settled amongst the rumpled sheets. She muted the television set so that she could think and tossed the remote as well. Veronica was always flighty, she'd been that way as a kid, and since she'd become a multimillionaire (heck, she was probably a billionaire by now) her mood swings had gotten even worse. She wasn't the charitable type, and she didn't even like kids, so why in the world would she want to build an orphanage half a world away?

For the same reason she wanted a vineyard, Vivian thought. It was the new "thing to do." If there was one thing she could say about her sister, it was that she liked to be in style, whether with her clothing, cars, boyfriends, or pet projects. A few jet-setters paving the way by helping the world's poor in disadvantaged places made people like Veronica want to do the same thing. *Ugh.*

Was it worth it to stay here and try to purchase Carson Creek? Vivian thought about the beautiful rows of vines, the mellow sun as it dropped behind the brown California hills, the amazing parties she could host as owner of a vineyard. She thought about the life she could have, and she had her answer.

Yes, it was worth it. *After everything I've done, I deserve Carson Creek.* She rummaged through the bed sheets to find her phone, locating the television remote in the process. She aimed it toward the TV and froze. There, on the screen, was Carson Creek's handsome red building, smoldering, part of it in ruins.

She turned on the volume and listened intently. An explosion in the middle of the night had destroyed half the structure; the rest was severely damaged by fire. The arsonist's body had been recovered following the blast and identified as Christophe Barton, Estate Manager for Contento Family Vineyards.

Barton! Vivian swore and put her head in her hands. *What in the world . . .* She grabbed her cell phone, noticing that her hand was shaking as if she was some kind of drug addict. She scrolled back through calls until she found the one she was looking for. She exhaled, trying to stem the feeling of nausea mounting in her stomach. Two weeks ago he'd phoned and offered his services. *I know a way to help you get the vineyard,* he'd promised.

Vivian tried to think. There was nothing tying her to him, was there? So they'd spoken on the phone a few times. She hadn't made any kind of a commitment to him, had she? She tried to recall her exact words, but the panic was mounting and she was having trouble concentrating.

His text last night—what had it said? *Our plan is in motion.* She felt the pit of her stomach tighten like a vise.

His apartment. He'd told her he lived in an apartment in Wyattville. If she could somehow get into his apartment...

She grabbed her pocketbook and stuffed the phone inside. As scenes of the vineyard continued to flash across the television screen, Vivian Allen headed out.

———

It was five o'clock at the end of a mild autumn Monday and Andrea Contento was exhausted. Preparations for the funeral had been more tiring than she'd anticipated, and the service itself had been a grueling blur. So many of the Gomez relatives had sought her out, both to thank her for Selena's lovely service, and to speak with her about their lost relative, that she had finally had to hide in the kitchen to escape. The enormity of Selena's death was finally hitting her, settling on her shoulders like an overloaded backpack.

And then there was the death of Christophe Barton.

Andrea leaned against her granite countertops and pictured the arrogant Frenchman, so cocky that he was almost a caricature of himself. Would she miss him? She hadn't enjoyed seeing his resentment toward Michael grow, his insistence that he, Christophe

Barton, was the one trained in the fields of Bourgogne, that *bien sûr*, he was the ultimate authority on everything having to do with a grape…

She put her head in her hands. Chris was gone, a victim of his own explosive device. *What a waste.*

Time heals all wounds, she whispered, recalling a saying that had hung on a small trivet in her parents' house. She sighed and wondered if she should go over her list of tasks for the annual wine auction. There was still so much to do, and it was only three weeks away. Now she and Margo would have to assume a few of Barton's tasks as well. *Face it, you'll never concentrate tonight*, she thought. Instead she left the kitchen for the patio, where she sat down with a magazine, determined to relax.

The air was still, as if waiting for something to happen. Not a breeze ruffled the olive trees, not a bird song broke the quiet. She opened the magazine, put her feet on a chair, and tried to block out everything else.

————

Sophie Stewart took her cell phone off the charger and called her grandmother's number. In their last conversation, the older woman had given kind, but vague, answers to Sophie's questions about her mother's death. Sophie knew it was a difficult discussion for the elderly woman, and yet she was fourteen and old enough to know the truth. She heard her grandmother's pleasant hello and her heart began to beat. Haltingly, she asked the question she could not stop pondering.

"You're sure you want to hear this, Sophia?" Her grandmother was the only one who called her by her full name, and Sophie couldn't resist a quick grin.

"Yes, Grandma. You know I can't ask Dad, and I think it's time I know the details."

Frances Kinney was a determined woman who had run the family farm almost singlehandedly for going on twenty years, and her granddaughter shared her chief character trait of persistence. Sophie hoped that her grandmother knew her well enough to sense that changing the subject or pussyfooting around wasn't going to work with this teen. She heard the older woman take a deep breath.

"Very well then."

Sophie waited, holding her breath.

"You know that your mother was having some troubles," she began. "A case of the blues, is what I thought at first, but it turned out to be much more serious. Her doctor was trying to help her come out of her depression by giving her some different medications." She paused and Sophie felt guilty for making her tell the story. "Well, one night Natalie couldn't sleep and went into the bathroom. She must have mixed up what she was doing, and she took too much of one of the medicines. Your dad found her the next morning. Poor Natalie was dead."

Sophie felt as if all the air had left her body. "She overdosed on some of her medicines, is that what you are saying, Grandma?"

"Yes." She made a sighing noise. "I'm sorry sweetie. I'll go to my grave convinced it was an accident, because your mother loved you too much to do something like that to herself."

Somehow Sophie managed to thank her grandmother, adding a story about needing to hang up so that she could meet a friend. Frances Kinney wanted to talk more, Sophie could tell, and yet the stricken girl could not bear to speak.

Instead her mind raced with thoughts of her father and Selena Thompson. The image of all those orange-capped pill containers filled her brain. What if Detective Nardone found out about her mother's death, so similar to Selena's? Would the search for a murderer begin and end right here in her own house, with her father hauled away in handcuffs?

He hadn't killed her, she was sure of it, just as he hadn't killed the love of his life ten years ago. But the police might come to a different conclusion. *Detective Nardone wants a murderer. She could finger Dad and be done with it.*

Sophie felt her fear turning to resolve. *I know what I need to do.*

———

Darby pondered her very limited wardrobe with a frown. Since arriving at Carson Creek with only a change of clothes, she'd allowed herself a trip to a small clothing boutique in Wyattville to find something for Selena's funeral, but now she was once more in need of an outfit. She glanced at her watch. The store was open for a half-hour more and it would take fifteen minutes to drive there. She gave a small smile. Fifteen minutes to find something fabulous? *Plenty of time.*

———

Andrea Contento was awakened from her doze at the patio table by a scream. Instantly she was wide awake, her senses alert for the source of the anguished sound. *The tasting room.* She sprang to her feet and began running.

Twenty yards from the building, she saw the door fly open and Margo Contento emerge, a wild look on her face. "It's Dad," she cried, her voice rising in hysteria.

Andrea pushed past her into the room. She glanced wildly around until she spotted a rumpled heap on the floor.

"Oh my God," she whispered, running to the prostrate form of Michael Contento. She wrapped her arms around him in an embrace. "Margo!" she screamed, her voice echoing off the tasting room's walls. "Margo, what the hell happened?"

———

The Mission Inn was a small, chef-owned restaurant tucked away from busy roads, halfway between St. Adina and Wyattville. The waiter showed Miles and Darby to a corner table bathed in the soft glow of antique candle sconces flickering from the walls. Miles waited for Darby to sit down, and then helped to push in her chair.

"You look absolutely stunning," he said, in a quiet, almost bashful way. "That dress..."

"Thank you." Darby had seen the raw silk sheath as soon as she entered the boutique, the emerald green color calling to her like a siren song.

She handed Miles the wine list and watched him peruse it, his face wearing an uncharacteristic frown.

"I keep hoping to see Selena's wines but once again, they aren't listed," he said. "Maybe that will be something the new owner will pursue when this murder investigation is over. I suppose nothing much will happen on the sale of the property until that is resolved, right?"

"I think you're correct, Miles. I can't imagine a sale occurring until the person who killed Selena is caught. Why would anyone purchase a property with such a dark cloud over it?"

"Any progress?"

Darby nodded. "Now that the funeral is over, Detective Nardone seems to be intent on making headway. I told you about Fritz Kohler. We know he was at Carson Creek that afternoon and that he had a prior relationship with Selena."

"And he told you he was chosen to purchase the property?"

"Yes. According to him, all he wanted to do was help Selena." She made a skeptical face.

"I gather you don't believe dear Mr. Kohler."

"Well, we know he's not telling the truth about going back to the property at four fifteen. That receipt from the drugstore proves he was there. So it's not hard to think he could be lying about his offer, too. Selena could very well have told him to get lost."

"Meaning he was not going to get the vineyard."

"Exactly."

"And you think he might have been motivated to kill her because of a long-simmering grudge, coupled with anger and frustration over not being able to buy Carson Creek?"

"Well said, Miles." She took a sip of water. "Then there is Vivian Allen, who has her pop star sister, Veronica, for a backer. She claims to have had a very friendly relationship with Selena, and says that Selena promised her the vineyard."

"Blast! Did Selena promise them all the bloody vineyard?"

Darby couldn't help but smile at Miles' outburst. "Either she was stringing them along, or not everyone is telling the truth."

"Okay, so if she told Vivian that she was getting Carson Creek, why would she have killed Selena?"

"I don't know. Someone like Fritz could have snapped, but that doesn't seem like Vivian. I suppose she could have thought she was helping Selena by giving her an overdose of beta blockers."

"A mercy killing?"

"Perhaps. And then we have the Contento family. None of them have made a secret of their desire to own Carson Creek. Between Andrea, who claims to have been so close with Selena for years, and Michael, who acts like he admired Selena, plus Tim and Margo—there are quite a few suspects. I guess the whole family was annoyed when she hired Dan Stewart out from under their noses."

"This whole thing with Barton blowing up the place baffles me. Do you think that is tied in with her murder as well?"

"Detective Nardone says it's not Barton's style, but that he could have been working with someone else. I find that intriguing, but until we see some kind of link between him and one of the other suspects, it's just a hunch."

Miles fished in his jacket pocket and pulled out his phone. "Speaking of hunches, I've got the story for you on the wine futures trading. It mentions Tim Contento and a few other people, several of whom were fined." He touched the screen to find the story and continued. "Turns out they were betting on the popularity of cult wines, and one or two local vineyards were involved."

Now it was Darby's turn to ask the questions. "Cult wines? Sounds satanic!"

Miles laughed. "You can be absolutely adorable, do you know that?"

She felt her cheeks redden. "Let's have your explanation before I take a look at the story."

"Okay. Cult wines are the unknowns that become classics almost overnight. With enough spin and excitement, a wine can be eagerly anticipated before it is even bottled, so much so that collectors are willing to shell out money for cases and cases of the stuff, betting that when it is released to the public, the bottles will sell for more."

"I don't see anything illegal in that. How did Tim Contento get in trouble?"

"Turns out one of the wines his club advertised didn't exist, for one thing." He handed her the touch screen. "It was a small vineyard in Sonoma called Sleepy Spaniel. Production problems caused them to miss a harvest so they couldn't deliver on their promises of a spectacular Syrah, but that didn't keep the blokes who set up the deal from pocketing the money after they substituted the bottles."

"Sounds like fraud." Darby scanned the story, looking for information. She caught her breath when she saw one of the names. *Harrison Wainfield.*

"Wainfield was implicated in this," she said, keeping her voice low. "That could have cost him his real estate license."

Miles peered over his shoulder. "You know him?"

"I've met him. He's the Contento's real estate broker. I think he wanted to get the Carson Creek listing as well." She scanned the story. "What kind of money did the investors lose?"

"Several thousand dollars each. Not big money, but enough to get feathers riled enough that they took the wine club to court."

"It sounds like the club paid damages to the Sleepy Spaniel investors."

"That's right. Of course, the damages were in excess of what they'd originally invested. The club paid out fifty thousand dollars, all told. It's unclear who ended up footing that bill."

Darby looked into Miles' eyes. "That is one piece of information I would love to know."

Miles gave her a quick grin. "Then I shall do my best to find out."

———

Andrea Contento held her stepdaughter's shoulders with both hands and gave her a hard shake. "Margo, listen! You've got to tell me what happened!"

The distraught woman nodded and made an effort to speak.

"Dad said he wanted to talk with me about something. I was in the office so I came to find him. He was—he was slumped in the chair, holding his chest. I ran to him and he said something and fell forward onto the floor."

Andrea wrung her hands. The tears would come, later, but now she was focused on trying to understand the chain of events leading to her husband's inert body lying four feet away.

She cocked her head. The ambulance was approaching, and they were using their sirens.

"What did he say?"

"I don't know! A few words, they didn't make sense." She hung her head and Andrea knew she was near hysteria.

"Listen to me, Margo; you need to pull it together and think because it could be important. What did he say?"

"Something about Ahab," she whispered.

"Ahab? As in *Moby Dick*?"

Margo bobbed her head wildly. "Ahab. Ahab's life."

Andrea exhaled. She felt the ridiculous urge to laugh out loud. *Melville.* How typical of her scholarly husband to reference literature with what might have been his very last breath.

She released her grip on Margo's shoulders and pulled her into an embrace. As the paramedics burst into the room to work on Michael Contento's body, Andrea continued to hold the sobbing woman, stroking her hair and comforting her as she had done many times and many years earlier.

———

The apartment door was locked. It was a small, one-bedroom place tacked on the back of a commercial building that sold computers in one office and offered dance lessons in a tiny studio, the kind of place that looked more like an afterthought than a home. *This is where Christophe Barton had schemed to blow up Carson Creek,* Vivian Allen realized, hoping the locked door would open. *Here in this depressing little ramshackle apartment.* She rattled the door knob in frustration. There was no other entrance and she did not have the strength to break in. She spun on her heel to leave.

The back of the building was littered with trash, some of which had probably belonged to Barton. *I'm desperate, but I'm not about to start rooting through garbage.* She spied a broken kitchen chair among the debris, along with several empty wine bottles. She recognized the Contento Family Vineyards label and smirked.

The western side of the apartment was visible from the street, and there Vivian spotted a slightly opened casement window. She stopped. Perhaps this was her way in. The window was small, but Vivian was a slim woman and she sensed she could wriggle through.

She marched back to the debris pile and grabbed the chair. It was missing a back cushion but all four legs and the seat itself appeared sturdy and intact. She carried it to the window and stepped gingerly on top. Her height was an asset and she could easily reach the window. So far, so good.

The window screen yielded with a simple push, clattering to the floor of the apartment. Vivian squirmed into the open space, relieved to see a ratty couch positioned just below. She pulled her lower body through and rolled onto the couch. A small cloud of dust rose as she landed.

The apartment had definitely been searched. Drawers were ajar, books pulled from the shelves, and even the kitchen cabinets, stocked with canned goods and boxes of packaged foods, appeared to have been inspected. Vivian surveyed the small space and the even smaller bedroom, wrinkling her nose at the poster of a nude woman that covered the grimy wall.

There was a stack of papers on a small table in the main room and Vivian leafed through them. *I don't know what I'm looking for,* she thought, *but I suppose I'll know when I find it.* She was about to leave when she heard a sound.

She glanced wildly at the apartment door. A few letters lay on the floor and through the side window she saw the retreating figure of a postal carrier. *Mail,* she thought. *They are still delivering his mail.*

She scooped up the envelopes and scanned them hurriedly. Bills, all of them, from various providers, including the gas and electric companies, cable, and American Cellular...

His cell phone! Vivian ripped open the envelope and scanned the list of calls. Sure enough, there were four or five to her number. Her heart thumped. She had to destroy this before it gave the police any ideas.

She clutched the bill and envelope in her hand, casting about for a match with which to burn them. A few peeks into his kitchen drawers yielded nothing. Maybe Christophe Barton was a non-smoker. Or maybe he'd used his last matchbook to light his pipe bomb.

Vivian tried to chuckle but the apartment was starting to give her the creeps. She noticed that the door had one of those cheap locks that did not require a key, so exiting through the window would not be necessary. She unlocked the knob and pulled open the door. There, wearing a patient look on her face, stood short little Detective Nardone.

"Hello Ms. Allen," she said pleasantly. "Any mail for me?"

FOURTEEN

"So, what do you think of this dessert wine?" Miles scraped his plate with a spoon, taking a last scoop of pumpkin cheesecake, and then sat back with a sigh. "That dessert was delicious. Absolutely sinful. Why is it that I couldn't get you to eat more than one bite?"

"I was totally stuffed from my risotto, that's why." She'd tried the restaurant's renowned venison and chestnut risotto and had not been disappointed with the earthy, mingled flavors. She took another sip of the cool white wine and let it linger on her palate.

"Stone fruits and honeysuckle," she said approvingly, "transitioning to apricot and hazelnut. I'm guessing it's a Sauvignon Blanc from Matanzas Creek?"

Miles sat back with an amazed look on his face. "Absolutely correct." He grinned. "I totally forgot about your amazing taste buds. Have you astounded any of the local winemakers with your prowess?"

"No. Between spending time with ET and Carlos, and worrying about Doug—"

205

"I know, there hasn't been any time for that sort of thing." His eyes lost their merry look. "Have you had any news from the Sunset Beach Police Department?"

Darby pulled out her phone and checked the display. "I called the station and they said someone would contact me," she said. "But so far, no one has."

"Try them again," Miles urged. "I don't mind, and maybe we'll find something out."

Darby found the last call she'd made to Hawaii and tried again. The same voice answered, and once again Darby relayed her request to report a missing person.

The dispatcher was taking down Doug's name when she stopped. "Henderson, you say? I think we just located the guy."

Darby felt her body temperature chill. "Is he okay?"

The woman hesitated. "He is now," she finally said. "He was beaten up pretty badly and for a day or two we didn't know who he was. Whoever mugged him took his identification and the poor guy couldn't say much until this afternoon." She paused. "I'm sure Officer Haina will be in touch with you, but at least you know Mr. Henderson is in the hospital and he's going to be okay."

"Is there a number where I can reach Doug?"

"I'd prefer to let Officer Haina speak with you first, but I promise to tell him that you are anxious for a call."

Darby thanked the dispatcher and hung up. After telling Miles what she had learned, she took a long drink of water and exhaled. Doug was alive. That was the important thing.

Miles put his hand over hers. It was warm, and she felt currents of heat radiating up her arm and through her midsection.

She looked into his eyes. Slowly he leaned across the table and gave her a tender kiss.

"It's going to be alright," he said softly. "I promise."

———

Detective Nardone looked like a bulldog, Vivian decided. A tenacious little bitch of a dog, the kind that would bite you in the backside if it had half a chance. She watched as the petite woman pursed her lips and looked back over the cell phone records of Christophe Barton.

"So," the detective began, taking a sip of coffee and placing the Styrofoam cup back on the scarred wooden table. "I certainly appreciate your agreeing to come down here to explain these calls to me, Ms. Allen. It's always nice when we can get some cooperation on these kinds of things."

Vivian inclined her head but said nothing. *Let's see where your questions go*, she thought, *and we'll see how cooperative I'll be.*

"Can you explain to me why you were receiving calls from Christophe Barton?" The detective's eyebrows were raised so high they were becoming one with her coiffure.

"He called me and said he understood I was interested in buying Carson Creek. I asked him who he was, and he told me he worked at Contento. He hinted that he knew some kind of inside track that would get me the vineyard, and I told him that I wasn't interested."

"Why was that?"

"Because I was already meeting with Selena Thompson and I felt I was building a good rapport with her. I didn't need whatever kind of help he was offering."

"Did you ask him what his type of 'help' was?"

"No." She paused. "Not that time."

The detective indicated the next call on the list. "Two days later—that would be one week ago—he called again."

Vivian nodded. "He asked me whether I had a signed contract. I said it wasn't any of his business, and hung up."

"It sounds as if his calls were becoming harassment." There was sympathy in the detective's voice, but Vivian wasn't falling for it.

"Just annoying," she said.

"Did you think of calling the Contento family and complaining?"

"No. He was like a pesky fly. Annoying, but not worth my time." She glanced at her watch. "Detective, I'm late for an appointment with my sister. Can we wrap this up?"

"Certainly." Detective Nardone consulted the list. "The third call was last Tuesday. Please tell me what happened."

"Christophe Barton called again. This time I didn't answer, so he left a message."

"Do you still have that message?"

She shook her head. "No. But he sounded—different."

"How so?"

"More insistent. He said he needed me to call him, so that we could talk about the vineyard."

"Did he say anything else?"

She nodded. "He said, 'I've got information about Carson Creek that you'll want to hear.' So I called him and told him to leave me alone."

"And what happened?"

"He said I would be sorry that I hadn't cooperated, and I hung up."

Detective Nardone made a steeple of her fingers. "The last time he called you was Thursday morning, the day Selena Thompson died."

Vivian bobbed her head. "He said he was planning something big and if I wanted in, he would guarantee that I'd get the property."

"What do you think he meant?"

She shivered. "How can I guess what some sick person was talking about? Maybe he thought that by blowing the place up, he was accomplishing something." She shrugged.

"And finally, the text message, which you received at three a.m. on Monday morning."

"Yeah, I didn't notice when it was sent, but that's when the buzzing woke me up."

"And that was the 'Our plan is in motion,' message, correct?"

She nodded.

"It certainly seems like Mr. Barton considered you a partner in his endeavors to destroy Carson Creek."

"Then he was delusional, because I was nothing of the sort." Vivian Allen stood. "I really must go now."

Detective Nardone rose to her feet. "Thank you for coming by, Ms. Allen. Given your cooperation, I think we can forget your little incident of breaking and entering."

Vivian Allen shot the woman a look. "Thank you," she mumbled, and hurried out of the room.

Darby and Miles returned to Carson Creek, relieved to know that Doug Henderson was safe, but puzzled by the sedan parked in the driveway.

"It's Detective Nardone's car," Darby observed, coming around the front of the farmhouse. "What could possibly have happened now?"

"Just looking for your time," quipped the detective, emerging from the old barn in a brisk walk. Darby marveled at the woman's range of hearing. She hadn't spoken very loudly and the detective had been at least twenty yards away. "I'm hoping we can talk about those offers on the vineyard Selena received."

Darby nodded. "I have them in a file inside. Come in, and I'll make us some coffee."

"Thank you." Detective Nardone seemed preoccupied, as if only a part of her were present in the conversation.

Miles glanced at Darby before opening the door of the farmhouse. "Do you mind if I stay awhile, Detective? I may have information that could prove useful."

Nancy Nardone climbed onto the top step, her face grim.

"By all means," she said. "Let's make it a party."

Darby shot Miles a look and he raised his eyebrows. They led the detective into the dining room and Darby hurried to put on a pot of coffee.

"Fritz Kohler," began Detective Nardone, pulling out his offer to purchase Carson Creek Estate & Winery. "Owns a successful yoga spa business. Knew Selena Thompson ten years ago as the owner of Off the Beaten Track Biking. In fact, they were more than acquaintances—they were on-again-off-again lovers with an explosive relationship that at times grew so physical Ms. Thompson phoned the authorities." She paused and looked up from the paper. "Twice."

"Do we have any evidence that they kept in touch over the past decade?" Darby wondered out loud.

"No. But we do know that Mr. Kohler became interested in purchasing this property about two weeks ago. He says the first face-to-face encounter he had with Selena was on the day she was killed. He drove up here around one-thirty that afternoon, passing Dan Stewart on the road, and although he told you he had a nice little chat with Selena in which she promised him the vineyard, he now says they didn't speak."

"He's changed his story!"

"Apparently so." Detective Nardone glanced down at the paper in her hand and continued. "At 4:15 he paid for a prescription for metoprolol at the Save-All Pharmacy in St. Adina. Mr. Kohler takes this drug to control high blood pressure and has for approximately a year. He then went back to Carson Creek to see Selena. According to what he told me yesterday, he spoke to Selena in the old barn—what they use for storage and such—and he admits that the conversation grew pretty heated. Selena told him he was not going to be getting the vineyard and that she'd chosen someone else. He maintains that when he left, she was alive and that he had nothing to do with putting metoprolol in her wine."

She paused, shuffling the papers. "Now, Vivian Allen claims that she was on track to purchase the vineyard and that every interaction she had with Selena was positive. However, she began receiving phone calls from Christophe Barton approximately ten days ago, with offers from him to help her obtain the vineyard. These calls became increasingly threatening, culminating in a text message she received the night Barton died."

"How strange! Why was Barton trying to get her involved in his activities?"

"I'm thinking blackmail. Vivian does not seem to know about the prior sabotage at Carson Creek—no one but Dan, Selena, and Barton himself knew about that—but I think that Barton found out about Veronica and sensed a business opportunity. All he had to do was implicate Vivian in some way, and then he would wring hush money out of her sister." She smoothed the paper with a hand. "Vivian was one of the few people who knew about Selena's illness. She may have even spoken with her about specific medications, including metoprolol. The question is: why would Vivian kill Selena if she believed that she had been chosen to buy the vineyard?" She pursed her lips. "Perhaps Selena's murder had nothing to do with the vineyard. It's possible Selena voiced to Vivian her desire to be pain free, and Vivian thought she'd help her along with an overdose."

Darby glanced at Miles. He rose and went into the kitchen for the coffee pot. "Where was Vivian when the poisoning took place?"

"She says she was at her hotel room in Wyattville. I've checked with the hotel staff and no one can verify that she was actually in the hotel."

"So she does not have an alibi." Darby pictured the tall redhead entering the farmhouse kitchen and adding the chemical to the bottle of wine.

"Correct."

"Okay, so who's next?"

"Harrison Wainfield. He represents the Contento family as their real estate agent, and yet Fritz Kohler told me Wainfield was also willing to put in his offer. The guy's trying to make a buck any way he can."

Miles returned with the coffee and poured a cup for Detective Nardone. "I'm sure you've heard about the wine futures scandal Tim Contento and Wainfield were involved in. Perhaps he's trying to recoup his losses from that?"

She nodded and took a sip of coffee. "There's a good chance Wainfield needs money. Whatever was paid to settle that lawsuit was a drop in the bucket for Tim Contento, but that wouldn't be the case with Wainfield. He may make large commissions when he sells property, but he appears to live way beyond his means." She plunked her mug onto the table. "Here's my question: how would killing Selena improve Wainfield's financial picture?"

"Perhaps he sensed that the vineyard was going to someone other than his clients the Contentos," Darby began. "He had no way to control the sale with Selena alive, but with her dead, the Contentos could shine as the helpful neighbors and have a shot at getting the property."

"Possibly." Detective Nardone glanced at her watch. "It's getting late. I'd better head out."

"Why not finish with the list of suspects?" Darby asked. "Miles and I don't mind."

The detective raised an eyebrow. "I would think you'd have better things to do than listen to me try to figure out this case, but fine, I'm glad to use the two of you as a sounding board. Goodness knows my department can always use extra help." She picked up the last offer. "The Contento family—Tim, Margo, and Andrea—

none of whom have solid alibis for that Thursday. Tim was in the fields, then back and forth to town for errands. Ditto Andrea Contento, except that she was working in the kitchen with a few short trips here and there."

She took another sip of coffee and ran a hand through her graying hair. "Margo was away on a business trip to Seattle. She flew into Ventano County Airport early afternoon—one o'clock—on an earlier flight than originally scheduled. Christophe Barton picked her up at six o'clock that evening and she claims she spent the intervening five hours shopping." Detective Barton raised her eyebrows at Miles and Darby. "Of course, we can't ask Barton to corroborate her story, and she has no purchases to show for all that shopping." She gave a long exhale. "Margo could have easily rented a car, driven here, and added metoprolol to Selena's wine. Any one of them could. Andrea and Tim could have added it that morning, knowing Selena would drink it in the afternoon."

"And Michael Contento?" asked Darby. "Have you eliminated him as a suspect?"

"At this point we have, yeah," Detective Nardone said drily. "And here's the reason. Michael Contento is dead."

––––––––

Dan Stewart put down the phone's receiver and sank onto an upholstered chair. Tim's voice had been clear and strong as he gave the news of his father's passing, quick to note that although the great man was lost to the winemaking community, his legacy at Contento and throughout the valley would continue. "And I want you to know, Dan," he said, his voice beginning to waver. "If things don't work out with Carson Creek's new owner, we'd love to have you back." He tried to chuckle. "Who knows? Maybe we will end up owning it after all, and you can keep on doing what you're doing."

Dan thanked him and hung up. His mind reeled with images of Michael at one event after another, or striding through the rows of his beloved grapes. He remembered Michael's joy at Selena's silly jokes. Both of them, gone in one week: two people he had respected and enjoyed.

Of course Christophe Barton was also dead, but Dan could feel nothing but anger for the man who had tried to ruin Carson Creek. Why had he acted in such a way? Was he motivated by greed? Revenge? Or was he just plain crazy? Dan doubted if he would ever know the reason for Barton's actions. The fact that the vineyard was still standing was a minor miracle.

Dan climbed the stairs and listened for noise from the other side of Sophie's closed door, but it was quiet. Too early for her to have gone to bed—most likely she was lying on her floor, listening to music. He could tell her in the morning about Michael Contento. No need to ruin her night at this point.

He continued down the hallway to his bedroom. Tomorrow at dawn the harvesting crew would be at Carson Creek, and he needed a good night's sleep in preparation. With any luck, they'd get most of the fields picked in a few days, and then wrap up what was left later in the week. Dan went over the details in his mind. Due to the damage caused by the explosion, the grapes would be crushed and the juice stored at a neighboring facility. It was a temporary solution and Dan hoped it would work.

He yawned and opened the door to his room, his sense of purpose back in focus. *My job is to produce the best wine possible, and I owe it to Selena—and to the memory of Michael Contento—to do just that.* With that thought in mind, he crawled into bed, and although it was early, soon fell asleep.

———

The door shut behind Detective Nardone and Darby turned an incredulous face to Miles. "I can't believe it. Michael Contento had a heart attack."

"It happens, especially when one is pushing eighty." He carried the coffee cups into the kitchen and began rinsing them out.

"You don't think it is at all strange given what's been going on?"

Miles shrugged. "No. Michael struck me as a vigorous guy in good health, but he did have a minor heart attack last year. And you can't say this past week hasn't been stressful for that family. According to what his daughter describes, it sounds like what happened was the classic myocardial infarction."

"Ummm." Darby put the cream back into the refrigerator. "I suppose I'm so frustrated by this case that I'm starting to imagine things."

"Such as?" Miles turned, still washing dishes, his face inquisitive.

"Maybe Michael discovered who killed Selena and that's why he died. He was arguing with Margo just before the attack. He might have been accusing her, or telling her about someone else."

"Andrea or Tim, for instance."

"Exactly." She shook her head. "I know she's trying, but Detective Nardone doesn't seem to be making any real progress. I feel like the investigation is stalled, and now the window of time to solve this case has come and gone." She made an exasperated sound. "Listen to me, like I'm some kind of expert detective or something." She ran a hand through her glossy black hair. "I shouldn't be critical, but I know this wasn't a suicide. Somebody added that metoprolol to Selena's wine." She pointed. "The bottle was sitting right there on the counter, Miles. Right there."

He turned off the water and followed her finger to the spot. "You realize that our poisoner could have come anytime during the day, or even the night before, for that matter. Does Dan recall anyone else coming by Carson Creek?"

"No, but he wasn't here the entire time. He was in the fields and also running errands in town."

"The thing is, that person may have waltzed right in with Selena's blessing, right? All the time they would have needed to poison the wine was a few seconds. She could have been in the bathroom, or getting something from the living room, and she wouldn't have known."

"That's true." Her brow was furrowed. She pushed her long black hair off her face and turned a troubled face toward him. "Who wanted Selena Thompson dead, so badly that they brought the crushed metoprolol to her property and put it in the wine?" She shook her head in frustration. "It's time to solve this murder before anyone else gets hurt."

He hung up the dishtowel and rested his hands on her shoulders, pulling her slender body toward his. "I know you want to figure out who killed Selena, and I know you'll succeed. But even the best detectives take breaks now and then. What if we forget about the murder for a while and get to know each other better?" He pushed a strand of hair away from her face. "I've only got a little time before I head back to San Francisco. That is, unless I'm invited to stay here?"

"Hmm ... I'll have to think about that."

"Maybe you'll think better after this?" He pulled her face gently toward his and kissed her on the lips. She felt his longing and wanted to melt into him.

"Miles, you know I would love your company, but not here. This isn't my home—it would be awkward."

He kissed her again. "Are you sure?"

She felt like slipping into the warm embrace of the kiss. *Forget the murder, Doug's disappearance, and the events of the past few days.* She felt like forgetting it all and losing herself in Miles' gentle touch. It would be so easy ...

Instead she pulled away. "I'm sorry—I just don't feel comfortable."

"Let me change that."

She couldn't help but smile. "I love your persistence."

"I'm glad somebody does, because I'm getting damn sick of it." He flashed a wan grin, but Darby thought she detected a slight edge in his voice.

"You know what I mean, Miles. There are times when it's right, and times when it isn't." The explanation sounded lame, even to her ears. "This place ..." She swept her hand around the room, taking in Selena Thompson's treasured possessions. "I can't."

"Okay, I get that. My dumb mistake. Let me find a little place, then."

Romance. She wanted it, too. She longed to brush her hand through his cropped hair, explore the planes of his chiseled face, and nestle into his woodsy, clean scent. She wanted it all—but not tonight.

She exhaled and saw a look of wounded pride cross his face. Gently he removed his hands from her shoulders and held up one finger.

"Don't say it, Darby, because I have a feeling I've heard it before." He rose to his feet with a long sigh.

"You have urgent matters calling for your attention." His tone was light, but the words sounded clipped. "I understand that, because believe it or not, I do, too." He walked across the room to the door. At the threshold, he turned slowly to face her. "Let me know when you can make me one of your priorities."

She watched him walk out the door and into the night.

———

A knock on her bedroom door roused Andrea Contento from her daze. She stood, shook her head a little to clear it, and went to the door.

"Hey." It was Margo, wearing a robe and slippers. "I went to my house and grabbed a few things. I thought I'd stay in one of the extra rooms tonight so you wouldn't be alone."

"Thanks." Andrea opened the door wider. "Come in. I was just sitting here trying to wrap my head around the fact that he's really gone. I know it's still early, but I'm exhausted."

"Me, too." Margo padded into the room and walked to her father's bureau. She fingered his pocket watch, which had sat in the same spot on his dresser since she was a little girl. "He loved this thing," she said, lifting the gold chain and feeling the heft of the timepiece in her hand. "It was his father's, I guess. He told me once that he never would have inherited it if his older brother hadn't been killed in Vietnam."

"That's true," commented Andrea, thinking of the vineyard itself. "David's death put your father on a whole different course, one which I know he grew to love." She gave a sad smile and wiped her eyes. "He wasn't pleased at first, we all know that. I know from the way he spoke about it that he loved his life as a university professor. But he was a part of this land and a part of this place. It was surely in his very being. I don't think he regretted the way his life turned out."

Margo nodded slowly. "I know he was happy. That's why it puzzles me so much to think about his last words. 'Ahab's life.' What did he mean? Was he saying he regretted not staying in academia?"

Again Andrea flashed a small smile. "I've been thinking about it as well. Captain Ahab spent his life chasing the white whale, right? So what was your father's 'white whale'? What was his biggest challenge?"

"Making the perfect Pinot?" Margo guessed. "Honestly, I can't come up with anything."

"Maybe that is part of what he was saying. His search for perfection as a vintner was as futile as the whaler's in chasing Moby Dick." She crossed over to Margo and put a hand on her shoulder. "Or maybe he was just having a passing thought. Maybe he didn't intend for us to be sitting here and analyzing his words."

"Maybe." She sighed. "Are you okay? Staying here, I mean?" Margo indicated the bedroom with a sweep of her hand.

Andrea nodded. "I miss him so badly it is like a physical pain. But I also feel his presence." She pointed at the top of the dresser. "Things like that watch. I saw him pick it up and hold it so many times. It gives me comfort in a strange way."

Margo sighed. She started toward the bedroom door but suddenly stopped.

"I told you that we were arguing just before Dad collapsed."

Andrea nodded. "Margo, I hope you don't think any of this was your fault. His heart was weakened by the last attack."

"I know. But we fought earlier in the day as well."

Andrea Contento frowned. "I don't get it. What was he so upset about? Can you tell me?"

Margo paused, considering the request. Finally she bit her lip and admitted, "He wanted to know why I killed Selena Thompson."

———

Darby brushed her teeth in a kind of a fog. First she'd heard the news about Doug, who was safe in a Honolulu hospital, although in what kind of shape she didn't really know. Next Miles had departed after issuing some strong words regarding their relationship. *Was that our first fight? Perhaps our only one if I never see him again.*

Is that what I want? She really wasn't sure. She liked Miles. She was very attracted to him and had been since the first time she'd seen him. He was kind, smart, and funny, not to mention sexy as hell. *Why would I risk losing such a good man?*

Darby knew that she kept a big chunk of herself behind lock and key. Since her teen years and her parents' accident, she'd mastered the art of keeping people at a distance. She remained friendly; but not really friends. She toyed with the idea of a serious relationship and yet never let anything evolve that far.

Miles was different. Rather than run from her barriers, he was trying to break them down. And yet even someone as patient as

Miles would have his limits. *Perhaps he's already reached his*, she thought. *That's why he left.* She rinsed out her mouth and regarded her reflection. Miles undoubtedly had other women who found him attractive…

Darby finished in the bathroom and walked into the guest bedroom. She picked up her phone and found Miles' number. As she willed herself to call, she heard a rapping on the downstairs door.

Darby frowned. The phone landed on the bed with a soft thump as she headed down the stairs.

———

The Power Yoga hour had begun and Harrison Wainfield sat transfixed before the television, watching his new client with growing admiration. The man was certainly flexible—he'd give him that—and yet he was incredibly strong, as well. Wainfield watched as Fritz Kohler effortlessly balanced on one arm, twisted himself into an impossibly contorted pose, and then sprang to his feet in a warrior stance, all the while encouraging his viewers to do the same. "Feel your inner strength," Kohler chanted. "Feel the power of yoga transforming your muscles and your life."

Wainfield reached over and shut off the television. *Inner strength my ass.* He looked at the offer he'd drafted for the purchase of Carson Creek Estate & Winery. This was the true power: the ability to purchase property without regard to cost. This was where inner strength really derived.

He lifted a glass of Contento Family Vineyards Reserve Merlot to his lips and took a satisfying swallow. It was going to be a pleasure to see someone besides the Contento family getting what they wanted. After they'd stuck him with paying off that Sleepy Spaniel mess! And now that Michael was dead…

A thought occurred to him that stopped him in his tracks.

Now that Michael was dead, Andrea was available. He stroked his goatee and pondered the lateness of the hour. Andrea was now a widow requiring comfort. Perhaps Fritz Kohler's offer could wait.

FIFTEEN

Vivian Allen stood in the darkness, knocking repeatedly on the weathered farmhouse door.

Darby pulled it open, immediately noting the woman's mussed hair and pale complexion. *She's frightened*, Darby thought.

"I know it's late, but I wondered…"

Darby moved to the side and beckoned. "Come in, Ms. Allen."

"Just call me Vivian." She took a hesitant step, glancing around the house as if hoping no one else was present.

"Let's take a seat in the living room, Vivian. Can I fix you a cup of tea?"

The tall woman followed Darby and perched on the sofa, clearly ill at ease. "No," she stammered. "No, thank you."

"What can I do for you?"

Vivian bit her lip and sighed. "I need to talk to someone about this whole thing." She motioned with her hand around the room.

"You mean your purchase of Carson Creek?"

"Yes."

"I'm happy to try and help but I do want to remind you that I represent the sellers of this property, Enrique and Carlos Gomez."

"I know, I know." She closed her eyes. "I understand all that and I don't think it really matters anymore."

She leaned back on the pillows of the sofa and was quiet for a few moments. "Remember when you asked me if I had a business partner?"

Darby nodded.

"I lied to you. My sister Veronica is my partner on this venture. Or at least she was."

"Go on."

She sat up and took a deep breath. "Veronica isn't too excited about owning a vineyard anymore, but I think I could swing it on my own if need be."

"I see."

"It's been my dream to do this kind of thing, even before I became sick. I love the idea of having my own business, of producing something that I can be proud of. I had some good long talks with Selena about it, and I know she felt comfortable turning over this place to me."

She sighed. "I wish she had signed the offer before she died. I wish she had told someone else—like Dan Stewart—that she intended me to be the new owner. I feel like you don't believe me and now that you know about Veronica, you'll hold that against me as well."

"It's not up to me, Vivian. It's up to my sellers."

"Oh, I know that, but I also know they're going to listen to you, which is why I hoped you'd hear me out."

"Were you keeping Veronica's involvement secret because you thought it would jeopardize the sale?"

She nodded. "I suppose the kind of celebrity my sister enjoys is frightening to most people. It's the kind of thing where her houses are protected by guards and yet paparazzi are always waiting when she pulls out the gated driveway. She can't live any semblance of a normal life. Did you see the little article in the paper? People in the valley are already panicked just thinking about having her here. And if I'm completely honest with myself, I guess I can see why. Veronica doesn't just move to a house. She *invades* a whole county."

"That can't be easy."

"Oh, she's used to it. It comes with the kind of high wattage stardom she loves, so there you have it." She stood and walked to a window, looking out upon the dark vines. "Selena knew about Veronica. She was worried her involvement would change the character of Carson Creek. I listened to her concerns and privately I agreed with them. I think I hoped my sister would lose interest and back out entirely, which is what she seems to be doing."

She turned from the window. "I may borrow funds from her, but I will be the sole owner of Carson Creek, and I'm happy to take it even with the damage to the red building."

Darby nodded. An insurance agent was due the next day to take a look at the wreckage. Knowing that Vivian Allen was still interested despite the explosion would be a comfort to Carlos and ET.

"What about Carlos working for Veronica?"

She colored. "You know about that?" Seeing Darby's quick nod, Vivian rolled her eyes. "Okay, so I don't feel good about using a job offer as a bribe, but I was desperate. And the truth of it is, Carlos is very good. He can have a job with Veronica if that's what he wants—regardless if I get this property or not."

"There is still the matter of Selena's death," Darby said quietly. "Until that is settled—"

"What do you mean? Surely now that the service is over, her brothers are willing to sell."

Darby remembered her admonition from Detective Nardone. Should she mention the circumstances of Selena's death, or stay quiet?

"There may be some investigation around Selena's cause of death," she said. "There was a high level of beta blockers in Selena's blood. An abnormally high level."

Vivian Allen walked slowly to the couch and rested her hand on it. "Ever since I heard she drowned in the hot tub, I've been wondering if that were the case," she said softly. "But I can't believe she would have done it."

"What are you talking about, Vivian?" Darby's tone was sharp.

"The beta blockers … and the hot tub …" she closed her eyes. "I read about it in a novel. A woman with a terminal illness ended her life by overdosing on beta blockers and then getting in a hot tub."

"Did you tell Selena about this novel?"

"I did. We joked about how it would be such a great way to go, to be relaxing in a hot tub and then just slip away."

Darby looked into Vivian Allen's eyes. "Vivian, do you really think that your telling Selena about this—this *technique*—would have influenced her so strongly that she would have committed suicide?"

Vivian's face was suddenly chalky. "I don't know."

"Did she say anything more about it after that conversation?"

"Yes," she said dully. "She asked me to lend her the book."

"And did you give it to her?"

She nodded. "I didn't have it with me, but I found a copy on sale at the big bookstore outside of Ventano. I gave it to her last week." She put her head back in anguish. "She said she needed something good to read. I never thought—"

"Come with me," Darby commanded, taking the farmhouse stairs two at a time. The saying Selena had stenciled on the old stairs —*With wine and hope, anything is possible*—seemed like a mockery now. In Selena's bedroom, Darby flicked on the light. Several books were stacked on the bedside table, and Darby picked them up.

"Well?"

"This is it," Vivian whispered, pointing at one of the books.

It was a paperback novel, what the publishers called "chick lit" from the look of the cover. Darby opened to a dog-eared page and scanned the text. Her eyes caught the words "beta blocker," "blood pressure," "hot tub," and "drown," before she looked into Vivian's stricken face.

"It's my fault," she said, sinking onto the bed. "I told her how to do it." She looked up at Darby. "I killed Selena Thompson."

———

Nancy Nardone closed the door behind Vivian Allen and regarded Darby Farr.

"Well?" she asked after a few moments. "Do you still think suicide is out of the question? It sounds like Selena was influenced by the plot of this book and decided to try it." The detective waved the novel in her hand. "She wouldn't be the first person to do something stupid that she read about."

Darby stood with a hand on her hip. She'd called Detective Nardone to come and speak with Vivian, and had heard the distraught woman relay much the same information she had told Darby minutes before.

"I know Selena was in a bad situation, dealing with a difficult and very painful illness, and I suppose she could have seen suicide as an alternative," she said carefully. "But I think several things are all wrong about it."

"Such as?"

"First off, the timing. I'm no expert on motives for suicide, but why would Selena end her life when she was just about to sell the vineyard and make a big pile of money? According to Dan Stewart, she wasn't morose about the sale—she was pleased. He said she was proud that she'd built up a business that could attract so many eager buyers."

The detective nodded. "True enough. What else?"

"Okay, the metoprolol in her empty bottle of wine. Why would Selena have added it to the bottle when it would be so much easier to stir it into her glass? Doesn't first pouring the wine, and then adding the chemical into the glass make the most sense?"

"Maybe she wanted more than one glass."

"We can check with Dr. Yang, but I think that was impossible. The amount in there would have worked quickly to cause light-headedness. Besides, Dan Stewart said she was pretty rigid about only having one glass of wine a night."

"Yes, but if it's your last night …"

"I see what you are saying, but I still don't think it makes sense."

"Maybe this wasn't her first attempt. Maybe she had tried the night before, which was why it was in the bottle."

Darby considered. "Yes, but then why not leave a note? Why leave the business of selling the vineyard unfinished? I tell you, Detective, I really do not believe that woman wanted to die."

Nancy Nardone sighed. "Then we are right back at square one. Who wanted Selena Thompson dead?"

———

Contrary to what her father believed, Sophie Stewart was not in her room sleeping, nor was she reading a book or flipping the pages of the latest teen magazine. She was quietly using her laptop to instant message her friend Whitney, a fellow candy striper whose mother was best friends with Margo Contento.

Whitney had started the conversation by dropping the bombshell that Michael Contento was dead, a statement that Sophie simultaneously corroborated by using another window while she was waiting for Whitney to instant message her back. The eager teen had then confided that Michael had argued with his daughter Margo before succumbing to his fatal heart attack, and that Margo was a basket case because of it. Thanks to her mother's penchant for repeating each statement she heard over the phone before pausing to respond herself, Whitney had eavesdropped on the entire conversation. She even knew the odd words Michael Contento had uttered with his final breath.

Ahab's life.

Sophie pondered the phrase after she'd signed off with Whitney. The famous winemaker had been a professor—that much Sophie knew by having spent time in his immense library. She recalled the twinkle in his eye when she'd stared, open-mouthed, at the tall shelves of books, and his genuine delight when he'd handed her a picture book and told her to choose a comfy chair. "Go ahead, read it," he'd coaxed. "I'll get Andrea to bring you some of her chocolate chip cookies and a glass of milk."

Sophie scanned the shelf where the picture book was stacked with a few others. Michael had insisted she take it home as a gift. "Books give many pleasures," he'd said. "One pleasure is in reading them. Another is in sharing them with others."

He had been a nice man. A very nice man, really. She knew that her father would be upset when he learned of his death in the morning. She shut off her computer, brushed her sandy hair from her face, and turned off her light. *I won't let this distract me,* she vowed to the darkness. *I won't let it stop me from finding Selena Thompson's killer.*

She thought back to the night she'd taken the wine bottle. Who had been at Carson Creek to pay their respects? More importantly, who had been missing?

———

Tuesday morning dawned bright and warm, and Darby opened her eyes to the first rays of the sun and the chatter of voices down in the driveway. She rose and peered out the window. Groups of men were clustered on the pavement, talking quietly and smoking cigarettes, their hands clutching cups of coffee. She watched as Dan Stewart strode up to the men, his body language relaxed and welcoming. He greeted a few of the men by name and even exchanged a few pleasantries in Spanish.

Darby pulled on some clothes and headed down the farmhouse stairs. She poured a cup of coffee into a pale blue mug and scooped some dry cat food into a bowl for Jasper. Then she slipped on a pair of sandals and a sweatshirt and headed outside.

Dan smiled when he saw her coming. A few of the pickers looked curious, even a little suspicious, but they said nothing and quickly resumed conversation among themselves.

"Come to see the start of the harvest?" Dan asked, shielding his eyes from the rising sun.

"I thought I'd check it out, yes." She indicated the assembled men. "Quite a few people here to lend a hand."

He nodded. "Some of these guys have been coming here for years. They make the rounds of the vineyards, helping out where they can. They're a hardworking bunch, all of them." His pleasant expression dimmed. "Michael Contento died yesterday," he said softly. "Heart attack."

"Yes, I heard. I'm sorry, Dan. I know he was your friend."

"Yeah. Well, his death is a loss, no doubt about it, but he lived a good long life. I'm glad he died at his vineyard, and with his daughter. You can't ask for much better than that."

Darby flashed to an image of Selena, alone in her hot tub, and wondered if Dan was thinking the same thing. She said, "I'm going to speak with Fritz Kohler today—at least that's my plan—and see where he's at regarding Carson Creek. The insurance adjuster will be here as well."

Dan exhaled. "Yeah, life goes on." He surveyed the fields, squinting against the sun. "Tim's coming by in a little bit. I think he just wants to talk. If he's having trouble reaching me, would you let him know to call my cell?"

"Sure." She watched as he gave a little wave and then whistled to get the attention of the pickers. They moved as a mass to follow him toward the old barn. The harvesting had begun.

———

The "send" button on his e-mail now pushed, Toby Bliss leaned back in his chair and let out a satisfying sigh. He'd pulled an all-nighter to get the Michael Contento Memorial tee-shirts designed, and now they were ordered and would arrive just in time for the Valley Wine Auction.

He allowed himself a long yawn. He'd made some good money off the Contento family over the years, thanks to their visibility in the wine world and their penchant for throwing party after party. He ticked off some of the more lucrative projects he'd mas-terminded: the posters he'd had printed up of various vineyard events, the sweatshirts advertising their charity run to benefit Ven-tano Valley Community Hospital, and even the hysterical calendar of snapshots of various wine country personalities in Halloween costumes. He smirked, remembering some of the memorable im-ages: Dan Stewart dressed in a werewolf getup; Nicole Franchi from Black Stallion Winery wearing a nun's habit; Tim Contento as Marilyn Monroe. The calendar had been a bestseller among the locals.

He took a look at his watch and sighed. Nearly nine a.m. If he conked out now he'd have a good five hours' sleep, and those ex-tra zzzz's would come in handy when he opened the bar later that day. Michael Contento's death would be the topic of conversation, usurping Selena Thompson's demise and even the explosion at Carson Creek.

It was not too late to come up with a special drink, Toby Bliss thought, as he switched off his computer and went in search of some rest.

———

Darby recognized Fritz Kohler's blue hybrid as it turned into the driveway and parked. She watched him emerge from the car, his powerful torso seeming to dwarf the little vehicle. He walked purposefully to the farmhouse and rapped on the door.

She greeted him, noting the manilla folder he clutched under one arm. "Come in. I'm glad you could come over on such short notice."

He nodded and indicated the dining room table with a nod of his head. "Shall we sit there?"

"Sure." Darby took a seat, noting the size of Kohler's hands. Those hands had dug into Selena Thompson's flesh, making bruises so intense her brother had seen them.

She looked at his eyes.

"I wanted to hear from you about your desire to own Carson Creek. I assume you are still interested?"

He nodded. "Yes, although I will be offering a slightly lower price due to the condition of the tasting room. Have you had estimates on the renovation?"

"Not yet, but those are underway." She phrased her words carefully. "The sellers have asked me to pose the same question to each of the buyers: Why are you the right person to own Carson Creek?"

He fidgeted in his chair and a look of annoyance flashed across his face. "I didn't realize I had entered an essay competition," he said smoothly. "I would have brought my number two pencil."

Darby gave a little smile but did not comment. *Let him squirm,* she thought.

"Here's the deal," said Fritz Kohler, spreading open his hands. "I have run two very successful businesses. Off the Beaten Track Biking, which I grew to be the largest bicycle touring outfit in the world, and Yoga World United, my current company. I know how to make a business work. Carson Creek, for all its charm and bucolic peacefulness, is a business. A business that I can take to the next level and beyond."

He paused, and Darby wondered if he was finished. Just then he cleared his throat and continued.

"I believe we discussed that I had some prior history with Selena Thompson. She was, if you'll pardon the phrase, the 'girl that got away.' I loved her, but I treated her badly. I suffered from an inability to manage my anger, and she got the brunt of it." He shifted his weight forward in his chair. "I had hoped to purchase Carson Creek as a way of helping Selena out of financial trouble. I thought that I could in some way pay her back for the pain I once caused her. But she made it clear that she had another buyer in mind for the property, although she did not say who. Now that she's gone, I hope her brothers will consider my very generous offer. I'd like to own this place and I'd like to make it succeed."

"It must have been very hard for you when Selena chose another buyer," Darby said quietly.

"You have no idea."

"I'm sure it made you angry."

"It did, but fortunately I have worked hard to master the art of self-control. When she told me she had another buyer in mind, I was able to use the techniques that have helped me and many others."

"Such as?"

"Deep breathing, visualization—listen, I don't think it's really any of your business."

"What about prescription medicines? Do they help with your anger management?"

"What are you talking about?" Darby could see from his balled fists and clenched teeth that his mood was changing.

"I'm talking about metoprolol," she said. "You'd filled your prescription the very afternoon you met with Selena. Is that one of your techniques?"

"That medication is for hypertension," he snarled. "I don't know what you're getting at."

"I'm getting at this: you were angry when Selena told you she wasn't letting you buy the vineyard, so angry that you obtained a bottle of metoprolol. You then came back here and put some of it in Selena's wine bottle. You must have known that she would help herself to a glass of that wine and sit in her hot tub. You hoped that she'd pass out and drown, and that's exactly what happened. You've been mad at Selena Thompson for a long, long time now, haven't you, Fritz? Ever since she was the girl who managed to 'get away' from your violent behavior—"

He lunged across the dining room table at Darby, his brawny hands aiming at her throat. She tried to dodge him, but his tremendous height had given him an advantage. She felt his knuckles grinding into the soft tissue of her neck and tried to cry out.

The living room door burst open and Detective Nancy Nardone busted in, gun drawn.

"Back off, Kohler!" she barked. The other officer, a wiry man wearing a uniform, grabbed Kohler from behind, yanking him away.

He subdued the enraged yoga instructor with a few well-placed tugs. Meanwhile Detective Nardone stood with legs akimbo, her gun trained on the suspect.

"You okay, Darby?" She surveyed the table with a practiced eye.

"Fine." Darby swallowed a few times; no damage had been done. She shuddered at the thought of those big hands around her throat. Her skills as a master of Aikido would have been sorely tested with Fritz Kohler. *Sometimes it's nice not to have to show off,* she thought.

Kohler turned an enraged face in her direction, interrupting her thoughts. "You set me up," he growled.

"Give me a break." Detective Nardone shook her head at him, her expression bemused. "You set yourself up when you came back to bully Selena. We found your prints on the farmhouse door and in the old barn."

"I never went in to the house," he yelled. "I came to the door, and I met her in the barn, but I never went in the house."

"We'll see about that. Let's go." Detective Nardone ushered Kohler out the door. She turned and nodded at Darby. "He's our man," she said. "Good work."

Darby watched as the law enforcement officials herded Fritz Kohler into a police car. His fingerprints were at Carson Creek; he'd purchased the drug used to kill Selena, and his violent temper had now been demonstrated in full. Detective Nardone seemed certain that Fritz Kohler was guilty.

Why, Darby wondered, *can't I bring myself to agree?*

SIXTEEN

"What is the yoga guy's car doing here?" Tim Contento asked, as he wandered into the kitchen at Carson Creek and took a deep breath. "Something smells terrific," he said. "Chicken?"

"Yes, it's nearly done and I'm bringing it up to your family when it's ready." She wiped her hands on an apron and turned to face Tim. "I'm so sorry about Michael."

He nodded his bald head numbly. "Me, too. He was a wonderful father, patient, and forgiving of my mistakes."

Darby thought about the wine futures scandal. In a gentle voice she said, "Such as what happened with Sleepy Spaniel?"

He looked downward and nodded. "Exactly. He thought I'd behaved like an idiot, but he surprised me by saying he understood why I'd taken the gamble. Dad said the wine business is all about risks, and that some pan out, and some don't." He tried to smile. "Tell that to Harrison Wainfield. He's still seething over that whole thing."

"Did he have to pay to settle with the investors?"

"Of course. We both did. But I don't think Wainfield ever forgave Selena for coming up with the whole thing. And then when she decided to sell this place herself, instead of hiring him, I thought he would go ballistic."

"What happened?"

"That's the odd thing. Nothing really happened. Somehow Wainfield got over it, I guess." He clasped his hands together. "I'm going to wander out and see Dan for a minute." He gave a quick smile. "Can't wait to eat this chicken."

Darby watched him go. So Selena hadn't been as well-loved as everyone insisted. She'd had her share of enemies, among them, Harrison Wainfield.

———

Darby was on her way to Contento Family Vineyards with the aromatic roast chicken when her cell phone rang. She pulled over and saw an unfamiliar area code and number. She checked her rearview mirror and pulled to the side of the road. "Hello?"

"John Haina here. I'm a police detective in Sunset Beach, outside of Honolulu, Hawaii, calling about Mr. Douglas Henderson?"

"Yes, Detective Haina. Thank you for calling. I've been very worried about Doug."

"I understand you are his friend and neighbor in Southern California, is that correct?"

"Yes."

"Okay then. I can fill you in on what happened here in Hawaii in a few moments. But first, I'm sitting with Doug right here in the hospital, and he wants to talk a minute."

"Great!" She waited while the detective passed the phone to Doug.

"Darby?" His voice was faint, but distinct. "Darby, whatever you do, don't sell my house."

"Don't worry, Doug. I'll take it off the market today."

"Good." He swallowed. "You were right about Rhonda—she was too good to be true. Everything she told me was a lie." He coughed. "The only consolation I have is that Detective Haina's gonna catch her. I don't want anyone else to go through this." He paused. "Are you still in wine country?"

"Yes, but I'll be back in Mission Beach soon. I'll help you settle back in to that great little bungalow."

He swallowed again. "Thanks. I'm putting Detective Haina back on."

In his clipped, no-nonsense fashion, John Haina described how Doug had fallen prey to a con artist known to him as Rhonda Starkle. "Unfortunately her scam has become quite common, thanks to the availability of so much information on the Internet," he said. "Rhonda sent him photos of what she claimed was her house, requested that he pay part of the rent, and then took off with the money. Meanwhile, she'd been given access to some of Doug's accounts, and needless to say she's cleaned those out, too. When Doug showed up, he discovered that the house belonged to someone else. He tried to track Rhonda down and came afoul of her boyfriend. That's the guy that beat him up, and pretty badly too. We'll catch him though, and we'll get Rhonda as well, and then Doug can help us put them both in prison."

Darby sighed. *Poor guy!* "Any idea when he'll be coming back to California?"

"I think the doctors will release him in a day or two, so he should be back home by the weekend."

"Great." She thanked the Detective. "Keep taking care of him," she implored as she hung up.

She gazed out the windshield of her Karmann Ghia. Outside, the day was sunny, and warm, and Darby thought wistfully of a long run through the countryside. It would give her time to process what had happened to her friend and neighbor, as well as think more about Fritz Kohler's arrest.

She glanced at her phone. *Call Miles*, she told herself. *He needs to know that Doug is safe.*

Since their last discussion, the one in which Miles Porter had basically told her goodbye, Darby had avoided even thinking about the tall, rugged reporter. But now, knowing she would soon hear his resonant voice, she was struck with angst. *What will I say? How should I say it?* Finally she told herself to stop being such a lovestruck high school girl and punched in his number.

The voice that answered the phone was resonant, although recorded. Darby left a brief message saying Doug was fine and would be coming back to California over the weekend. When she hung up and began driving once more, she expected to feel relieved that she'd not spoken with Miles. Instead, she felt keen disappointment.

––––––

Andrea Contento opened the front door, saw the covered casserole dish Darby was carrying, and gave a tired smile.

"How nice of you to bring something," she said.

Darby handed her the enameled pot. "Dan wanted me to convey how sorry he is about Michael. He'll drop by as soon as he can, but in the meantime, I thought I'd bring this."

"It's heavy, and it smells heavenly. A roasted chicken?"

Darby nodded. "A recipe my mother used to make from Julia Child's cookbook. *Poulet Poele a l'Estragon*. It was one of my favorite dinners growing up."

Andrea waved Darby inside the house. "Thank you so much. Let's put it in the kitchen."

Together they walked into the welcoming space. "What a lovely, professional kitchen," Darby said, noting the eight-burner commercial stove and the oversized refrigerator. A gleaming stainless steel pot rack hung over a large granite island, the copper-bottomed pots glinting in the sun.

Andrea smiled. "Yes, it's terrific, isn't it? When we decided to start hosting cooking classes and holding large events here at the vineyard, I lobbied Michael to expand this kitchen rather than building another one. The new cave space has a small commercial kitchen for events that are held there, but this one serves the tasting room and anything that happens in the garden or in the house." She ran a hand over the smooth surface of the granite and grinned. "Consequently I end up doing a lot of the prep work, but I enjoy it. I'm much happier behind the scenes. Michael is the one…" her voice caught. "He was the one who liked to be front and center. Luckily his daughter has the same sensibilities."

As if on cue, Margo Contento entered the kitchen, blinking at Darby. "Oh, hello," she said. She wore a blank expression as she turned and walked out of the room before Darby could reply.

Andrea sighed. "Forgive her, Darby. She's quite upset." She placed the chicken on the counter. "It's getting so warm that perhaps I need to refrigerate this." She rearranged something in the refrigerator and placed the chicken on a shelf. "There." Placing her hands on the granite-topped island, she faced Darby. "I'm glad you came by. I heard from someone downtown that the fitness expert, Fritz Kohler, has been arrested for the murder of Selena. Is that true?"

"Yes, it happened this morning."

"That seems crazy to me. Selena died in her hot tub. Are they saying he killed her first and then put her in the water?'

Darby shook her head. "No. Selena was poisoned."

"What? How can that be?"

"Detective Nardone believes that Fritz Kohler put a drug called metoprolol in Selena's wine. The overdose caused her to pass out and drown."

"My God." Andrea Contento gripped the countertop. "Poison. I'm so relieved that Michael didn't live to hear this news. He would have been heartbroken. It was tragic to think that Selena died of natural causes, but murder? It's just unthinkable."

The front door slammed. Andrea frowned and peered out the window. "It's Margo. Wonder where she's headed." She sighed. "Michael's death has been very hard on her. They argued several times yesterday, including just before he had the heart attack. She feels guilty, I think, even though I reminded her that she and her father often argued. Sometimes it seemed that was the only way they knew how to communicate."

"So they had a stormy relationship?"

"I wouldn't say that at all. They had a very loving relationship, actually. They're just passionate types who liked to debate. Whether it was because they were so much alike, or both on the headstrong side, I don't know, but their discussions could get pretty heated."

"What did Margo and her father argue about yesterday?"

Andrea seemed to consider whether she'd answer or not. Finally she said, "Michael wanted her to take over Christophe Barton's position as Estate Manager, and Margo didn't want to."

"Why not?"

Andrea shrugged. "I think she was concerned about her brother's feelings. She's a softie when it comes to him, and Michael's never understood that. For him, it's all about family obligation and duty. And so, they argued. It was just their way."

"What about Tim?"

"Oh, he's not the type to bicker—too easygoing. He doesn't have his sister's confident personality, either, but we can't all be the same, now can we?"

The phone rang in the background and an answering machine picked up.

"That's probably the twentieth call I've gotten today. Lots of them are from the press, the people who write the wine blogs, and old connections of Michael's. It's crazy." Andrea put a hand through her brunette bob. "I'm sorry I haven't offered you anything, Darby. It's just that I'm kind of overwhelmed right now—"

"Please don't apologize. I totally understand. I'm going to take off and head back to Carson Creek."

Andrea nodded, her eyes brimming with tears. "First Selena, and then that bastard Barton, and now my Michael." She swiped at her eyes and took a deep breath. "And still life goes on. The wine auction is in two weeks, we've got Michael's funeral to plan, and an excavator comes tomorrow to work on the old cave. Life insists on humming along." She walked toward the door with Darby. "Thank you for the chicken. The last thing I feel like doing is cooking, so it is much appreciated."

Darby told Andrea she was welcome and said goodbye.

———

From her vantage point in the woods by Contento Family Vineyards, Sophie Stewart observed Darby Farr driving out of the estate and down the driveway. She crept out of her hiding place and, sticking close to the trees, continued walking toward the house. She had taken only a few steps when the murmur of voices made her freeze. The soft lilting sounds of Spanish met her ears and she exhaled. It was just the Mexican workers on a break. They were in one of the outbuildings and would never notice her.

Sophie trudged along, her shoulders aching from the heavy backpack she lugged back and forth to school each day. She shrugged it off and placed it by a flat rock where it wouldn't be seen from the road. So far, her plan was going well. She'd boarded a bus at school, but instead of going home, had requested to be dropped off at a stop near the vineyard. The walk had been a long one, but it was the only way Sophie could get around without her father knowing.

She resumed walking stealthily toward the Contento's house. The driveway was clear, and she was about to bolt across it when the door opened and Andrea Contento stepped into the sunshine.

Once more Sophie became immobile, her heart thumping in her chest. Andrea Contento glanced at her watch and then walked briskly toward her car, a white Explorer. She climbed in, started the engine, and drove slowly down the driveway.

Slowly Sophie let out her breath. She hurried to the door and entered the house, listening for sounds within. The place was silent. *As silent as the grave*, she thought. She headed up the stairs, her footsteps muffled by the plush carpeting.

In contrast to Carson Creek's humble farmhouse, the Contento family's home was palatial. Sophie wasn't sure which style it was, but she always thought of it as a manor house. Although furnished casually, the first floor's parlors were grand. There was a cozy library with a fireplace, an amazing kitchen, and a wide stairway leading to five big bedrooms. Quite a bit different than the simple home Selena had cherished.

Sophie knew from exploring the house as a child that Margo Contento's room, the one she'd lived in as a kid and now used when visiting the vineyard, was at the end of the hall. Softly the teen pushed open the door and crept inside.

A surprising darkness met her eyes. Heavy drapes at the windows were pulled closed but even in the murky light Sophie could see the room was a mess. Bunched on the floor at the foot of the bed lay a puffy comforter, along with a pillow or two, and a solitary sneaker. Stretched diagonally across the bed she saw a tangle of sheets and blankets. A pile of clothes spilled over a chair, and the lone sneaker's mate peeked out from under a dresser.

Had Margo been this messy as a kid? Sophie imagined heaps of stuffed animals, crooked posters, and twin beds in a constant state of disarray. Maybe she'd had a maid to pick up after her, because somehow Sophie couldn't picture Andrea doing much housework. Perhaps Margo had been allowed to be a slob.

Sophie turned on a small lamp and looked at the items on the dresser. A lipstick, some change, a folded piece of paper... She opened it up. Scrawled in loopy letters was what appeared to be an address. *2738 Redwood.* Sophie groaned. That could be just about anywhere in northern California, she thought. Every single town had a street named after the state's famous tree.

Once she had the numbers memorized, Sophie refolded the paper and put it back on the dresser. She moved silently toward the bathroom door and pulled it open.

The vanity held a polka-dotted makeup case, a toothbrush and toothpaste, contact lens solution and a plastic contact lens case. A nightshirt and robe were draped on the edge of the tub, and a quick look in the wastebasket showed nothing of interest. Sophie peeked inside the makeup case. Another lipstick, blush, mascara, and some moisturizer—nothing out of the ordinary.

Disappointed, Sophie backed out of the bathroom, turned off the little lamp, and crept back down the hallway. She was nearly down the stairs when she heard the noise of the front door opening. Somehow she managed to jump noiselessly down the stairs and position herself in the hallway as if she'd been waiting there.

"What are you doing here?" Margo Contento tossed a slouchy pocketbook onto a nearby bench and gave Sophie a puzzled look.

"I was looking for my dad." It was the first thing Sophie thought of, and she hoped it sounded plausible.

"Your dad? Why would he be here? Isn't he starting to harvest?" Margo had started to walk toward the kitchen, giving Sophie the chance to peer into her pocketbook. Beside a pink wallet was an orange-capped plastic bottle. Sophie nearly gasped.

"I don't know," she said, a little too loudly. "I thought he might have come over, you know, because of your dad."

At the kitchen threshold, Margo Contento stopped. Her back stiffened. She turned slowly around.

"I'm sorry about that," Sophie said. "I mean, I'm sorry that Michael died. I liked him."

The corner of Margo's mouth twitched. "Thanks." She frowned. "Do you need a ride home?"

"No. I'm going to walk down the hill and call my dad."

"Okay. I'll see you later, Sophie." She resumed her path into the kitchen and Sophie heard the clatter of a cabinet door opening. Gingerly she tiptoed to the bulging leather pocketbook and grabbed the prescription bottle.

It took her only a second to read two of the words typed on the label.

Beta blocker.

Sophie Stewart dropped the pills into the purse. With shaking hands she opened the door of the Contento's house and took off, running, until she'd reached the safety of the woods and her backpack.

———

Harrison Wainfield sat at the desk in his office, checking e-mails, when one from Ann Johnson caught his eye. She'd sent it only minutes ago: *Heard about the arrest of the yoga guy. Is Carson Creek still available?* Wainfield gave an exasperated sigh. Why in the world was she asking him about Carson Creek? Didn't Ann know he didn't have that listing? He shook his head in irritation. She really was out to lunch.

He was about to delete the e-mail when the words "yoga guy" registered. Fritz Kohler had been arrested? Quickly he scanned the on-line edition of the *Wyattville Tribune*, reading the news with disbelief. Kohler was a suspect in the murder of Selena Thompson. He swore and slammed his hand upon the table. *There goes that sale! He won't be buying a vineyard if he's going to jail.*

Wainfield sat back in his chair, his heart thudding in his chest. According to the article, Kohler had known Selena before she'd moved to the valley, and had been charged twice for assaulting her.

He took several deep breaths, and when he felt calmer, shut down his computer.

You can never tell about a person, Wainfield thought. Kohler had seemed so controlled and together. And yet even controlled people could snap.

He gave his goatee a few strokes. Most people would think poison was a woman's weapon—clean, easy, and no strength required. A man choosing to murder via poison seemed strange. Or was it strategic? Kohler could have thought it all out as well as anyone. His mind raced. Maybe the loss of Fritz Kohler as a client could turn out to be a very good thing after all.

————

Darby Farr hung up the phone with ET and sighed. He'd been saddened at the news of Michael Contento's death, and then shocked at Fritz Kohler's arrest, but relieved that there would finally be some closure around his sister's death. "I'll call Carlos and tell him," he promised. "And I imagine we will want you to offer the vineyard to the Contentos and Vivian Allen, if she is still interested." He'd paused. "You know, I don't really care what happens to Carson Creek, but I keep thinking of Dan Stewart and his daughter. I'd like the new owner of the vineyard to treat them well."

Darby asked ET to call her with Carlos' feedback. "Or ask him to get in touch with me if he'd like to discuss it," she offered. Darby then filled him in on Doug's situation, and asked him to alert Claudia to withdraw the bungalow from the market.

"Do one more thing for me?" she asked ET. "Ask Claudia to drop off a bag of Sugar Babies at Doug's house. The biggest bag she can find."

"No problem." ET was quiet a moment. "Thank goodness your neighbor is safe. He will want to see you when he returns to California, and we need you here at the office as well. I will make sure Carlos calls you, and then I think you should pack your bags and return to Mission Beach."

Sitting at the dining room table at Carson Creek, Darby pondered ET's advice now that their conversation was through. She was ready to be home, and knew her real estate work needed her, but she had the nagging feeling she had unfinished business at the vineyard. *Selena's killer*, she thought. *I don't believe Fritz Kohler is guilty.*

She felt the brush of fur against her legs and looked down to see Jasper, his amber eyes gazing up at her. Stroking his soft coat, she reflected on what she knew about Selena's murder. Everything was a jumble—nothing made sense. *Maybe if I write it down,* she thought. *Maybe then I'll see some sort of pattern.*

She found the little notebook she'd used once before in Selena's kitchen drawer. Settling back at the table, she began a list of the facts she knew:

1. Selena drowned in her hot tub while drinking a glass of wine.

2. Residue from the wine bottle showed its contents had been spiked with the beta-blocking drug metoprolol.

3. Selena suffered from hypertension.

4. Selena was reading a novel that described the way she had died.

Darby paused. Was that really all she knew? She sighed. There was the evidence about Fritz Kohler: he'd gone to the pharmacy, filled a prescription for metoprolol, and come to Carson Creek, where he'd spoken to Selena.

Had someone else been watching their interchange? She thought back to Michael Contento's reaction at the news of Selena's murder. Had the old vintner seen something on one of his walks? Had he seen someone else at Carson Creek?

The ring of her cell phone brought her out of her reverie. She looked down at the screen. *Miles Porter.* She made her voice calm as she answered the phone.

———

Finding the location of the address written on the scrap of paper had not been as difficult as Sophie Stewart imagined. After her heart-pounding experience at Contento Family Vineyards, she'd taken the bus to the library, where her search on one of the computers had given her two possible choices: a factory in San Francisco, and a small house in Ventano.

Getting to the house in Ventano would be an issue. It was a long bus ride, and she really had no clue as to what part of the city it was in. Sophie loved a mystery, but she had no desire to wander into a strange neighborhood as the afternoon sunlight waned.

Perhaps she could find a phone number. She tried a few different ways, finally coming up with a directory that gave the information, and scrawled down the number. At least she could try to find out who lived there.

The library had a no cell phone rule, so Sophie packed up to leave. Passing by the circulation desk, she spotted a display encouraging library patrons to read the classics. She paused and glanced at the titles. *Pride and Prejudice, The Great Gatsby, Animal Farm*, and others were arranged around the table. Behind *To Kill a Mockingbird* was a worn copy of *Moby Dick*.

Sophie picked up the book. On an impulse she returned to the computer to do one more search.

———

Miles Porter thanked Darby for the message about Doug. "It's great to hear that he is safe," he said, with real feeling in his voice. "I've yet to meet the man, but I know you value his friendship."

Darby's heart did a little leap. Miles had said, "yet to meet" Doug. Did that mean he was hoping for a future that included meeting her friends? She pictured his face, the hard angles, his cropped hair and kind hazel eyes ...

"I'm sure you've heard about Fritz Kohler."

"Yes, I read about it on the wire. What does this mean for the sale of Carson Creek?"

"It means I can move forward with offering the property to Vivian and the Contentos. I spoke with ET, and I think he and Carlos are ready to wash their hands of the vineyard." She paused. "It's time for me to go home, but I can't shake the feeling that Detective Nardone has arrested the wrong person."

Darby expected Miles to remind her that she was a realtor, not a detective, and that surely the police knew their jobs. Instead he paused and said thoughtfully, "You possess a kind of special sense for this kind of work. If your instincts are telling you something is off, I'd put my money on you."

Emotion welled up in Darby and she struggled to keep her tone light. "That's probably one of the nicest things anyone has ever said to me," she admitted. "You really know how to charm a girl."

"Do I? Then I daresay this will mean even more." He paused. "I love you, Darby. I know you may not be ready to hear me say it, but nevertheless I must. I love you."

She swallowed and said in a soft voice, "I don't know what to say."

"You could tell me that you love me back," he offered, without any bitterness in his voice. "And I'm confident that one day soon you'll say exactly that. And you know what? I've decided that I'm prepared to wait for that day. It's not going to be easy, but there you have it." He waited a beat and then cleared his throat. In a different tone he said, "Now, I've gotten a little writing assignment here in San Francisco that's going to keep me busy until the weekend. Are you perfectly safe there, or should I show up with my considerable brute strength and debonair charm and keep you company?"

Darby smiled. "I'm fine." She knew for certain it was the truth, at least for the moment.

SEVENTEEN

Dan Stewart wiped the sweat from his brow and regarded the steel vats holding Carson Creek's pinot noir grapes. Amazingly, the harvesting was going along smoothly. No machinery had broken down, no swarms of bees had attacked, and although the day was unseasonably warm, progress had been substantial. The men were focused and fast, so determined to complete the harvesting in record time that they had offered to pick until the sun went down. Dan Stewart had been touched at their kindness to the memory of Selena.

He looked up now as Darby Farr strode across the driveway, a smile on her face as she regarded the piles of glossy purple grapes.

"How's it going?" She flicked her hair over her shoulders. "Has it been a productive day?"

"Tremendous. I think the curse on Carson Creek died with Christophe Barton." He frowned, thinking of Selena, wishing she could witness the harvest. Her delight last year had been contagious. He felt the familiar pain in his gut over her death. Would it ever get easier?

Dan swept a hand over the gleaming vats. "We're not done yet—in fact, the pickers are going to work with me until dark—but we've made great headway." He mopped his brow with his shirtsleeve. "I'd like to wrap it up tomorrow, and if we keep going at this pace, it's possible." He gave a grimace. "With all that's been happening here, I've seen very little of that teenage girl of mine. I don't like that."

"What's she up to while you're here now?"

"Hanging out with friends, I guess. She said she has plans for dinner and a study session at another kid's house, so that's good. Still, I don't like to think she's running around on her own."

"She's a good kid, Dan. I'm sure you have nothing to worry about."

"Thanks. She is a good kid, I know that, but she's all I've got and I do worry about her." He sighed. "One night's not going to make a difference, I know. It's not like she's going to put herself into any unsafe situations or anything."

"That's right." She glanced at her watch. "I'm trying to reach Carlos because I think he and ET are ready for me to offer the vineyard to Vivian and the Contentos." She paused. "May I tell both the parties that you are interested in continuing on as winemaker?"

He looked at the vats of grapes and nodded. It was a crazy job, but one he loved. "Absolutely."

———

The ornate building housing the bank in Ventano sported a large poster announcing the Valley Wine Auction. Vivian Allen stopped to look it over, noting the date so that she could attend. *I won't own my vineyard then, but hopefully I'll be close*, she thought. She pulled open the heavy door of the building and nearly collided with Andrea Contento.

"You're Andrea, aren't you?" Vivian could see fine lines around the woman's eyes and bluish shadows beneath them. "I'm sorry about the loss of your husband."

"Thank you." Andrea looked away for a moment.

Vivian hesitated. "I'm Vivian Allen. I'm glad to run into you, although I wish the circumstances were happier. You're the one who asked Mr. Deschaines to call me, right? I wanted to thank you."

Andrea gave the redhead a tired nod. "Yes, you're correct. Dominic is an old and dear friend. When I heard he was thinking of selling Deschaines Cellars, I thought of you."

"The vineyard sounds lovely," Vivian said. "I'm going to meet Mr. Deschaines and take a look tomorrow. I love Carson Creek, but there's too much sadness for me." Her words trailed off.

Andrea nodded again, looking off to the side. "I know, believe me, I know." She gave Vivian a direct look. "I'm sure you realize that I have an interest in your deciding not to bid on Carson Creek."

"Of course," Vivian answered smoothly. "I get it. But if I can purchase Deschaines Cellars before he hires an agent, I'll get a better deal. So this benefits me as well."

Andrea gave the ghost of a smile. "Exactly." She extended her hand. "Good luck, Vivian."

"Thank you." Vivian watched the widow glide out of the bank and thought, *I'll see you again, Andrea Contento. You'll see.*

———

The phone line for the house on Redwood Street was continually busy and Sophie Stewart was becoming frustrated. She dialed again, expecting to hear the familiar and annoying signal, when to her surprise it rang through.

A male voice answered. "Hello?"

Sophie listened to the static on the line, momentarily at a loss for words. She then remembered the lines she had practiced. In a clear voice she said that she was calling from Contento Family Vineyards.

"Yeah, yeah, yeah," the guy said, his words muffled and faint. "You're looking for Jim."

"Jim?" The reception was terrible and Sophie felt like she was shouting.

"Yeah, Jim. He's staying here while his place gets repainted." More words followed but they were garbled. "He's gone to the vineyard to have dinner with his sister. Try him there."

"Okay, thanks." Sophie hung up, relieved to have the connection terminated. Who the heck was Jim? She could swear that was the name she'd heard, and yet "Tim" was what made sense. Was it possible she'd misheard? She flashed to the game "Telephone," a childhood diversion she and her friends had once loved. After relaying a message around a circle, the end result would be markedly different from the original words, in frequently hysterical ways. She grinned. It was definitely possible—and highly probable—that he'd said "Tim" and she'd just heard it wrong.

The house on Redwood was a temporary address for Tim Contento, a place to crash while his house was repainted. As Sophie walked away from the Wyattville Public Library, she thought about the fact that what one heard was not always accurate.

Your ears could play tricks on you.

———

Darby hung up the phone with Carlos and dialed Contento Family Vineyards. The clear voice of Margo Contento answered and Darby explained the call.

"I'd love to speak with you about buying Carson Creek, Darby, but there's so much happening here that I'll have to squeeze you in. Do you mind meeting me somewhere? I have an appointment in downtown St. Adina that shouldn't take long. Can you meet me in half an hour?"

Darby looked at her watch. "Sure. Where is convenient?"

"There's an old mission just outside of town. Do you know it?"

"No."

Margo gave directions while Darby listened. "It's a quiet, peaceful place," she said. "We're working on funding its restoration through the wine auction. I think you'll like seeing it."

Darby hung up. With all that was happening, no wonder Margo Contento craved peace and quiet. She took a quick check of her messages. Claudia Jones from the office had called ten minutes earlier. Fearing there was something wrong with ET, Darby quickly dialed.

Claudia's voice was reassuring.

"No, no, nothing is wrong here. ET is sad, naturally, but time will make things easier. The Henderson bungalow is off the market and I explained to the young couple what happened. They completely understand. In fact, I showed them another property and it looks like they may bite on that one."

Darby could not resist a smile at Claudia's use of a fishing metaphor to describe her clients. She fought the urge to respond, "I hope you hook them."

"That's great. Anything else?"

Claudia paused. "Yes, actually, the reason I called is that you had a visitor this morning. A Mr. Kenji Miyazaki from Gen—"

Darby could tell Claudia was having trouble pronouncing the company's name. "Genkei Pharmaceuticals." She pictured this Mr. Miyazaki, imagining a frail, elderly gentleman in a tailored suit. "That's odd that he came all this way to see me." *Especially after my e-mail to him,* she thought but did not say.

"He was competing in a hang-gliding competition," Claudia offered. "Out at Point Loma."

"Hang-gliding?"

"Yes. Apparently he's quite good—he has a shot at winning the whole thing, I guess. And he is very handsome, too! I don't know if you've ever dated a Japanese man, but this guy is adorable. I didn't see a ring, either."

Darby was astonished. "He's a vice president of the company, right?"

"*Senior* vice president," she said, sounding like a proud mother. "Beautiful straight teeth, gorgeous suit, and lovely manners. And of course, Ken's English is flawless. It ought to be! He went to Harvard, after all."

Ken? Darby was trying hard to reconcile the image she'd formed of Kenji Miyazaki with the new and improved version put forth by her employee.

"Did this amazing creature say why he wanted to see me?"

"Yes," Claudia said. "He has information about your family." She hesitated. "Your *Japanese* family."

Darby thanked her and hung up the phone. Who was this Kenji Miyazaki and what kind of information did he possess? She shoved her phone in her pocketbook and sighed. Obviously she was going to have to talk with this mystery man at some point.

She grabbed her pocketbook and let Jasper outside into the late afternoon sun. Thoughts of her business in San Diego, Doug Henderson's condition, and even ET and Carlos were put on the back burner as she jumped into her sports car and started the engine.

Darby was headed to the Mission.

———

Harrison Wainfield cradled the bottle of Sleepy Spaniel Syrah in his hand, feeling the heft of the glass. This was the wine that had started it all, the one that Selena Thompson had said was a runaway favorite. "It's a vineyard that's just getting better and better," she'd insisted, a glass of Syrah in her hand. They were on the patio at Contento Family Vineyards—she, Tim, Harrison, and Margo. Andrea and Michael were in the kitchen, putting the finishing touches on dinner. It had been a scorcher of a day—late July, or August—and the women were wearing sundresses and sandals. "Plums, blackberry," Selena had gushed. "It has such a wonderful smoky finish. Can't you just imagine pairing it with food coming off the grill?"

Wainfield could imagine it, that was the problem, and he'd fallen for her charming predictions as he sipped more and more of the captivating wine. Later, while he and Tim smoked a joint as they walked among the vines, Harrison convinced the Contento heir to snap up some futures on the Sleepy Spaniel winery. Not that the sales job had been too difficult. That summer Tim Contento would have gone along with anything Selena said. He was entranced by her vivacious spirit and voluptuous body, and no doubt was enjoying the afternoon hot tubs at Carson Creek in more than a neighborly fashion.

Of course, there had been other investors—plenty more. Ventano Valley was full of people who had money to risk and loved the idea of taking a chance. "There is a saying about making an investment in the wine business," Michael Contento used to say. "To make a small fortune, start with a large one." Indeed, most of the investors in their newly formed wine club had large enough fortunes that they could afford to gamble on a fresh, exciting wine.

All except one.

Nicole Franchi was an assistant winemaker at a new winery located on the grounds of a historic equestrian center in St. Adina. She was cute, young, and easily influenced, a friend of Tim's from the Valley Wine Auction committee. Perhaps to impress him, she raised a substantial amount of capital to invest in Sleepy Spaniel's production—and, when the whole thing went south, lost it all.

"Nicole is pretty pissed off," Harrison Wainfield remembered Tim saying. "She's threatened to go to the press."

Wainfield had felt the prickly beginnings of panic. "She can't do that," he said. "You have to stop her."

"And how do you suggest I do that?" asked Tim. "Any bright ideas?"

Wainfield shrugged helplessly. He was out of bright ideas.

Now he fingered the bottle of Sleepy Spaniel, wondering what had happened to Nicole Franchi. She'd been fired from her job at the new winery shortly after news of the scandal broke. Wainfield suspected she'd left the area after Tim had mandated that no one else in the valley hire her.

He grabbed the bottle of Syrah by the neck and brandished it like a club. It would be easy to smash on the back porch, but what was the point of that? The time for anger was long past, and the only one he really blamed had already been punished. Instead he found an opener in the drawer, pulled out the cork, and poured himself a glass.

———

The Karmann Ghia's tires crunched the sand surrounding the Mission San Francisco Ventano. Darby parked in the nearly empty lot and came outside into the late afternoon sun. She looked across the dusty stretch to a long, white adobe building, punctuated on one end by a handsome, although crumbling, chapel. Her eye followed a series of arches, some intact and some in disrepair, curving down from the roofline, providing a shaded corridor that had no doubt sheltered hundreds of Franciscan monks. A bell tower—or the remains of one—reached heavenward from one end of the chapel. A pile of rubble on the other end indicated there may have been twin bell towers, but that was a long time ago.

Darby looked around for Margo, noticing that the lot's sole car appeared to be empty. She raised her face toward the sun for a moment, enjoying the warmth and the mission's silence. The place was practically deserted, a far cry from other historical sites Darby had visited, where gift shops, ice cream vendors, and hordes of tourists were the norm.

She decided to start her tour of the old mission without Margo and began crossing the lot. Straggly weeds managed to poke up through the sand, their pale green leaves covered with a thin layer of dust. Her feet made a muffled sound, barely noticeable against the stillness, which was starting to feel less serene with every step. Darby glanced around, pulled out her cell phone, and called Nancy Nardone.

The detective's curt message played and Darby left an equally brief response, stating where she was and why. Years of meeting real estate clients in strange places had taught her to be cautious and to pay attention to her surroundings. As a woman in law enforcement, Detective Nardone would understand.

Darby surveyed the buildings looming before her.

The widest archway appeared to be the main entrance. She paused on the cracked terra cotta tiles to read a bronze plaque announcing she was about to enter one of California's northernmost missions. A sign below the plaque implored visitors to donate funds to help restore the structure to its original glory. Darby fished a twenty dollar bill out of her pocketbook and stuffed it into a locked box marked "Thank you." *Vaya con Dios*, she thought.

Quiet voices approached. A young couple, their arms linked, strolled by her, headed toward the only other car in the lot. Darby watched them wistfully, wondering whether they'd come to meditate or had enjoyed another form of spiritual awakening. Judging from the girl's tousled hair and smudged lipstick, it had been the latter. *The place is certainly private enough to do either,* she thought, heading through the arch and into the covered hallway.

Under the shelter of the old adobe overhang the temperature was much cooler. Darby gazed down the long corridor, enjoying once more the total silence of the place. Most missions she had visited were in the center of bustling towns and cities; many still operated as active parishes with regularly scheduled services. For some reason this one had yet to enjoy the restoration efforts so lovingly lavished on its more fortunate brothers and sisters farther down the California coast.

She came back into the sunlight and approached the attached chapel. A large wooden door with huge iron rings was the entrance, and Darby felt sure it would be locked. She pushed on it gingerly and to her surprise it swung open with a load groan. She stepped into a dimly lit space.

This had been the heart of the mission, the place where the missionaries and their converts had gathered to worship. Once sacred space, the chapel was now free of ornamentation, as if it had been stripped years earlier of its artifacts. The back wall bore a gaping hole out of which Darby could see the darkening sky.

She glanced at her watch. Margo was running very late. Perhaps whatever appointment she had mentioned had thrown off her schedule. Darby wondered if she should continue to wait. *Even though I called Detective Nardone, I'm here all alone, in an isolated spot. Not exactly a wise move.*

She fingered her cell phone and checked to be sure there were no messages. *I'll give Margo another five minutes, and then I'm out of here.*

Darby continued to the back of the chapel where another wooden door awaited. *I'll see the back of the property and then head back to the vineyard.*

The creak of the second door's metal hinges made a shiver run down Darby's spine. It was a sound from countless horror movies, the kind she and her father used to watch on the rare nights Jada Farr wasn't home. No matter how scary the movie, Darby had never felt frightened wrapped in her father's strong arms.

Unlike now. There was a strange feeling in the mission's back garden, or maybe it was just that the abandoned site was starting to wear on her nerves. Here, piles of adobe bricks were scattered in what looked like an old foundation, creating troughs that looked as if they could hold water. Around the edges of the adobe rectangles were narrow canals with weeds sprouting through the cracked bricks.

"Know what it is?" A voice cut through the silence, making Darby shiver. She turned toward the sound, momentarily blinded by the sun.

Margo Contento strode across the parched ground and tilted her head at the ruins. "It's a *lavanderia,* Spanish for what we would call an open-air laundry. This is where the missionaries as well as people from the village gathered to wash clothes and bathe their bodies." She pointed into the distance. "Years ago, water from the Wyatt River was diverted here. It filled up these basins, as well as irrigating the surrounding fields." She pointed at a mound of curved stone that looked as if it had been carved. "See that thing right there? Believe it or not, that was a gargoyle. Water used to spurt from its mouth, back in the day."

Darby looked at the *lavanderia* with new eyes, picturing the tiled rectangles filled with refreshing water. She imagined the monks scrubbing their robes against the adobe, talking quietly or praying as they did so. "For a place that was so lively, it has a melancholy feeling." She looked up at Margo, who nodded somberly.

"I'm amazed that you sense that, Darby. You see, this place was also the site of a horrific massacre. Twenty monks and a dozen or so villagers were slain here, surprised as they bathed by a group of disgruntled natives. It was said that the water ran red for years after the slaughter."

"That's a terrible story."

"I agree. Terrible, and yet true." She shook her blonde hair away from her face. "I'm sorry to be so late. Dr. Yang was running behind, and I didn't have your number to call. Please accept my apology."

"You are a patient of Dr. Yang's?"

"That's right. Me and most of the female population of the county, it seems." She shrugged. "Anyway, I needed to see you because I felt when we spoke earlier that you have some doubts about Fritz Kohler's arrest. I sensed that you seemed to feel as if he could be innocent."

"I do think the evidence against him is pretty flimsy, but I guess that will be for a jury to decide."

"Sure. There's another piece of evidence that they'll know about, something I'm prepared to tell Detective Nardone in the morning." She hesitated. "My father told me something just before he died." She stopped and took a deep, steadying breath. "Dad saw a stranger by the cabana next to Selena's hot tub. It was Fritz Kohler."

Darby exhaled, blowing air through her mouth. "Wow. That changes everything. Why didn't your father tell the authorities?"

"He didn't think it mattered. Dad figured Kohler had been at Carson Creek to see Selena before her accident occurred. We all thought Selena had died naturally, remember?"

Darby nodded. Margo had a point. There would have been no reason for Michael Contento to tell anyone about seeing Kohler, and since no one had asked, he'd said nothing.

Except to his daughter.

"Why did he tell you, Margo?"

She lifted her hands in a gesture of incomprehension. "He was annoyed with me for not coming home that night, more to the point, for being out with Christophe Barton. He said if word got out that I was linked to him, there would be a scandal. I told him that he didn't know everything that went on, that he was an old man, and he countered with telling me about seeing plenty. That's when Dad said that he'd seen Fritz Kohler at Carson Creek."

Darby looked down into the troughs where the missionaries had once cleaned their clothes. Was it her imagination, or did she see a ring of dried red blood around the tiles? She looked back up at Margo. "Detective Nardone will welcome that information. It perfectly corroborates her theory that Fritz Kohler is the murderer."

"That's because he is, Darby. You must see that now." She looked down at her watch and swore softly. "I've got to get back to the vineyard. Listen, we still want to purchase Carson Creek, despite all that has happened over there. I hope you'll be in touch about that soon."

Darby followed Margo as they walked around the chapel and back to the parking lot. She still had not heard from Carlos and was not going to proceed until he called. "Tomorrow," she said. "I promise I'll let you know tomorrow."

She climbed into her car, first texting Detective Nardone that she was on her way back to Carson Creek. A few seconds later, she received a reply.

IN THE MIDDLE OF A MEETING. YOU OKAY?

FINE, Darby texted back. *Just fine.*

On the drive from Ventano back to Carson Creek, Darby pondered Margo's assertion that her father had seen Fritz Kohler at Selena's hot tub. She claimed Michael had been taking one of his walks along the perimeter of Contento Vineyards, and from the vantage point he had once described to Darby, seen the yoga guru on Carson Creek's property. Fritz Kohler was certainly distinctive looking. Even from a distance, his unique shape and sheer size would have been easy for Michael to discern.

But why had Kohler been at the hot tub? He would have added the metoprolol to the wine in the kitchen, and by the placement of the drugstore receipt, they knew he'd been in the old barn. But why the hot tub?

The answer came to Darby in a rush.

He wanted to make sure Selena was dead.

The chilling sentence caused goose bumps to rise on her arms. Michael Contento had been a witness to the murder. If what he'd told Margo was true, Michael had seen Fritz as he crouched by the hot tub, watching Selena Thompson take her last breaths.

"Whew!" Dan Stewart took a long drink of water and placed the glass on the kitchen counter. "That was a very long, but productive, day." He glanced at his watch. "Think I'll go and collect my daughter—wherever she is—and call it a night." He glanced up at Darby. "What time are you taking off in the morning?"

"Probably around ten. I'll see you, but I won't see Sophie, so please say goodbye for me."

"I'll be sure to do that. Now you and I can save our goodbyes for the morning, right?"

Darby nodded, knowing she would not be at her most coherent if she and Dan began a conversation. For some reason she was feeling the strange sensation that she was underwater, struggling to rise to the surface and gulp air.

Dan grabbed the keys to his jeep and regarded Darby with a furrowed brow. "Are you okay?

Again she nodded. "It's this whole thing with Fritz Kohler—his arrest and now Margo's information. He never seemed like the killer to me, and I can't figure out why."

"Maybe more evidence will come to light during his trial," Dan suggested. "After all, it does seem that he and Selena shared a pretty violent past."

"That's true." She took Dan's glass and placed it in the dishwasher. "Go on home to Sophie, Dan. I'll see you in the morning."

He grinned. "Good night."

The crunch of his wheels on the driveway receded as the jeep eased down the hill. Darby prepared herself a simple salad and ate it, deep in thought. Finally she took her phone and called someone she knew would be a wise and sympathetic sounding board: Miles Porter.

"As always, I'm happy to aid you in your detection efforts," Miles quipped once she'd described her doubts about Fritz Kohler. "Why don't you start by telling me exactly what it was Margo said to you at the old mission?"

"Okay." Darby thought back to the conversation, wanting to get the details straight. Had it been only an hour ago that she and Margo had spoken? She took a deep breath and began.

"Margo told me that Michael said he saw Kohler at Selena's hot tub. I asked her why he did not tell anyone, and she said he figured Kohler had been at Carson Creek to visit Selena. She pointed out that everyone had assumed Selena's death was an accident. The only reason he told Margo before he died was that he was trying to prove the point that he saw a lot that went on. I think it was his way of saying that he was still on top of his game."

"Now, you spoke to Michael that same day, right? Isn't that when he told you that he could see part of Carson Creek when he took his walks?"

"You are a good listener, Miles. I spoke to Michael and I met Fritz Kohler." Again she had the sensation that she was trying to swim up to the surface for air. She closed her eyes and tried to relax.

"Sweetheart, are you alright?" Concern deepened Miles' question.

Darby considered her answer. She felt like confessing that no, she was not alright, that in fact she was going certifiably crazy. Instead she hedged and said, "I'll be better when I figure out why I think Margo is lying."

"You actually think she is making the story up?"

"I do. That's exactly what I think." She thought back to her conversation with Michael Contento at his vineyard. He had grown upset with her, had told her to pack up her bags and go back to Mission Beach. His anger had flared because she had told him...

She snapped her fingers. "I've got it Miles! Margo said Michael did not know Selena had been poisoned, but he did know. He knew because I told him. I told him exactly what I knew about the metoprolol. He was furious, and I had the distinct impression that he was scared as well."

"Scared for whom, that's the question? His children?"

"Certainly not Fritz Kohler! Miles, this is it. Michael told Margo something, but it wasn't about Kohler, I just know it." She rose and put her salad bowl in the sink. "I'm going over there right now to talk to Margo. I'm going to make her tell me the truth."

Miles exhaled. "Listen to me, Darby. Don't put yourself in danger."

Darby didn't reply. She was already headed out the door and into her sports car.

———

The sky was taking on a more somber note as Darby parked her Karmann Ghia in the Contento Vineyards' lot and strode to the front door of the farmhouse. Calling Margo was out of the question. Darby needed to see her face to face and find out why she had lied.

"Come in!" A male voice rang out as Darby entered the farmhouse. She heard it call out again. "I'm in the kitchen!"

Darby crossed the hallway and walked through the vineyard's spacious dining room. The scent of sage perfumed the air, mingled with a hint of garlic. Darby entered the Contentos' gourmet kitchen.

The space was brightly lit, reflections shining off the copper bottomed pots and pans hanging over the island where Tim Contento worked. His back was to Darby but she could see a large pot simmering on the stove, the source of the delicious smells.

Tim turned slowly, his bald head shiny in the light, and smiled. In his hands were two gleaming butcher knives.

"What brings you here?" he asked. Methodically he began stroking one knife against the other in a rhythmic motion.

"Margo," she stammered. "I'm looking for Margo."

The muscles in Tim's arms bulged as he sharpened the knives.

"Huh. She's feeling kind of nostalgic tonight. Off on a goodbye visit to the old cave. You know where it is? The one Vincenzo built a hundred years ago? She's probably still there."

Darby shook her head. The flash of the knives' silver blades was hypnotic.

"It's in the old barn behind the tasting building. Margo's two ponies are kept there—for tonight at least. In the back of the barn is a wooden door, and stairs leading down to the cave. Watch out because they are really punky. There's another way down from the outside, but it's even more rotted. Wish I could take you over there and say goodbye to it myself, but I'm kind of in the middle of things. Want a flashlight?"

Darby nodded. She managed to thank Tim when he handed her a battery operated flashlight from a kitchen drawer.

"Tell her I'm going to be about half an hour with this risotto and the chicken you so thoughtfully cooked," he said, pulling the dish Darby had brought out of the refrigerator. "Andrea's out for a walk and should be back any moment." He looked up. "You're welcome to stay for dinner if you'd like."

"Thank you. I've already eaten."

"Okay, then." He put down the knives and stirred the contents of the pot. "Another time, perhaps." He cocked his head. "You feeling okay?"

"Yes, I'm fine." Darby backed out of the kitchen and headed for the old barn, the flashlight gripped tightly in hand.

EIGHTEEN

DARTING BLACK SHAPES FLICKERED across the darkening sky as Darby hurried across the grass to the small wooden barn. Perched on the side of the Contento's rows of Chardonnay grapes, the little structure was charming, although in dire need of repair. Was it to be destroyed along with the cave? Darby wondered why the family would demolish such an important part of their history, but then, the whole vineyard was their heritage. Maybe one compromised building wasn't worth renovation.

She heard the soft snuffling of the ponies as she approached. She whispered calming words to them, hoping to ease their anxiety over a strange person in their midst. "Easy, easy. It's okay." She'd never had a horse as a girl, but one of her clients outside of Mission Beach had invited her to ride several times, and she found she had a natural affinity for the powerful animals. "Ssshhh, it's okay." She stroked the soft muzzle of one of the ponies, wishing she had brought along apples as a peace offering.

Darby took a deep breath. Her heartbeat had finally slowed to a normal rhythm.

He freaked me out with those knives, she admitted to herself, wanting almost to chuckle at the absurdity of her fear. *I'll laugh about it when I'm back at Carson Creek,* she thought. Now it was time to find Margo.

She whispered once more to the ponies and began searching for the wooden door. It was located in the corner of the old barn, as Tim had described, and Darby saw that it was ajar. Calling out to Margo, she flipped on her flashlight and peered into the door and down the stairs into darkness. "Margo?" she called again.

"Down here." The voice came from below. Darby began descending the steps, testing each step for rotted wood as Tim had recommended. One plank sagged nearly completely under her weight; she yanked back her foot and found sturdier purchase. When at last she touched the solid earthen floor of the cave, she swept the beam of the flashlight around the dark walls, shiny with moisture, and cautiously straightened up.

She could stand, but just barely. Water trickled down her neck and a constant faint dripping punctuated the quiet. Jumbled in one corner, Darby saw what looked to be the decomposing remains of several wooden barrels, no doubt for aging wine, along with a few broken bottles scattered about the dirt floor. Webs from long-dead spiders made a lacey design against the moist rocks. The air was musty and damp, like a very deep hole.

"Margo? I need to speak with you. About what your father told you before he died."

"I'm saying goodbye to these caves." Her voice was distorted. Darby shivered and edged toward it. Finally her flashlight flickered on Margo's blonde hair.

"Let's go back up where we can talk." It was a good thirty degrees colder underground, and already Darby was chilled.

Margo pivoted slowly toward Darby. Her arm was extended, almost as if she was pointing. She was holding something shiny.

"Let's not." The thing in her hand was a revolver, trained directly at Darby's chest.

"What?" Darby gasped. "What are you doing?" She looked up at Margo's face. What she saw made her heart nearly stop.

The person holding the gun was not Margo Contento. Darby watched in horror as the imposter's free hand ripped off a blonde wig to reveal a chic brunette bob.

———

Dan Stewart was experiencing every parent's worst nightmare: he could not find his child.

From the moment he'd entered the house, he'd sensed something was terribly wrong. Sophie wasn't in her room; nor was she anywhere in the small but comfortable house that they shared.

He checked his cell phone. No calls from her; no responses to his text messages. No answer when he dialed her phone.

He swallowed the panic that was rising like bile in his throat. This was his fault, this was because he was a terrible parent; this was because he was too focused on the vineyard and not on this real job of raising a daughter safely to adulthood. He wanted to cry out in anguish. Instead, Dan forced himself to make a plan.

First he called Carson Creek. Darby did not answer. Next, he phoned all of Sophie's friends, but no one knew where she was. He tried to ignore the pity in the voices of their moms when they offered to help.

What could they do? What could anyone do? It was time to call the police, and time for Dan Stewart to jump in his jeep and roam the valley's twisting roads.

———

Andrea Contento tossed the blonde wig to the ground and kept the gun trained on Darby. "Get on your knees," she said, as calmly as if she were ordering a pound of prosciutto at the deli. "Get on your knees and put your hands behind your back."

Darby's mind raced. Getting on the ground was not an option the trained Aikido student wanted to take, but the gun-toting Andrea was too far away for Darby to fight. *If I'm closer, I can overpower her.* She decided to try that tactic first.

Darby took a step toward Andrea, her hands raised in submission but at shoulder height where she could quickly maneuver them. "Andrea, I think there has been some misunderstanding."

"I said, get on your knees," Andrea barked. "Do it or I swear to God I'll shoot."

Darby peered through the darkness into the other woman's eyes. They were cold and calculating—unflinching. *The eyes are the windows of the soul,* she recalled her Aikido sensei saying as he paced the floor of San Diego's Academy of Martial Arts. Darby recognized the look of total malice in her opponent's stare. Those eyes were the eyes of a killer.

She made a quick calculation.

The distance between me and Andrea is too far to knock the gun out of her hands without it going off. I'll have to wait for another opportunity to disarm her.

Darby sank to the damp ground, her knees against the dirt. She'd practiced self-defense many times in the *hanni* position, but it was not one of her favorites.

"That's better." Andrea remained where she was, the gun aimed at Darby's heart. "Drop the flashlight." The device fell to the ground with a thud, its beam aiming into the darkness. "Now I'm coming over with some duct tape, and if you move a muscle I will blast your internal organs all over this cave. Understood?"

"I don't get it, Andrea. Why the blonde wig?"

Andrea lowered herself slowly and picked up a roll of tape. She moved toward Darby.

"Was the wig to make me think you were Margo? Is that it?"

Andrea was about two feet away from Darby, still standing above her with the gun.

"Margo isn't down here with you, is she?" Andrea was coming within striking range. *Don't hit the trigger finger,* she remembered her sensei instructing. *If you hit the trigger finger it will cause the gun to be fired.* Darby steeled her resolve, all the while keeping her face calm and watching Andrea's eyes.

With lightning speed, Darby brought both of her hands down hard on the wrist holding the gun, driving it in a swift counterclockwise move. It was a last resort tactic, but Darby had to take the chance. With her right hand grasping the handle of the gun, she punched with her left at Andrea's jugular. In a second she was on her feet with Andrea subdued.

"Now you're the one who's going to her knees," Darby commanded. "Get down."

Andrea sunk to the ground, moaning. "My neck," she groaned, her arm massaging the place where Darby had punched.

Darby grabbed the duct tape and ripped off a strip. "Hands behind you, let's go."

Andrea put her hands behind her, wincing in pain, while Darby advanced with the duct tape. She bent over, ready to secure Andrea's wrists, when a force struck, hard, and the damp floor of the cave rose up to meet her.

Andrea had coiled herself into a powerful spring and unleashed pure fury on Darby. The realtor lay on the ground, the gun skittering into a dark corner.

"You little bitch," Andrea breathed. She gave several savage kicks to Darby's stomach, and then ripped off a long strip of duct tape. "Stick out your arms," she commanded. "Now!"

Darby ignored the piercing pain in her midsection and, acting as passively as possible, stuck out her hands, her wrists touching.

Andrea wound the tape around and through Darby's wrists until she was satisfied. She then wrapped her ankles, grunted, and slapped a long piece over Darby's mouth.

"Now you listen to me. I'm the one in charge of this little party here, so don't get any more stupid ideas." She was breathing hard, her chest heaving with the exertion of having bested the younger woman. "You think you're pretty damn smart, don't you? You come down here looking for Margo. Well, she can't help you. She's tucked away in her office, selling case after case of Contento wine."

She rubbed the spot on her neck where Darby's punch had connected with soft tissue. "Luckily you didn't get me in the face where Tim and Margo might notice," she spat. She patted her hair. "I've been out for a walk, so if I look a little worse for wear, that's no big deal." She turned again to Darby. "I was perfectly content to let you head back to San Diego. But you're like a little dog with a bone. You just won't give it up."

She picked up the flashlight and began walking toward the stairs. "Contrary to what you might think, I'm not a bloodthirsty killer. I'm more—opportunistic. So, just like I knew what would happen to Selena, I've got a pretty good idea of how you'll die." She paused at the first step. "Tomorrow the excavator will come to tear down the barn and you'll be buried in tons of rubble. Old Vincenzo's cave will be filled in and you, my darling Darby, will be part of the fill. No one will find you for hundreds of years—if you're ever found."

She sighed and put a foot on the stairs. "I'll be back as soon as I've had dinner with the kids. Wouldn't want them to come looking for me, now would we? I'll bring you a little bedtime snack that will guarantee you'll sleep peacefully through the night, despite the nocturnal creatures who'll be nibbling on you like an old sandwich." She climbed gingerly up the rotted stairs. "See you soon, Darby."

Darby wasted no time getting to work on her constraints. She'd deliberately placed her wrists in one of the easiest escape positions; still, it would take time to loosen the tape's sticky hold so that she could slip her hands free. The strip across her mouth was causing her to gag, but Darby willed herself to ignore it, just like she would not let herself focus on Andrea's revelations. *My hands are the top priority. I've got to get them free.*

The tape bit into her flesh as Darby worked single-mindedly to loosen it. She was so intent on making progress that she did not at first feel something brush against her thigh.

A rat.

Darby squirmed and the animal skittered into the darkness. It would be back, she knew that, and the next time it would be bolder. More determined than ever, Darby rubbed her wrists.

———

Sophie Stewart scrambled in her pocket to turn off her cell phone. It was her father, his ring a bad rendition of the reggae hit, "Red, Red Wine." She knew she should just turn it off, but she couldn't bear to. "I'll be home soon, Dad," she vowed. "Right after I see what's so interesting in the old barn."

She'd watched Andrea Contento head into the structure, and then to her surprise seen Darby Farr go in as well. Minutes later, Andrea had come back out—alone.

Once Sophie saw that Andrea was back in the farmhouse, she headed for the barn. The ponies gave nervous whinnies, lifting their heads in protest, and Sophie soothed them as best she could. Using her cell phone to light her path, she spied a stairway in the corner of the old barn and hurried toward it.

Old farm tools were piled by the stairs, long since replaced with newer and more modern implements. Sophie put a tentative foot on the first stair. It was springy, the wood damp and rotted.

Descending slowly downward, Sophie strained to see anything in the darkness. When her feet were on solid ground, she swept the feeble light around her surroundings. *The cave.* She remembered coming down here once or twice when her father had worked at

Contento Vineyards. It was super creepy during the day; at night it was positively horrible.

There was no sign of Darby Farr, and Sophie was about to climb back up the stairs when her cell phone illuminated a long shape. She crept closer. It looked like a human body, a moaning body that was undulating like a caterpillar. Sophie wanted to scream.

Instead she crept closer until the creature raised its head. Sophie leaned closer with the phone's feeble light and nearly yelped in astonishment. The pupa-like shape was Darby Farr.

———

Detective Nancy Nardone squinted her eyes at Dan, trying to get something out of him that would help her find his daughter.

"Can't you tell me anything that might shed some light on Sophie's whereabouts?" she said. "What does she like to do, what are her hobbies? Nicknames?"

"Sophie Doo," he said softly. He ran a hand through his hair. Maybe this had been a mistake, coming to the police station and asking for Detective Nardone, but Jesus, it had been several hours and there was still no sign of Sophie.

"She used to love the cartoon *Scooby Doo*," he explained. "It's about a dog who solves mysteries…"

"I know what *Scooby Doo* is about," snapped Detective Nardone. "Why didn't you tell us this earlier?" She twirled a pencil in her fingers. "Sophie fancies herself an investigator, and we don't have to think about it too hard to realize which crime she's trying to solve." She snapped her fingers at a nearby officer. "Get on the phone with Contento Vineyards," she ordered. "Tell them we're coming over." She got to her feet and pointed at Dan. "Let's get going. I have a feeling our *Scooby Doo* hopeful thinks she's on the trail of a mystery."

––––––––––

Darby winced as the duct tape was yanked off her mouth with a surprisingly hard pull.

"Andrea did this, didn't she?" The teen felt the tape around Darby's wrists. "I need something to cut this tape." She jumped to her feet. "There's an old piece of metal in the barn," she breathed. "I'll be right back."

"Hurry," Darby implored. "But be careful on the stairs."

The thump of Sophie's footsteps receded as the teen climbed up the stairs. Moments later she was pounding down them and back at Darby's side.

"Here, maybe this will work." She rubbed a rusty corner of an old blade against the tape. It slipped and cut through Darby's flesh.

"Ow!"

"Sorry! You've had a tetanus shot, right?"

"Probably, but truthfully tetanus is the least of our problems. Keep up the good work, Sophie, you're making headway." Finally the tape gave way and Darby pointed at her ankles. "See what kind of damage you can do to my feet," she said.

Sophie sawed at the tape with the rusty blade. "I figured out today that it was Andrea who killed Selena Thompson," she said, a hint of pride in her voice. "I've been watching her like a hawk."

"Well, you did better than me," Darby said, looking toward the old stairs with trepidation. Her hands were finally free and feeling normal. "I thought it was Margo."

"I did, too, until I realized what Mr. Contento *really* said when he died."

"What was that?"

"Well, Margo said it was 'Ahab's life,' so of course you think about Moby Dick and Captain Ahab. Today I started thinking that she heard him wrong. What if he said, 'Ahab's wife?'" Sophie sat back on her haunches, and Darby could sense that she wore a triumphant smile.

"Okay, you're going to have to explain this to me, but first give me that blade for a while." Sophie passed her the rusted metal and Darby began sawing at the tape. "Fill me in. Who's Ahab's wife? I don't remember anything in *Moby Dick*."

"That's because it's not from *Moby Dick*," Sophie said. "Ahab was also the name of a famous king in the Bible. His wife was called Jezebel. She had their neighbor killed because the King coveted something the neighbor owned. Know what it was?"

"No." Darby had nearly freed her ankles.

"A vineyard. Jezebel got her neighbor stoned to death so that they could scoop up his vineyard." She paused and let the words sink in. "See, Michael Contento was a professor. He said, "Ahab's wife," because he wanted us to know that Andrea was just like Jezebel."

"Why didn't he just say that Andrea had done it, save us all a lot of time?" Darby gave a last push with the blade as the tape finally gave way. She wriggled her ankles and scrambled to her feet as the loud blare of a cell phone playing "Red, Red, Wine," split the silence.

"Crap! It's my dad again."

"Answer it!" Darby said. "Maybe he's nearby."

"Hey Dad? It's me, Sophie, and I'm—"

Thwack! A hard blow sent the cell phone flying from Sophie's hand. Darby tensed, ready to spring, when she saw the situation.

Sophie was trapped in a headlock. Andrea had managed to sneak down the stairs and locate the gun and now its barrel was pressed against Sophie's skull. She dragged the girl to the phone, lowered herself down, straightened, and then heaved the phone into the darkness.

"Looks like I did the right thing in turning down dessert," she muttered. "Who would have guessed you'd have a little teen side-kick to help you out of jams?" She jerked her head toward the corner. "Get on the ground, Darby."

Darby crouched, her hands feeling for the rusty blade.

"Get over there next to your friend," Andrea commanded, shoving Sophie. "She's the one who'll keep you company while you both die."

Darby's fingers scrabbled along the dirt in search of the blade.

"They won't find you down here, and even if they do, I'll be long gone," Andrea said, almost as if she were convincing herself.

"I told my Dad," Sophie insisted. "He's on his way!"

"You did not, Sophie. I heard you." She waved the gun. "You've left me no choice but to shoot you both. It's not my style, but I've got to do it."

"You don't," Darby said, stretching her hand and searching for the blade. "Let us go now and the courts will show leniency."

"Right! After I poisoned Selena? I don't think so."

"Selena was sick. You felt sorry for her." Darby's index finger found the edge of the blade. She strained to pull it closer.

"That's the argument my lawyer would take, if I were going to be tried. Which I'm not, because I'm getting on a plane and disappearing as soon as I kill you both." She waved the gun. "Say your prayers."

Darby did say a quick prayer for an accurate throw as she hurled the blade toward Andrea's chest. Diving at Sophie, she pushed the girl out of the path of danger. The gun went off, its roar echoing in the darkness, but Darby was already on her feet, the years of training in Aikido flooding through her brain.

Without wasting a second, she grabbed Andrea's forearm, twisting it backwards and removing the gun. A well-placed kick to her assailant's calf sent the woman sprawling face first onto the floor of the cave.

"Wow," Sophie breathed. "That was pretty cool."

Darby's heart was pounding. Keeping the gun trained on Andrea, she asked, "You okay?"

"Yeah." Darby could hear Sophie struggling to her feet.

"I'll stay here with her. Go on outside and find some help."

Sophie moved warily past the prostrate Andrea and toward the stairs. Darby heard her climbing the rickety structure and was just about to remind her to be careful when there was a loud crash.

The stairs had collapsed.

NINETEEN

DAN STEWART HEARD THE gunshot as he jumped out of his jeep and began running across the Contento's lush lawn.

"What's going on?" Tim Contento stood on the porch, his hands in a questioning gesture. His bald head glistened under the porch's light. "What is it, Dan?"

"That shot—where did it come from?"

"I don't know. Probably a hunter looking for quail or something. What's going on?"

Dan paused, his heart pounding. "I'm trying to find Sophie. She's been missing for several hours."

"She's not here."

"Who is?"

"Margo and I are inside, and Andrea just went out to check on something."

Detective Nardone emerged from the shadows. "Where is Andrea?"

"She's in the old barn," said a clear voice from the porch. Margo Contento had a strange expression on her face. "I think I may know why you want her."

———

"Crap!" Sophie yelled into the darkness.

"Are you hurt?"

"I think I broke my foot." Darby heard the girl's muffled movements. "Ahhh ... Ahhh ... I'm sure I broke my foot."

"Are you bleeding?"

"A little."

"Where?"

"I hit my head."

"Okay, listen to me. You may have a concussion, Sophie, so I don't want you to move too much. Can you find where you are bleeding?"

"Yes."

"Can you put pressure on it until I get there? I'm going to see if I can find that cell phone of yours and call for help." She didn't voice her real fear: what if Sophie had sustained a severe neck or head injury?

"Ow!" Sophie moaned. "Okay, I'm applying pressure to the bleeding."

"Good." Darby glanced at the huddled form of Andrea, still motionless on the basement floor. If she had the duct tape readily available, she could restrain her, but she didn't want to waste precious time searching for the duct tape. Sophie needed help, and quickly.

Still clutching the revolver, Darby moved to the edges of the cave, using her toe to probe the dirt floor. She hit something and it clanged against a rock. She knelt to touch it. Was it the cell phone? *A bottle.* Staying on her knees, she reached with her hands until she located a rectangular object.

Sophie's cell. Now Darby prayed that the thing would still work.

"I found your phone," she called out. It was the flip type, but Darby didn't want to waste time trying to figure it out. "I'm coming over to you so we can call your dad." She took a step toward Sophie. Suddenly her ankle was seized and yanked with an inhuman strength. Darby fell heavily to the ground.

Andrea Contento loomed over her, her hands stretched toward Darby's throat. Like an apparition from a bad horror flick she intoned, "You are dead…"

Darby held out the gun and pulled the trigger, expecting the recoil to slam her head against the dirt. *Nothing.* She tried again.

Andrea was upon her, shaking her with rib-cracking force, and the gun skittered out of her hand. Darby fought to flip Andrea and succeeded, the two wrestling along the damp earth floor. Andrea brought her knee into Darby's chest and for a moment the realtor was winded. Darby let go of Andrea and groped on the ground for some kind of weapon.

Her hand closed on the broken wine bottle. *Smash!* She brought it down upon Andrea's skull and the impact shattered the glass into hundreds of tiny shards. Andrea went limp.

"Darby?" Sophie's voice sounded small. Scared.

"It's okay, honey," Darby said. "It's finally over."

———

The voice of Dan Stewart echoed off the damp cave walls. "Sophie! Are you down there?"

"Yes, Dad." The teen's voice was feeble, and Darby knew she needed medical attention, and fast.

"Dan, it's Darby. Sophie's taken a fall and has at least one broken bone, probably a concussion as well. Have you called an ambulance?"

"On the way." Dan mumbled something to someone else in the barn. "Tim and I are going to get a ladder down here just as soon as we can."

"Dad?" Darby could hear the panic in Sophie's voice. "Dad, don't go."

"I'm not going anywhere, Sophie Doo," he said soothingly. "Tim has gone to get that ladder and I'm staying right here." He raised his voice. "How about you, Darby? Are you okay?"

"Yes." *Bruised, battered, and chilled to the bone, but alive and well*, she thought. And Andrea? Darby could hear nothing from the woman, not even a moan.

"Sophie, I'm coming over to see how you're doing," Darby said in a confident voice. "Okay?"

"What about—"

"She's not going to bother us anymore." Darby picked her way along the cave floor and through the rubble that had been the stairs. Sophie was lying on her back, a mound of debris on one leg. Darby was careful to keep her voice neutral.

"Okay, we're going to get you out of here just as soon as we can," she said. She reached down and touched the girl's shoulder. "You hanging in there?"

"Yeah."

"Can you wiggle your toes?"

"Sure. That was the first thing I did, Darby. I am a candy striper, remember."

In the darkness Darby smiled. "Oh, yeah." She bent and grabbed a chunk of wood. "Then let's see if we can get some of this pile off you."

———

Only later, after Sophie was safely lifted from the cave and loaded onto a stretcher, and Darby herself had climbed the ladder and emerged into the barn, did Darby think about Andrea Contento's condition. A second team of paramedics was attending to her, with Detective Nardone hovering alongside.

———

As the paramedics began loading her into an ambulance, Andrea Contento managed to open one of her eyes. Though her vision was blurry and bloodied, she knew the person climbing into the vehicle beside the gurney was Detective Nardone. "She's a flight risk," Andrea heard her explain to the technician. "I'm not taking the chance that she escapes."

Andrea's whole body ached and her head pounded from the encounter with the wine bottle. She thought about the private jet waiting to whisk her to a remote Caribbean island and gritted her teeth. *I must escape.*

———

The cup of coffee was warm in Darby's hands, although it was doing nothing to banish the chill that seemed to have settled in her bones. She looked across the table in the Contento kitchen, where Margo and Tim sat in stunned silence. Moments before, the last of the ambulances had exited the property, sirens wailing, on its way to Ventano Valley Community Hospital.

"When did you figure it out, Margo?" Darby asked quietly.

Margo sighed and looked up. "I didn't," she admitted. "I never suspected Andrea." The shrug of her shoulders was a tired one. "She and Selena had been such good friends."

"What was it your father said to you the day he died, when you argued?"

Margo frowned. "He said that he saw me crouching by the cabana on the afternoon Selena died. He said he knew it was me because he saw my blonde hair."

Darby took a sip of the coffee. "Why did you tell me that Michael saw Kohler?"

She shot a guilty look at her brother. "Because I knew Dad had seen someone else, wearing a blonde wig, and I was afraid ..."

Tim Contento put his hands on his head and gave a snort of disgust. "You suspected me? Thanks a lot!" He scowled at Margo. "I can't believe you could think for one minute that I'd kill anyone, much less Selena."

"I realize now it was stupid," Margo admitted sheepishly. "But I remembered you from Halloween. You made such a convincing Marilyn Monroe ..."

Tim shook his head, looked back at his sister's face, and suddenly barked out a laugh. "You jerk!"

Margo looked relieved. She gave a helpless smile. "Plus you take those beta blockers. I found them in your car."

"I take them for stage fright, before I have to make one of those Contento corporate talks." He rolled his eyes. "Not everyone can be as self-assured as you, Margo."

Watching the interaction between the siblings, Darby realized the family dynamic was an old one. Margo had acted as she had throughout her life—she'd protected her twin. ET and Carlos had tried to do much the same thing for their sister.

"You both should know that Andrea was planning to run away somewhere. She's undoubtedly gotten hold of some money."

"We'll alert the banks tomorrow," Tim said ruefully. "Not much we can do tonight."

Darby took a last sip of coffee and stood on shaky legs. "No, there's not much any of us can do but try to get some rest. Thanks for the coffee."

"Let me give you a ride back to Carson Creek," insisted Tim. "It's the least we can do."

"No, I can manage," she said with a tired smile. "I'm looking forward to a nice hot shower and a good night's sleep."

"Me too," Margo said, "Except I don't think it's going to happen. I'm absolutely stunned. How could Andrea have killed Selena? Why?"

"It was just like Sophie said," Tim intoned. "She wanted that damn vineyard."

———

Forty-five minutes later, Darby lay in bed in Selena's guest room and dialed Miles. He was silent as she relayed the events of the evening.

"You could have been killed," he said. "That maniac could have shot you and that young girl as well."

"I know." What else was there to say, really? It was all too true: Andrea Contento had nearly ended both their lives. "If it hadn't been for Sophie, I might still be lying in that cave." She recalled the duct tape across her face and the bristly feeling of the rat against her thigh and shuddered.

"Listen, I can jump in my car this minute and motor to the vineyard," he said. "I'm only an hour or so away."

"You're too good to me." She sighed. "Maybe I'm overly optimistic, but I feel as if I'm actually going to get some sleep tonight." She paused. "Will you drive up in the morning?"

"Absolutely. You get some rest, and I shall be there when you awake."

Darby smiled and turned out the light.

————

Dan Stewart shook hands with the orthopedic surgeon and headed back to the ER waiting room. Dr. Beaumarron had scrutinized the x-ray and assured him that Sophie's ankle would be fine, that the break was fairly clean, and that her young bones would heal splendidly. "She'll be ready to go home in a half-hour or so," he assured Dan. "Go get yourself a cup of that awful hospital coffee and watch some CNN. We're taking good care of Sophie—she's one of the staff's favorite candy stripers."

Dan smiled as he walked back to the waiting room with its plastic chairs and tired magazines. As he passed the curtained-off exam areas, he glimpsed a thickset police officer standing guard next to someone lying flat on a stretcher.

Andrea Contento.

Dan's jaw tightened and he stopped, mid-step, paralyzed by a rage he didn't know he could possess. She had killed Selena, she had tried to kill Darby, and most important—she had been ready to take the life of his fourteen-year-old daughter. And for what? For a stinking twenty acres of land?

He felt the tenseness of his entire upper body, as if he were a spring ready to uncoil, or a tiger at a watering hole, ready to pounce on an unsuspecting antelope. *I could crush her with my bare hands. And it would feel good...*

Just then he registered a light touch on his elbow. He turned in a jerky motion toward the sensation, and saw a young intern peering at his face. Concern clouded her eyes. "Hey," she said softly. "You're Sophie's dad, right?"

He nodded numbly. His eyes slid once more toward the exam room, and then back to the young doctor.

"I just left Sophie. She's feeling so much better and is excited to be going home." Now her eyes darted to the patient lying behind the curtain. She nodded imperceptibly, as if she understood the whole tense tableau, and placed her hand once more on his arm. "Come with me," she coaxed, giving his shirt a gentle tug. "Let me tell you about the funny thing that happened the last time Sophie was volunteering. I was doing rounds and there was this lady from L.A.—"

He felt himself guided down the hallway, away from the malevolent form lying in the exam room, and into the cheerless waiting room that suddenly didn't seem so bad.

———

Darby awoke to sunshine peeking through the windows, followed a split second later by Jasper jumping on her chest. He fixed his penetrating amber eyes on her face and gave a loud yowl.

"Jasper, you've finally made a noise," Darby said. "What's the big occasion?"

Miles entered with a tray of food, graced by a few asters in a small vase. "I'm afraid our feline friend likes salmon," he said. "I've never seen him quite so animated."

Darby giggled. "Did he let you in, as well? I could have sworn I locked that door last night."

"You don't have to be in America too long to realize that you Yanks always put a spare key under the flowerpot," Miles quipped. "Besides, I didn't want to wake you."

She sat up, smoothing her old Chargers tee-shirt, wishing she'd worn an attractive nightgown, and surveyed the breakfast before her. "Umm … a spinach frittata with salmon? Miles, you are amazing."

He grinned. "I like the sound of that. Would you mind terribly saying it again?"

She acquiesced. "Miles, you are amazing."

He leaned forward, careful not to spill the tray, ready to plant a kiss on her lips. She held up a hand in alarm.

"I haven't brushed my teeth," she protested.

He brushed the hair from her face. "Darby, I don't give a toss."

"Is that sort of like what Rhett Butler said to Scarlett?"

He nodded. "Exactly."

———

Nancy Nardone emerged from her sedan, slammed the door, and crossed over the pebbled driveway to the unfamiliar car in Carson Creek Estate & Winery's lot. She peered in the window, spotting a tweed jacket folded neatly on the passenger side seat. *It's the British guy, Miles, the one who's head over heels for Darby,* she reasoned. She glanced at her watch. Nearly noon. Whatever they'd been up to was undoubtedly over by now.

Her rapid knock on the door was answered by the glossy-haired realtor. "Detective Nardone," she said, her almond eyes looking more rested than usual. "Come on in."

The detective stepped into the farmhouse kitchen and spied the tall British journalist sitting at the dining room table. He nodded hello and rose quickly to his feet. "Good morning," he said. "I heard you had a little excitement over at Contento Vineyards last night."

Nancy Nardone huffed. "I guess you could call it that, Miles." She looked over at Darby with concern. "How are you doing?"

"I think I'm actually okay," she answered. "A little sore, but not too bad. Just tremendously relieved the whole thing is over."

The detective nodded. "It may hit you more as the day goes on," she said. "Post-traumatic stress, that kind of thing. At any rate, I wanted to let you know that we've released Fritz Kohler, although I don't think he'll be in the market for any Ventano vineyards." She looked down at her hands. "Sorry about that."

"It's okay. I don't think he really wanted Carson Creek—or at least not for the right reasons. It seems to me he felt guilty about how he'd treated Selena, and thought that by buying her property he could somehow make amends."

Detective Nardone nodded. "And Vivian…she's done a few slippery things, but I don't think she sought out Christophe Barton, or aided him in any of the damage he caused." She paused. "I can't prove it, but I think he was influenced by Andrea. I have a feeling that she financed his little reign of terror, and probably suggested he contact Vivian as well. You can bet I'm going to look hard for evidence to connect Barton and Andrea."

Miles raised a finger as if in a press briefing. "What about Michael Contento's death? Did Andrea have a hand in that as well?"

"Good question. Obviously he suspected his wife of wearing that wig and crouching at the cabana, or he wouldn't have made that cryptic reference to Jezebel. Another loose end we're going to have to try and tie up." She rose from her chair. "I imagine you'll be heading back to San Diego, is that correct?"

Darby nodded. "Dan is making dinner here tonight and I'll leave after that." She grinned. "We'd love for you to join us."

Nancy Nardone's mouth twitched in what seemed like a smile. "Just so happens I'm not working, so perhaps I'll stop by." She stood up and leaned against a pressed back chair. "There is one more thing. Early this morning, Andrea Contento tried to escape from Ventano Valley Community." She saw the shocked faces of Darby and Miles and put up a hand. "I said she *tried* to escape. She did not succeed. The suspect is now safely behind bars at the Wyattville jail."

Miles put a rugged hand over Darby's slender one as Detective Nardone saw herself out.

———

A soft pop signaled the uncorking of a bottle of Carson Creek Pinot Noir. Miles poured Darby, Dan, Detective Nardone, and himself each a glass. He stuck a striped straw in Sophie's ginger ale, handed it to her, and raised his wine glass in a toast.

"To Sophie, for saving the day," he said, giving the teen a wink. "We are all extremely grateful for your inquisitive mind and grasp of obscure Biblical references."

"I'll drink to that," Darby said, sipping the ruby-red liquid. She stopped her brain from analyzing the taste. *Not now,* she thought. Instead she asked, "How's that ankle feeling?"

"Better, now that I can't move it." Sophie looked down at the plaster cast encasing her left foot and grinned. "Wait until people ask me how I broke it," she said. "Oh, I was in an abandoned cave with a homicidal maniac and a martial-arts kicking real estate agent." The others chuckled. Cracking jokes after such an ordeal was undoubtedly a healthy sign.

"I think you could have a great career in law enforcement." Detective Nardone offered. She was off duty and looked very stylish in navy Capri pants and a fitted white blouse. "After all, you cracked the case with your deciphering of 'Ahab's wife.'"

"Thanks, but I've already figured out my career." Sophie held up a hand. "First, I finish high school." She ticked off one finger. "And then I go to the University of California at Davis to study viticulture." Another tick. "When I graduate, I'll get Darby to sell Dad's house and we'll move to my grandmother's farm in New York State." Tick number three. "And then he and I start a winery."

Dan Stewart raised his eyebrows in surprise. "This is starting to sound like my kind of plan."

"Right? It's not Wyattville, Napa, or Sonoma, but there is pretty land out there, and New York is producing some great Chardonnays, and even Pinots." Sophie's earnestness was palpable.

Dan laughed. "I'm sold, Soph. You and I can make it happen." He turned to the others. "Meanwhile, I guess I'll be running Carson Creek for the foreseeable future. Carlos and ET feel like they need to let the dust settle before making any decisions."

Darby smiled. "The vineyard couldn't be in better hands than yours, Dan. Did they tell you their thoughts for the new barn building?"

He nodded. "Something about a restaurant serving Mexican cuisine, right?" He glanced toward his daughter. "I'll admit I was a little distracted when Carlos explained it."

"They want to honor the culinary tradition of the Valle de Guadalupe, where their grandfather worked in the vineyards. Apparently one of the cousins who came to the funeral is quite a talented chef."

Sophie plunked down her ginger ale. "Do I hear lucrative summer job, or what?"

Dan grinned and Darby could not help smiling as well. "We'll just see what time brings," he said, ruffling her hair.

"That sounds like a brilliant idea," Miles said, his hazel eyes fixed on Darby.

She felt herself blushing as she turned to Nancy Nardone. "And what about you, Detective? Any plans in store for you?"

"Actually, yes. I'm taking a vacation this summer, something I haven't done in a long, long time." She looked pointedly at Sophie. "After I eat in the new restaurant with Sophie as my waitress, I'm going to visit a place I've always dreamt about."

"Where's that?" Sophie asked, taking a sip of her soda.

"Maine."

Darby smiled in surprise. "That's where I grew up."

"No kidding!" Detective Nardone pursed her lips. "I thought you were from Mission Beach."

"I am now, but I was born and raised on the rocky coast of Maine."

"Huh! You aren't by any chance a sailor, are you?"

Darby flashed on the sleek Alden 48 she'd grown up sailing, the boat that had vanished with John and Jada Farr on that tragic August afternoon. She waited for the familiar feeling of sadness to overtake her mood, braced herself for the pain that always came when she thought of their deaths. To her great surprise, instead of sorrow, she felt excitement at the prospect of once more giving herself to the unfettered freedom that was sailing.

Miles was gazing at her intently. Darby met his eyes and then turned to answer the detective.

"Yes," she said, with a genuine smile that lit her lovely face. "I am a sailor, and a darn good one. I'd love to meet you in Maine for a cruise."

THE END

© William von Wenzel

Top-producing Realtor Vicki Doudera uses a world she knows well —high-stakes, luxury real estate—as the setting for her suspenseful series starring crime-solving, deal-making agent Darby Farr. A broker with a busy coastal firm since 2003 and former Realtor of the Year, Vicki is also the author of several non-fiction guides to her home state of Maine.

When she's not working, Vicki enjoys cycling, hiking, and sailing with her family, as well as volunteering for her favorite charitable cause, Habitat for Humanity. She has pounded nails from Maine to Florida, helping to build simple, affordable Habitat homes, and is currently president of her local affiliate.

Vicki belongs to Mystery Writers of America, Sisters in Crime, and the National Association of Realtors. She serves on the board of the New England chapter of Sisters in Crime and is available for signings and book events. Read more about her at her official website, www.vickidoudera.com.